The Last Cannoli

Printed and bound in Canada

On the cover, Rosanna Musotto Piazza's "Terribile duello tra Chiaramonte Bordonaro e Notarbartolo di Montallegro" from *Rosanna Musotto Piazza* (Milano: Giorgio Mondadori & Associati), 1989. (Via Marchese di Villabianca, 4, 90145 Palermo, Italy).

The Last Cannoli

A Novel

A Sicilian-American Family Comes of Age through the Ancient
Power of Story-telling

By

CAMILLE CUSUMANO

LEGAS

Library of Congress Cataloging-in-Publication Data

Cusumano, Camille.
  The last cannoli : a novel / by Camille Cusumano.
    p.cm.
  ISBN 1-881901-20-3
  "A Sicilian-american family comes of age through the ancient power of story-telling."
    1. Italian American families--Fiction. 2. Sicily (Italy)--Emigration and immigration--Fiction. 3. Italian Americans--Fiction. 4. Storytelling --Fiction. I. Title.

PS3553.U782 L37 1999
813'.54--dc21

                                                    99--052660

Acknowledgments

The publisher is grateful to Arba Sicula for a generous grant that in part made the publication of this book possible.

For information and for orders, write to:
Legas

P.O. Box 040328	68 Kamloops Ave	2908 Dufferin Ave
Brooklyn, New York	Ottawa, Ontario	Toronto, Ontario
11204, USA	K1N 8T9 Canada	M6B 3S8 Canada

Or call toll-free: (877) 670-5800

Web site: home.earthlink.net/ ~ocaramia

Accomplishing the way of great peace has no sign. The family style of peasants is most pristine, only concerned with village songs and festal celebrations. What do they need to know of the benevolence and virtue of the ancestors?

Adapted from the *Book of Serenity*, an ancient Buddhist text.

Donitella Family Tree

Maridona Delvecchio m. Pasquale Coniglio   Concetta Provenzano m. Nicolò Donitella
Gemma Leonforte m. Franco Coniglio   Lucia M. Conforti m. Mario Anthony Donitella
(1920)   (1915)

Maria Magdalena Coniglio m. Vincenzo Giuseppe Donitella
(1941)

Mario Anthony	Lucia Maria	Vincent Joseph
(1942)	(1944)	(1946)
Carmine Anthony		Franco Joseph
(1948)		(1949)
Maddelena Christina		Nazarena Rosalie
(1954)		(1955)
Maria Anna	Teresa Santa	Carmela Lisa
(1958)	(1959)	(1963)

Partial Glosssary

Italian	Sicilian	English
Acidità	àcitu	stomach acid
Bella	bedda	beautiful
Bello, m.	beddu	handsome
Brutta, f.	laida	ugly
Brutto, m.	laidu	ugly
Capocollo	capicollu	a type of Italian ham
Capisci	capisci	understand
Cardoni	carduni	cardoons
Che vuoi?	chi voi?	what do you want?
Compari	cumpari	baptismal relative**
Cannoli	cannoli	cannoli (pastry)
Guarda	talè	look
Lui	iddu	he
Lei	idda	she
Me ne fotto	minni futtu	I don't give a damn
Questo qua	chistu ccà	this one here
Vieni qui!	veni ccà!	come here!

**Untranslatable.

Table of Contents

Dedication

For my parents Charles Anthony and Carmela Madeleine and my brothers and sisters, Jimmy, Terri, Chuck, Sal, Grace, Tommy, Lisa, Tina, and Donna.

Mario (1957)

In the beginning there was terrible darkness. Light, love, and all things good lay frozen in ice as hard as a stale biscotti, as still and cold as Great Grandpa's breath the day we buried him.

But then, a sun was born to the universe and a pulse, a sleepy heartbeat quickened deep in the Earth. When the solar heat radiated down to Earth and the buried heart began to writhe, the salt of the Earth began to eat the ice.

When these things came to pass there flowed over the Earth all the great green and blue waters of the world, our oceans, seas, rivers and streams. And of these great waters of life, none was bluer or more beautiful than one that flowed near the warm half of the world. It was called Mediterranean. For this warm sea was like a plate of church glass, a mirror for the sun. It kept the deep blue that had once glowed in the caps and caverns of ice.

Now, in addition to love and goodness, many things were freed as the ice melted: gloves, hairbrushes, teething rings, old teeth, old bones, fossils, old sweatshirts, and a dancing hat and boot.

When the sleepy tri-cornered hat and the boot awoke, they had so much rhythm and happiness and soul that they began to dance to-gether. Later, some would say that the hat was all heart and the boot was all soul. They danced and danced, together, floating around the world until they were absolutely danced out.

Guess where they came to rest.

They lay down in the Mediterranean Sea. The boot came to be called the Land of Italy and the hat the Land of Sicily.

And from Earth's womb came the mountains of Italy and Sicily.

Now, Italy was nice.

Ah, but Sicilia! Sicily was the most spectacular place on Earth. Its coast was blessed with warm sandy beaches and rocky bluffs. Tongues of sapphire water lapped at the sweet, pure land and the sun poured warm gold over the rugged red cliffs. For Sicily was the

9

most wild and free, with a spirit so full of music and rhythm, even the rocks, even the wind sang!

"Even the rocks, even the wind!" My father was a genius for this sort of stuff. He missed his calling. My father strung words together the way I, his firstborn son, strung musical notes together. He had never set foot in his ancestral *Land of Sicilia*. But its praises tumbled from his mouth with a fierce melody. The stories were his only title to the land of his parents, and had shaped his every thought, his every sigh. This land he had seen only in the shifting landscape of his own wild imagination.

When my father sang, when my father told stories, everybody —even I— listened. It meant he was in a good mood and everybody relaxed. Everybody felt comfortable. The whole universe seemed to go along with him. Things went right.

He had laid down his French horn many years ago when he married my mother. Slowly, the notes rose to his tongue. Stories became his music:

Everything worth living for grew and flourished on this island, every beautiful flower, every succulent fruit and vegetable.

His stories. His name. Such was the burden I was ordained to bear. Was it not enough that our Donitella name—round and mellow, showing off its every soft and hard sound, hiding nothing of its nature—echoed the eminence of a Renaissance sculptor?

No. That was not enough. It had reached us through the sweat of Sicilian peasants. My legacy was sealed not long after we moved from the Peterstown neighborhood of Elizabeth to Rahway. It was a warm evening in May 1957. My father came home from his produce stand, threw the tomatoes and *cucuzza* on the kitchen table and said I could not play my music that evening. All seven of us children had to come sit and listen to him after supper.

On this spring evening he started to tell the stories with the force of Moses on the Mount.

We had moved from Peterstown, the Italian enclave where my four grandparents had brought their peach trees, tomato and eggplant crops, even their grapes, on the boat from Sicily. And where my mother and father and the first seven of us were born. We had moved into this house in Rahway, where the background music of Italian voices was gone.

Now, we lived in a quiet Protestant suburb, with softer voices, more discreet tones. Homes were a little farther apart, a little farther from the smokestacks, and a little bigger than the railroad flat in Peterstown. The wooden house on Kristyne Street there, owned by my mother's parents, seemed to "split its sides after the seventh child," said Mercy, our neighbor.

Here at 2724 Creek Street in Rahway we had four bedrooms to divide among the 10 of us, including Nonnie. Two dormers upstairs, each slightly bigger than a tool shed, fit four boys and three girls. My parents had a real bedroom with a door and privacy. They were glad no longer to have Grandma and Grandpa Coniglio living right above us as our rent collectors. But after about six months my father missed his people. That did it. He began to wonder if he had made a mistake.

And on this day in May his longing became our evensong.

If grief had not turned up the volume of his words, he would not have become tone deaf to my music.

My father's preamble: "The stories and my name, these are the fruits a humble fruit and vegetable vendor can give his children."

That evening each of us found my mother picking weeds in her little vegetable garden by the creek that ran through our backyard. You could hear her deep, monotonous resignation: Sorry, Lucy, you can't see Joe tonight, tell him to wait till tomorrow; No Rena and Maddelena, no catching lightning bugs; no stick ball, Vinnie, Carmine; Frankie, no *Million Dollar Movie*.

And no band practice for me.

As she tugged at crab grass around the green peppers in the patch, she gave reason to each of us to be happy even as our wishes were denied. "Be thankful that there is no new threat of war with the Communists." Tug. "Be thankful you don't have to pray the rosary." Tug. "Be thankful you don't have to go to the Novena tonight." Tug. "Be thankful God gave us the means to buy this big new house." Tug. "Be thankful you're alive." Tug. "Now go wash your hands and sit around the supper table. All of you. You too, Mario."

I had already attended Novenas to save the souls of all my ancestors. I had amassed plenary indulgence to save the world. All I wanted was to play my piano with the guys. My father knew we always had band practice on Thursday nights. Spaghetti and band practice. Always!

My mother picked a couple of green peppers for the salad and put them in her apron pockets. She cradled a few plum tomatoes in the crook of her elbow and brought them inside to ripen on the kitchen's sunny window sill.

For what it was worth I made my plea. "Mom!" I cried in desperation, following on her heels, "this could be another break. Have you ever heard of Greenwood Lake? I've been waiting for this...The SilkTones are getting known on the circuit! We could play Greenwood Lake upstate New York someday! Ma!"

She told Maddelena and Rena to put their dolls away so Lucy could set the table. She ordered Carmine to help Vinnie gather chairs to put around the table. She turned to me.

"Mario!" she said as if she had just recognized which one of her kids I was, "You know your father."

We were both hard-headed, my father had said. Tones, pitch, scales, the chords we struck, we both had our own ideas about these.

"Tell the boys to come Friday night for pizza," she added, "Bring their instruments, you can eat and practice down the cellar. What's the difference if you wait a night."

What's the difference!? My mother, who thought pizza could fix everything, would never understand.

We squeezed around the kitchen table and ate, glum about having to stay inside when there was still light outside. Light by which to pitch balls, to run, sweat, and shout with new friends.

When we could fit no more spaghetti and meatballs in our bellies, we moved our chairs into the small parlor. Vinnie brought the Singer sewing machine chair for my father. Outside the air was warm and silken. The sticky nights had not yet begun. It was that brief window of time in New Jersey when the weather was comfortable. There was new scenery in our lives this first spring. The maples on Creek Street had begun to leaf out. The confetti of their early buds still carpeted the streets, fringing the curbsides. Up and down the block, bikes were abandoned on lawns. Neighbors sat on porches reading the late edition of the *Elizabeth Daily Journal*. To all this we added our Peterstown trademark, laundry hung on a backyard line. Two 30-foot lines were strung from a pulley on the back of our new house to the trunk of the mulberry tree near the creek.

Although we hated our father for not letting us go out, for resolutely ignoring the symphony of our pleas, we rallied around him. His voice tapped some internal metronome that lulled us into submission in spite of ourselves. And we sat and actually listened to his words:

The scent of lemon blossom prickled the air. The sweet almond tree sprouted its gentle, soft flowers.

I could hear the kids in the street. Unrestrained laughter and frivolity. They were playing stick ball, oblivious to the ritual going on almost within earshot, behind our red brickfront. At first we were distracted by the squeals that sifted through the screened windows. The squeals of our new friends. Kids who had been allowed to sit at card tables in front of televisions and eat frozen dinners, fishsticks or pot pies—hurriedly—so they could run outside and play. We were so jealous of them.

Even as my father told his tales, a train of freshly bathed children, the three youngest, Frankie, Rena, and Maddelena, tumbled from my mother's arms. She had lined up the little kids to step into their snap-on pajamas. Hair dripping wet, they crawled like four-legged animals to a vacant patch of rug.

My mother got a little behind in the assembly line bathing. My father would interrupt himself now and then to call, "Mary Magdalena! C'mon, you're missing out." There were no stern notes in his voice, just coaxing, as if he were dishing out ice cream cones. She called from her chores. "I'm coming Vincent, one more minute, please!" It was a long minute. She had to wash the dishes and bathe the little ones before she could relax, because once she stopped she was immobile for a long time.

She was always late in settling down on the oak rocking chair that was reserved for her. She was like a silk garment tossed and falling in a maelstrom, at last coming to rest in a still pile of random folds. When she landed in the rocker all she seemed to do was breathe—and finger her rosaries. She was exhausted. Not just from bathing children, but from the behind-the-scenes exchanges that my father never saw, the fielding of so many deadend pleas.

The crimson blush of the prickly pear and the magenta of bougainvillea blazed everywhere.

My father told the stories from a stool, his back against the wall that held two gold-encrusted frames. At what might have been the right hand of God was a painted studio portrait of my father. Pitch black hair and bronze skin framed a white smile and forbidding eyes. In the frame at the left hand of God was, in pulsing red with gold-embossing, the Sacred Heart. Our next door neighbor, Dana Krause, pointed out to me that they were uneven. My father's countenance was hung an inch-and-a-half higher than the Sacred Heart. I assured her the ranking was correct and understated.

The supple ground smelled with olive, tomato, artichoke, grape, and cardoon. The splendor of the island's fertility was almost too painful.

In the armchair sat Great Grandma Maridona Coniglio. We called her Nonnie. She coiled and uncoiled her long grey plaits as she listened. Her braided hair reached below her waist. She always wore the same green and white checked smocked cotton dress. She'd finger her rosary beads piled on her lap and her lips would move. Or, she would snort a pinch of snuff from her silver case. Nonnie, my mother's grandmother, had come with us to Rahway. My father insisted we have a Sicilian relative nearby. His sisters kept his mother and we got Nonnie. He considered Nonnie a paragon because she listened without questioning. During a story he turned and spoke to her in Sicilian. She answered him the way we answered the priest in Church and he continued with his sermon.

Eventually the people who stayed here knew an easy, happy life and this rugged place of great diversity nurtured every whim, need, and dream. Body and soul could not find a better place on Earth Simple pleasures sustained the people—coarse bread, sweet grapes, hand-rolled macaroni, and home-cured olives were daily indulgences. Occasionally they had cannoli, the cream of all Sicilian pastry! They also had a genius for stuffing foods; they stuffed meats, they stuffed fish with currants and pignoli, they made the best ices in the world and they made lovely almond candies.

Time passed and your ancestors multiplied and built their villages from stone in the mountains. Over the years these villages came to be so deeply embedded they seemed to have grown of their own will from the rock. They were hanging temples, with steep winding streets laid out for the hoofed beasts of the Earth.

Many children were born, but only the very strong survived.

As dusk deepened, I glimpsed flashes of fireflies through the screen. Maddelena and Rena sat wide-eyed in their corner. They would have been out in the backyard catching the lightning bugs in cupped palms. They'd store them in canning jars with holes punched in the lids, hiding them in the bushes that separated our house from the Krauses'.

Frankie would be turning channels on the mahogany Emerson television that someone had just passed down to us. Carmine and Vinnie must have wondered who was in on the stick ball game —probably Tim, Ken, and Ed. There could be no spunk in the game without my brothers, who were half the team.

I had outgrown stick ball games. I no longer cared to talk on the phone every night like Lucy about who was dating whom, who had gone all the way with whom, who was cheating. I thought about music, rhythm and blues, the rock that I loved. I thought about my own future. A month earlier we had gotten a break. We had played the Alibi Lounge down the shore. Joey D. and Fats and others had performed there before they were famous. I was the only member who wouldn't show up at band practice. All because my father had a story in his head.

I had waited until the right moment to ask my father if I could go. He seemed to be in a good mood. But he darkened when I asked as if asking alone were a sin. He said, "Mario, don't think you're too good to spend a night with your family. When was the last time? You've been thinking too much that other things are important."

"But, Dad," I had said, "my friends will be disappointed..."
He stiffened. That was the wrong chord to hit. "Don't tell me about
your friends. You have no friends. They are acquaintances, at best.
Family comes first before anyone and don't forget it. You can count
your friends on one hand or less." He spat the last word at me, then
added that if I didn't want to sit in on his stories I could lock myself
in my bedroom and study since I was going to be a doctor or something great someday because my name was Mario A. Donitella.
Then he spoke the phrase that meant the conversation was over: "I
have spoken."

I could have studied for my organic chemistry exam, but I was
too distracted to concentrate. So I sat and listened to my father talk,
while the rest of us attended raptly, drawn into his orbit like planets.

We didn't have to worry about the phone ringing. My father
had pulled it off the wall a few nights ago. Lucy had been planning a
party for her fourteenth birthday. She was getting a lot of calls. Her
chatty girlfriends were calling to find out which boys were coming,
would my band be playing music. Patty, her cute blonde friend, had
called three times to find out if I'd be there. I knew she had been
hoping I'd answer the phone. Lucy broke my father's rule on
phones. She talked for more than five minutes on Patty's third call.
My father gave Lucy two warnings. She was a fool not to heed. But
Lucy was never taken to the wall in the cellar where the other boys
and I were whipped. My father just pulled the phone out of the wall
and said we didn't need one. Lucy told me that Joe Kelley, her new
boyfriend in Rahway, almost broke up with her the following day.
She knew he was going to call, he said, so why hadn't she answered?
Joe didn't believe her story about my father. Joe had never seen
strange bedfellows—violence, rage, and love—compressed into one
stare, either.

In Peterstown, everyone knew everyone's business and you
walked in anyone's house any time of day or night. But, for the lon-
gest time, the neighbors hid behind closed doors on Creek Street,
and peeked from behind lace curtains watching the scenes unroll at
2724. I felt their eyes on my back when I left in the morning to take
the bus to St. Benedict's Prep School in Newark. I felt their eyes
when I returned at night. The neighbors seemed courteous, but distant, not like my mother's and father's people, who made it neces-

sary to walk five blocks out of your way to avoid getting stuck in a conversation.

The likes of you! Spectacle on Creek Street! Our Lady in Blue and all! poured from Dana Krause, the girl next door. Lucy and I became good friends with her. Dana was 13 like Lucy, a couple years younger than me. She was an artist and understood my piano music. She took the train to Greenwich Village every Saturday and said someday she would live there. She had wild ideas, but she was honest. She said that the neighbors found us Donitellas loud and curious. She said that they had watched the steady stream of my father's and mother's cousins, aunts, uncles help us move in.

"The hands," said Dana, "when they were empty, swiped, slashed, and carved the air. We had not seen the likes of you folks on Creek Street. Ever."

One day when her parents and brother and sister were out, Dana brought me into her bedroom. She showed me the most astonishing painting. On a large stretched canvas she had painted nothing but hands. My relatives' hands, she told me. She, too, had peered through sheer curtains at first and here she had frozen the movements that captivated her. I immediately recognized what she had done and it sent shivers down my spine. I saw Aunt Rosie's hand coming off the canvas and Uncle Vito's hairy paw leaping with emotion. I must have looked upset, because Dana assured me, "They're very beautiful hands. You should be proud of them. However, I haven't really done them justice—it's hard, you know, when your subject won't sit still."

We laughed and I looked at the backs of my hands. It took an artist like Dana to love our family like no one else in the neighborhood. And my parents loved her, adopted her as our eighth Donitella. My father nicknamed her Madonna Caruso. Dana came over every Friday night for pizza. She said it did her Presbyterian blood good to abstain from eating meat with us Catholics.

What intrigued me most about Dana's painting was seeing what she and perhaps others saw. Something I'd never seen before, not from a distance: the bold outlines of who we Donitellas were. The borders at which we stopped being us and other people started being who they were. And what about the deep gulf between? I wondered how much more I didn't see. What else was hiding? What else did the neighbors see magnified through their sheer curtains? *What did my father's pride look like to people on the outside?*

Mrs. Lear must have seen it. She lived on our north side. She was the only one who was never fond of us. And she did nothing to hide it.

"She thinks there is some kind of voodoo in all your hand movements, dark malicious curses in the loud voices of dark people who come to see you. It's in your family gatherings, your tight-knit behavior," Dana told me. My parents said that no matter what Mrs. Lear said or did, we were to be nice to her and pray for her soul.

Mrs. Lear's suspicions must have been confirmed when we placed the statue of the Virgin in the middle of our lawn. "Our Lady in Blue and White Robes, with Red Lips," Dana called her. Dana painted her and contributed offerings of fresh flowers each week along with my mother's tulips.

Occasionally Mrs. Lear dropped her suspicions and was a regular neighbor. And everybody tried to like her, to welcome her into the fold.

That Thanksgiving after the stories started was one such occasion. I was sitting on our front porch, leaning against the black iron railing as I read Poe's "Cask of Amontillado" to Frankie, Maddelena, and Rena for the umpteenth time. I heard the scraping of rakes gathering brown leaves on dead lawns. The autumn sky was like frosted glass, behind which lurked dark, crouching shapes. The acrid aroma of burning leaves tickled our nostrils and it was chilly enough to see big clouds of our breath. But there was no place to sit inside the house. It was getting steamy with cooking food and the hot breath of so many relatives from Peterstown. They arrived in small groups, stepping over the kids and me into the parlor.

Mrs. Lear watched from her window as the guests arrived for the Thanksgiving dinner. This time I saw how they used their hands to cut and slash the air, while their lips moved and twitched. Every last one a spectacle. I glanced at Dana's window and saw her watching, too. She blew me a kiss, perhaps remembering our last visit. Every time a car pulled up Mrs. Lear got up from her chair and peeked through her front window. She hated when our relatives parked in front of her house.

I continued reading Poe: *"A succession of loud and shrill screams bursting suddenly from the throat of the chained form, seemed to thrust me violently back..."* when I felt a shadow above me. I looked up and saw her jowly face trying to look pleasant. "Your mother in there, Mario, well is she? I'd like to borrow some sugar. I'm making Russian walnut cookies and I ran out, now can you find out for me." She jiggled a measuring cup at her side and I wondered if she beat her son and daughter with a wooden spoon. She had a shrill voice whether she was trying to be nice or mean.

"Go right in, Mrs. Lear," I said politely, moving aside so she could pass us. I caught Frankie's gaze, but too late to stop what I knew he was going to blurt out: *"Mala femmina!"* He repeated what he had heard an adult call her. He didn't even know what it meant. Fortunately, the front door opened and the clamor masked Frankie.

My father and mother's people were squeezed into every corner of the kitchen and parlor. My father's cousin, Alfonso, who had come from Sicily just two years before, had Mrs. Lear's attention. He spoke little English. He was short and stocky with thick silvery hair that floated on top of his head like a dollop of mercury. His hooded eyes drooped toward his temples, ever at half-mast. He had been a prizefighter. I was almost six feet at 15, yet he had lifted me five feet off the ground to show me who was stronger. He was Aunt Sofia's second husband, my father had confided in me. Aunt Sofia's first husband was murdered in Sicily after being married to her for only a year. His body—various parts of it—was found around the village. Nobody knew who had cut him up, but everybody said he deserved it because he used to beat Sofia.

Alfonso smiled at Mrs. Lear and said, *"Chi?"* in his gravelly voice. She recoiled. Then Uncle Val called Alfonso away and he was swallowed by the parlor crowd. Mrs. Lear eyed my father's sisters Angela, Santa, Antoinette, Marialia, and Rosalia—and my great aunts—Vita, Lina, Tina, Jenny. They were sitting on benches drinking coffee and anisette, gesturing and talking about their kids, changing diapers on the floor.

19

My parents were out of sight for the moment. My father was setting up the long tables in the cellar for the day-long feast. My mother was stuffing the mushroom caps that Uncle Al loved and filling the cannoli shells.

Grandma Donitella, Dad's mom, saw Mrs. Lear's empty cup and empty look and pointed to the stove. *"Talé"* she said, *"voi na tazza di cafè?"* Mrs. Lear understood Grandma's hand, as if it could speak. She shook her head vigorously. Frankie whispered to me that we could lure Mrs. Lear down the cellar and bury her behind the wall. He was right. I had never seen her look so vulnerable. Then I realized how her distant expression was like Dana's canvas, reflecting the foreign outlines of my mother's and father's people. For a flickering moment I saw through the eyes of this witch. I saw the world that kept me from my music, kept me from the solitude I needed to organize the sounds in my own head. For a brief second I heard nothing but saw everything exactly as it was. I shivered.

Then the kitchen became warm and toasty again and I saw that my parents' people had gone back to what they were doing. Lucy offered Mrs. Lear a huge platter of antipasto—provolone, pepperoni, prosciutto, sticks of celery, braised fennel, marinated carrots and broccoli, Grandma Coniglio's cracked green olives. Mrs. Lear considered the tray's contents as if they were jigsaw puzzle pieces. I thought for a moment she would dare to try something. But then several little cousins squeezed by, reached up onto the tray and grabbed whatever their fat fingers wrapped around. I saw her recoil again. The tray almost tumbled on her as she turned her attention to Grandma Coniglio whose voice was dominating the room.

Grandma was singing Santa Lucia. She had been rolling a final batch of ravioli in case we ran short. At one end of the kitchen table, she kneaded and rolled the dough on the big pastry board with a long narrow stick. Her pudgy hands sank into a huge flour bag, then came out white to dust the dough. She rolled some more. Carmine was sticking a finger in the parsley-speckled ricotta mixture. Rena, Maddelena, and cousins were fighting over who would bless the dough for Grandma.

"Gram, I want to make the cross, Rena did last time," said one.

"No, me!"

"I want to!" they all squealed, pressing in on Grandma, who was only 4 feet 11 inches, though round and solid. Overwhelmed, she bellowed out a few lines from her favorite song. Then she let each child make the cross in the ravioli dough and added one herself, to the dough and to her forehead, where she left a flour smudge.

At last, I spotted my mother. She was in a corner between the refrigerator and counter, throwing salt in a puddle of olive oil on the counter. She was deep frying more cannoli shells—everybody's favorite dessert. I called to her, she turned, saw Mrs. Lear and wiped her oily hands on her flowered apron. She told Mrs. Lear to take the whole bag of sugar and tried to offer her coffee, homemade wine, or anisette. Mrs. Lear declined all but the cup of sugar and turned to leave with it. She thanked my mother, calling her Mrs. Donitella, not just Magdalena like all the other neighbors.

Mrs. Lear squeezed past Alfonso and four of my uncles, who were passing time playing *murra*. The five men faced each other in a tight circle, raising and lowering their voices, reciting numbers in Italian. What would it have meant to her? They were throwing fingers at each other. When they raised their voices on the last number it was piercing. The fingers in the middle of their circle meant something only to them. When two men made it to *capu* and *sutta-capu*, they dropped their intensity, laughed, and drank.

Mrs. Lear left and a few days later went back to being suspicious and unfriendly. She kept balls that landed in her yard. During the night she poured black shoe polish on cars parked in front of her house. She called the cops when my band played too loud. She pulled up rose bushes that my mother planted near her fence. She was very likely the one who, that winter, removed the Madonna during the night from the pedestal on our lawn and tossed her face-down in the snow in front of the wheels of our blue '52 Ford. Who else would have committed this sacrilege? My mother wept. She and my father made us pray extra hard for the soul of Mrs. Lear.

But after seeing Dana's canvas and after Mrs. Lear's Thanksgiving visit, little things I didn't see before began to annoy me. Olive oil dripping from my lunch sandwiches at school in front of my friends was one. "Make me bologna with mustard or peanut butter and jelly on white bread," I told my mother. Piling the nine of us into the Ford for Sunday mass was another. I began to walk to an earlier mass by myself to have time alone. I began to think of changing my name.

Then the SilkTones got the break we'd been waiting for. An offer to play warm-up at Greenwood Lake on Christmas Eve! I'd have to get fake I.D. to prove I was 18, but Barry had connections. More of a challenge was getting my father's permission to play my music. I had to find the right moment to ask him, because he was always in a bad mood around Christmas.

One afternoon I spoke a couple of minutes on the phone with Barry, our band leader. We discussed changing my name to Don Tell or Mark Dell or Dean Tell, maybe. We weren't sure which had more stage presence. I said we should think about it, hung up, and ran back upstairs to my room to study. My father's footsteps followed. It was unusual for him to enter my bedroom. I thought for a long second that I had done something wrong. He asked what I was reading.

"Astronomy," I answered, putting my slide ruler in the book to mark my place.

"What about astronomy?" he asked.

"I'm reading about stars that are so many billions of years old that they are gone.

"How do we know about them if they're gone?" He seemed genuinely interested.

"Because their light is just reaching our galaxy and scientists can make calculations from the speed of light and distance, even though the star itself has burned up."

He thought for a few seconds and then said, "Hmmm. I get it. Stars are like parents. Their light only reaches home to their kids' galaxy when they're gone."

I laughed, but he didn't, so I stopped short. I looked at him and waited. Finally, he said he needed my help at his produce stand the next afternoon after school, would I help out? I almost protested, but then realized this would be a golden opportunity to ask about Greenwood Lake, because he usually was in a good mood around his customers.

But when I arrived the next day at the stand at North Broad Street in Elizabeth, he was strangely quiet and reserved. He moved around furtively and ordered me tersely to do a few things—unpack crates, break down boxes, spray the lettuce. He showed me exactly how he wanted me to arrange fruits in pyramids, trapezoids, or at obtuse angles on the sloping plywood boards. He made sure I did it right and left me alone. But he came back once and scolded me for not separating the male eggplants from the female ones. I had to re-stack them so that customers could see the bottom ends right away.

"Some customers actually prefer the female, beats the hell out of me," he said. "They like the bitter seeds."

Customers came and went. He gave them his favorite one-liners but was not as chatty as usual, unless he took time to explain to them how to cook the dandelion or *luppini*. One regular wanted to know how to cook the escarole with meatballs and kidney beans. He told her in one breath, "Add some crushed fennel to the fried onions, then add the escarole greens and some water. For the meatballs, to each pound of ground chuck, you add two eggs, handful of grated Parmigiano, seasoned bread crumbs, chopped parsley, or mint if you have." He kissed his bunched-up fingers and opened them up heavenward and said, "Bonissimu!"

He turned to do some paperwork and I handled the steady stream of customers. He whistled *Oh Marie!* and I felt better.

Just as I was preparing to ask about Greenwood Lake, he said, "So the Reds have put Sputnik up in outer space. The Americans can't be far behind. It's a shame they beat us, the lousy Commies."

"Yeah, I guess so," I remarked, drumming my fingers on the counter. It had been almost a month since Sputnik went up.

"I'm glad you and Carmine are good in science and math. Both of you got good heads. One of you will make a doctor."

I put my hands in my pocket and whistled *Oh Marie!*

He picked an overripe tomato off the pile and ate it like an apple.

"I wouldn't be surprised if some damn spies—like those Rosenbergs—gave the Russians documents so they could beat us with that satellite," he said. "Damn Rosenbergs, they got what they deserved. Electric chair was too good for them. Lousy traitors." He threw the stem end of the tomato into a cardboard box.

"Some people don't believe they were guilty," I said about a case that was several years old.

"Ahhh, for crying out loud don't tell me about the shenanigans of your intelligentsia. Bleeding heart intellectuals! They'll be the death and ruination of this country. Mark my words. You be careful when you go to college. I know I raised you right but they'll try to corrupt you, too. Don't let them take away your manhood and make you a sissy." He straightened some cabbages and I almost pulled out the bottom tomato and sent the pile of them rolling. We both had something on our mind.

I decided against telling him that Jimmy Bartolo was responsible for our getting the job at Greenwood. Barry was on social terms with Jimmy, who would get a big cut of our booking. Jimmy had done time, but he was clean now. We were just eager to play. Warm-ups to the Coasters. What a break!

We closed the stand at 4 p.m. before dark. We packed the crates, lowered the canvas awning. As I hosed down the pavement, he said suddenly, "Mario, you never give away your luck."

I stopped hosing. I didn't know what he meant.

He put the cash in a strong box and locked it and banged the box down. He looked up and said, "You don't change where you came from and you don't change your name, hear me?"

So, he had heard me talking to Barry. I decided not to argue with him. Tackle one thing at a time.

"OK, Dad, I was just thinking of possible stage names," I said, trying to close the subject.

"Don't even think of it. You know you were named after a great man, my father. Your grandfather Mario Anthony left his village, Cammarata, Sicily, when he was only 15 to come here. He never went to school a day in his life. He didn't need any textbooks. By the time he died he was very smart and wise. He'd lived a full life. He sold hay, oats, and coal for a living. He worked his way up to a good paying job. He got work in construction. He poured asphalt all over Kenilworth, that town would be in the woods without him. He ran a delicatessen and delivered soda and beer. Then he got a white collar job selling insurance. He took a lot of guff from the Irish boys there, too. They told him, 'This place is not for you and your kind.' They called him Dago, Wop, Ginny right to his face. I heard him telling my mother one day. He was crying, he didn't know I was there or he never would have cried. He held his head high and he never gave away his luck. Never changed his name to make things easier for himself. So don't do it, either."

He took a few breaths and then said, "I only begrudge him one thing. He should have lived to see his first grandson." He slammed a rotten tomato into the woods behind the stand.

"My father appeared to me last night," he said. He moved the cabbage around, putting it stem-side down. Then he changed his mind and put it stem-side up.

"You mean you had a dream about him again?" I asked.

"If I would've meant a dream, I'd said 'I dreamed.' I'm telling you he appeared. Don't talk to your father like he's a dummy."

"OK, OK, Dad. He appeared." I picked up and tossed some cabbage leaves that had fallen to the concrete.

"Yeah, that's right."

"Where...uh, how...when...uh, what did Grandpa want this time?"

"It was in the kitchen. He was there. Yeah. I'm telling you sure as my name is Vincent Joseph Donitella. I haven't told your mother. She takes these things very seriously."

"I won't tell her. What did Grandpa want?"

"Check the hot peppers for any spots, we'll take 'em home."

I bagged the bruised peppers and asked again, "What'd he want?"

"My father doesn't talk to me like I'm talking to you. Here's what happened. I come in late last night from work. You're all asleep. I put a little pot of coffee on to have with some eggs, pepper, and sausage before I get into bed. I sit down at the kitchen table to relax and read the paper. Next thing I know my father's standing there. He starts shaking me, telling me get up, my time isn't yet. I jump out of the chair and see that the coffee's perked over, doused the flame, and the kitchen smells of gas. God knows how long it was leaking. I'd have gassed the whole bunch of us if my father hadn't come. I shut the gas, turned around, and he was gone, but this is the God's honest truth. The back door was ajar and I know I had closed it. He was there, Mario. This wasn't like a dream."

"OK, Dad. I believe you." I really did.

"Don't tell your mother about this one. She worries about these things. She'll think it's a birth or a death on the way. God knows we don't need either right now." We turned to leave, but he stopped a moment. He looked back over the awning, into the darkening sky, as if he were looking for a sign—from God, or maybe from his father again.

My father told me to drive the Ford, even though I didn't have a license yet. I stalled out a few times and bucked it really hard before I could get the hang of the clutch and the gears.

"It's that damn music your generation listens to," he muttered. "It has no rhythm. You kids would be coordinated if you danced a waltz or the fox trot or the Peabody once in a while. Forget that noise you hear today. Won't last. Now drive."

We drove down Broad toward the Harmonia Bank to deposit the day's earnings. Christmas lights and decorations flashed on stores and utility poles. A Salvation Army man and woman rang their bells for donations.

"Hit the horn!" my father yelled suddenly. "There's Fletcher and Hampton, the colored boys from Magnolia Avenue." He waved to them, rolled down the window, and yelled, "Hey fellas! See you this Saturday!"

"Hey Vinnie!" they yelled back, smiling broadly and waving.

"Those boys work hard for me on weekends, Mario," he said. "I gotta remember to bring a box of Argo starch for Hampton. He likes to chew on the stuff when he works. Those boys respect me. They know I pull no punches and I treat them right like decent human beings. But they know how I feel. We gotta stay on our own side of the fence. They're happier with their own kind, too. Like us Sicilians."

"But, Dad, isn't that the same thing the Irish always said about the Italians?"

"Mario, don't confuse the issue—I want you to have your own opinions, which I will respect when you've had as much worldly experience as I have. But listen to me, I've been around the block and it's not the same. It's just not."

He told me to stop at the Villa Roma so we could say hello to Frankie, his boyhood friend. That meant my father wanted a drink. Inside there were only a few people at the bar and the juke box was playing *I've got the World on a String* by Frank Sinatra. My father had two shots of whiskey and I had a Coke.

He hummed along with Frank Sinatra and tapped on the counter, then said, "SilkTones oughta do a version of this song. This rock stuff will never last. Mark my words."

Frank said, "Vincent, is this your oldest son? He's gonna be taller than you."

"Yeah," said my father, "but he'll never be able to take my place, he knows that, all my sons know that. I raise 'em right. Mario's gonna take after his grandfather." He told Frankie how smart I was and how I would probably be at least a doctor. Then Frank got busy and my father told me again how my grandfather sold hay, oats, and coal. He said my grandfather had told stories, too, good ones, and wrote poems and songs.

I knew that talking about his father made him feel good. The time had come to ask him about Greenwood Lake.

"Dad?" He looked straight at me. What came out of my mouth was, "Can I give you a hand at the stand again tomorrow?"

He broke into smiles, "Sure, Mario, that'd be nice." He turned away and continued to talk to Frank, who put another shot in front of him. If he said no, nothing, not the Pope, not my mother, not a shot of whisky could reverse it.

"Dad?" He turned to me again. His face gave me no hint which way he'd go. "You're right. I'm not gonna change my name."

"Say it, Mario, say it"

I didn't want to blow my luck, so I said it. "My name is Mario Anthony Donitella."

"Say it again," he ordered fiercely. I said it as loud as I could. Frank turned around and clapped and said, "Good for you."

27

My father grabbed me in a bear hug and said, "Don't think you'll ever be too old or too big, or too smart for me to hug or rap. I raised you right. I don't have to worry. You'll be like your grandfather." Who sold hay, oats, and coal.

I drove home without stalling once. My father said it was because I had just been listening to Frank Sinatra.

That evening he told a story. It was *Four Directions*: I kicked myself for putting Greenwood Lake on hold. Once again my father's pride was louder than my music.

When the First People arrived in Sicily, they believed that this was the hidden Garden of Paradise. They all arrived by the great water highway that surrounded Sicily. Many and diverse were the tribes who trod this island. For every major civilization from Four Directions was drawn to the mysterious beauty of Sicily, the island in the sea of blue. The Greeks and Phoenicians brought their high civilization, their temples, their astuteness. The Romans their enjoyment of sensual pleasures. There were visitors from the lands of the cold arctic regions and from the warm, sunny places. The Serbs, Saracens, Huns, Moors, French, even the Jews, the Goths, Barbarians, all of them, this island was a magnet for them. Thus did people from all lands mingle dark and light flesh and blood. There were fair and dark-skinned people, those with eyes as blue as the sea, as green as the prickly pear cactus pads, or as dark as olives. There was hair as golden as semolina and honey and as dark and shiny as a roasted chestnut or eggplant. From the northern tribes came your intellect and courage. From the southern tribes came your sensuality and love of life, from the east came wisdom and great artistic notions. And from the western peoples came your stupidity—to round things out.

Sicilians had it in their blood to be or do anything they wanted, my father said. And so, on that evening, I learned that no matter how poor we were, how humble the blood in my veins, how simple my beginnings, I, bearer of my grandfather's name and my father's stories, could be anything that I wanted.

Anything. Except better than my father.

Back when a prayer and a song and a hymn and a story were one and the same and when Sicily was still known as Zizily, the Siciliani knew how to throw a feast with all their body and soul. They knew how to lay down their tools and rolling pins and leave servile labor for another day. They celebrated the harvests of the three branches of life—the grape, olive, and wheat. For the grape harvest they mixed warm blood of the lamb with the first vintage of the season. For the olive picking, a live serpent was entwined around a branch to guard against bad fruit. And for the wheat harvest, the peasants danced the tarantella wearing blindfolds in honor of the great Santa Lucia.

Patron saints presided over each of these and every season saw a feast of huge proportions to celebrate the abundance of such a good life.

There were feasts for St. Joseph, St. Philip, St. Rosalia, St. Lucia, and many others. There was great fanfare for all. The saints were brought to life with floats decked with frills and crosses and statues of pure gold of the Madonna, and Jesus of Nazarene, for whom Rena was named. St. Rosalia's bones were carried through the streets, for she had been a Norman principessa, patron saint of Palermo, who had run to the Monte Pellegrino to live in a cave outside of Palermo. This cave became a shrine and miracles are still performed there. These were the days when Sicilians honored the ancient rhythm and beat of their soul. There was singing and dancing and prayers of thanks. The streets were filled with brightly painted red, green, and yellow carrette, pulled by handsome donkeys, who danced on their hind legs when no one was looking.

The Sicilians would eat and eat at a typical feast. There was rabbit or hen fattened with bread stuffing. They had fat chickens basted with garlic and olive oil, and if they were lucky, braciola stuffed with prosciuttu and hard-cooked egg. There were cardoons dipped in egg and herb-flavored bread crumbs and fried in bubbling olive oil, artichokes stuffed with Parmigiano and fresh herbs. There *was finocchio, fresh crisp strips between every course. And there was plenty of biscot' scented with the sweet anise that grew everywhere and almonds grown in their fertile fields. And, on very special occasions, there was cannoli.*

One of their favorite feast days was for Santa Lucia, for whom Lucy was named. Lucia had been a woman with beauty of classic proportions. Everyone in her village of Siracusa said she had the most beautiful eyes. Her eyes were so beautiful they lit up the night when there was no moon, and no torch was needed in the dark streets. Her eyes were big and blue as the Mediterranean. Here's how she became a saint: when a passing sailor flirted with her, she gouged out her eyes, to guard against a sin of impurity and to avow her love for God and God only, whom she could not see, but her faith was grand. Rest assured this worked. She was canonized a saint when she died.

Even before she performed her first miracle she was a saint! Her feast was celebrated from the year 283 A.D. by villagers in her hometown. At that time famine struck Siracusa. The people went to the Duomo and asked the Archbishop to invoke the aid of Santa Lucia. Santa Lucia! the Archbishop had only to raise his arms to heaven. No sooner had he done this when suddenly, lo and behold, three ships filled with wheat pulled into port—with no crew! (In later years some cynics said that the early Mafia had killed the crew.)

The news of the miracle spread to all of Sicily. And in Lucy's honor, to this very day, we Sicilians eat la cuccìa, the ceci beans cooked with whole wheat berries, bathed in warm milk, honey, and cinnamon. You kids love it.

Consider Saint Lucy's solution. Had she only known *Blue Moon!*

As Saint Lucy of Siracusa, my patron saint of light and sight, I held my eyes in the palms of my hands. Like my father's mother, Lucia Donitella, I was named for this astonishing woman.

In the St. Mary's All Saints' Day play I used two black olives to symbolize my eyes yanked from my head. I closed my eyes so everyone thought they saw only the empty craters. I held my eyeballs in my hands and I heard the sounds of disgust. But I honored my namesake. I held my laugh.

I've feared in darkness like Saint Lucy. The first year we lived in Rahway I had rabid nightmares. Wild fears! But I kept them to myself. I was the oldest girl named for a woman of such courage, honor, and strength. I was ashamed to talk of the shadows. For I knew I had to be a model—a patron saint—for my younger brothers and sisters. Mario, my older brother, would have made fun of me. Our father taught him to make fun of his own fears.

I saw the shadows, big and menacing, coming toward me as I climbed the stairs to my room alone at night. I took some comfort in sharing my bed with my sisters, Rena and Maddelena. But their sleeping bodies were too still. Besides, sleepers are prey to all sorts of wild things!

When I was told to fetch canned tomatoes in the cellar I saw the shadows and I imagined the figures that cast them. They came out of the dark opening behind the staircase to grab me. When I passed the wall where my father meted out punishment, I heard the crack of his belt. I blessed myself hurriedly. Three times! I had night sweats and whole nights where I slept not a wink. I heard the hangers in our closet jingle. The shadow again. I shut my eyes tight, so I wouldn't see what was going to come out of the closet and get me.

I considered Saint Lucy's solution. If I couldn't see it, it couldn't get me—not sin, not demons, not my own desires, not my own fears. But then even without eyeballs I'd still hear the creaks and footfalls, the brushing of the shadows, the rustle, the static of the night moving about me. I pressed the pillow over my ears. Sometimes I thought the stealing figure was my father. He had had enough of us and the striving Father Herman told him it was necessary to make ends meet. I was sure he was coming upstairs to do away with us, one by one, me first.

I tried everything: praying to God Himself, entreating Mary, my mother's intermediary. I talked to Rena's and Maddelena's patron saints, to all the saints on our vanity and throughout our entire house. St. Jude, St. George, St. Anthony, please! And then after I entreated everybody in heaven to save me from the horror in the dark that was going to rip out my heart, my eyes, my ears, and all my bones, I found my own solution. If it hadn't been for what Mario had taught me the year he was exiled from his music, I might not have found it.

Poor Mario. He taught me to sing when he was not allowed to. He found a way, like the slaves cut off from their drums found that their feet could beat out rhythm. Mario was kept from his music—a whole year!—after he snuck off to Greenwood Lake. How could he have forgotten? Our father read every printed word in the newspapers. It would have been so great that the SilkTones made the entertainment section of the *Star Ledger*—if only Dad hadn't thought Mario was at a local party that Christmas Eve. Going to the wall was the least of Mario's pain. No band practice for a whole year! It nearly destroyed him.

But the piano couldn't talk and the rest of us wouldn't. We all protected Mario's secret when my father was out. Mario would help me baby-sit. He played the piano and Vinnie, Frankie, or Carmine kept watch for my parents' return. Mario let me accompany him and taught me and the kids to sing *Blue Moon*. We even worked out a little back-phrasing, a little stylizing.

This was my solution when the shadows came. I started to sing my part in *Blue Moon*, low and to myself, over and over. And in so doing, all the faces of my younger brothers and sisters singing their parts passed before me and I heard them singing their harmony. It was perfect. We pooled all our awful sharps and awful flats and in-betweens and they came out full and perfect. We were like Seraphim Angels in a heavenly choir.

And so I came to believe in my brothers and sisters above all else, in all these children my mother bore. I wanted her to have more and more children even though we could barely afford those we had. We could barely pay the food bill after each week's shopping, after we had paid for the five-pound tins of peanut butter, three-pound cans of coffee, 10-pound bags of flour and sugar, the 20 pounds of this, 15 pounds of that. But one more mouth to feed also meant one more mouth to sing. And I knew God would protect me from the horrible things lurking in the dark. I knew that God would not punish my brothers and sisters by hurting me. I sang *Blue Moon* every night after I said my prayers. When God tested me with fear, I relaxed and hummed. And my fear of the dark diminished, thanks to our song.

I don't know what took me so long to find this solution. I didn't add *Blue Moon* to my prayers until three years and two babies—Maria and Teresa—after we had moved to Rahway. Mario had been allowed to resume the band. There was more chaos than usual.

There had been a death in the family, Lou Cataline, one of Mom's or Dad's fourth or fifth cousins. Perhaps a blood tie, perhaps not. Lou had passed away suddenly from a heart attack. He was only 51, but my father said he died because he kept too much in and his wife let too much out—she was *chiacchiaruna*, a chatterbox. That's what really killed him, my father said.

It was a Friday night and Mario's band, the SilkTones, was coming over for practice after supper. Mom and Dad rushed around so they could go to the wake and view the body at Cardoni's Funeral Home in Peterstown. They were excited about getting out alone. Last time they took all nine of us kids to a viewing at Cardoni's was for our Great Uncle Sal. Carmine had tried to touch the body and the babies, Maria and Teresa, both started wailing, trying to outdo Aunt Marietta. Then Rena, who had stared at the black iron eagle over the red-velvet-papered doorway, began to scream that the eagle was trying to get her. My father's sisters and aunts had to calm her down.

So Mario and I would baby-sit. I was glad for my parents' chance to get out and see their people. The widow would serve sandwiches, cake, cookies, and coffee at her home after the wake. But Mom and Dad would sit and eat with us children first.

It was my job to gather up my brothers and sisters so my father could tell a story before we ate. I called Mario in his room. He said he would be down as soon as he finished a logarithm. I looked out back, where I knew I'd find Vinnie and Frankie. They were restricted to the backyard for the whole summer. They were late for supper a week before, a grievous offense. They had gone to Squire Island Park with Kenny and Eddy. They took the path back deep to where the brush was thick by the riverside, where the earth and water smelled so sweet in the summer, where Joe and I went to see the wild irises. Surely the big boys must have been there skinny dipping, swinging from the loose branch of an oak. Vinnie and Frankie had forgotten time and all manner of law and order that guided their life. The days had just begun to lengthen. It was about 8 p.m. when they noticed it was pretty dark. I wondered what could have happened—nobody ever forgot my father's number one rule, to be home on time for supper. Vinnie and Frankie must have run home, the whole ten blocks together. They came through the door flushed, panting, and happy, as if the outdoors, their red cheeks, the tadpole in the bucket would redeem them from what they must have known was coming.

They were greeted coldly in the empty parlor by my father, the Sacred Heart and his own portrait hovering above them.

A simple question first: "Where were you two?" My father gave them one chance to explain. He always did that. The rest of us waited in the kitchen, food in our mouths not going anywhere. We had tried to stall dinner for them.

"Fishing," came a small voice from so far away, I wondered if they were really there.

"Down the cellar," my father said with the kind of quiet that comes before a storm.

Vinnie didn't say a word. Only Frankie pleaded for mercy, which was worse, because it meant he needed extra beating to toughen him up so he wouldn't have to beg in the future. How many screams? How many lashes? Who kept count? One would have done the job of many. He left them there without supper. Down the cellar against the wall, the one within a few feet of Mrs. Lear's windows. It got real quiet. I imagined their bodies, lifeless, oozing blood.

My mother murmured over and over about the screams. "The neighbors, the neighbors." We knew she meant Mrs. Lear. My father left them and came back to his food. He ate no more. He went to his bedroom. It was so quiet you could hear dry mouths trying to swallow.

Nonnie grabbed the broom and started sweeping the kitchen floor. My mother and I did the dishes. Everyone else went to bed, bathed or not.

But I couldn't sleep. About 10 p.m. I saw that Maddelena was fingering the bedspread and Rena was wide awake.

"Come with me," I whispered to them. We crossed the hall to the boys' dormer and saw that Frankie's and Vinnie's bed had not been slept in. We tiptoed downstairs to the kitchen to look for their bodies. I tripped over something in the parlor—it was the bucket with the tadpole. I heard it swish.

I took bread from the bread box. I groped in the dark for the long screwdriver, which, sunk into the right place, would open the broken refrigerator door. I found some *capocollo*. I told the girls to grab mustard and a butter knife. The light from the refrigerator showed the way. We brought the food down the cellar quietly. We found Vinnie and Frankie wide awake lying on a blanket, playing Knuckles with a deck of cards. They smelled like fish. They were both bloody—but just their knuckles. They had inflicted the only visible wounds on themselves with the deck of playing cards.

I gave them food to eat. They acted flip, as if they were not very hungry.

"Here's your tadpole, too." I handed them the half-formed creature. They giggled and could hardly contain themselves.

"Shhhh," I said sternly, "You'll get us all in trouble. Don't be late anymore. Just be quiet and eat."

"You sound like Nonnie," said Frankie, "That's all she knows how to say." He gobbled down the sandwich and so did Vinnie. They fed some crumbs to the tadpole. The girls and I crept back to our room. I thought I glimpsed a shadow of someone for a second. But perhaps it was only Nonnie, praying in front of her votive candle.

Vinnie made the most of the restriction and transformed the yard into a stage where he performed for Frankie, Rena, Maria, and Teresa. They loved his disappearing finger trick. Appearing to cut his fingers off, he'd make them disappear and then magically reattach them, a trick that impressed the little children.

"How did you do that, Vinnie?" Rena asked.

"Tell us!" said Maria and Teresa. "Where's the blood?"

"A true magician never ever explains his tricks," Vinnie smiled.

"Do giant-midget," begged Maria and Teresa.

Vinnie walked around on his wooden stilts that Carmine had made for him, with a long coat on. Then, with the coat on still, he slid around on his knees, stuck into shoes too big for him. He had salvaged the costumes from a bin in the cellar where my mother stored all the used clothing neighbors gave to us. Vinnie could enjoy himself entertaining the little kids all summer long like this. He taught them to dance. He seemed always to come up with new tricks and jokes for them. From behind a sheet or old bedspread hung over the clothesline he would come on stage, announcing, "Ladies and gentlemen and children of all ages, introducing the greatest show on Earth and even Creek Street, Amazing Vinnie!"

"C'mon Vinnie, wrap up the greatest show on Earth," I yelled as soon as one of his acts was over. "C'mon Frankie, Rena, put on Maria's and Teresa's shoes and bring them in. Everybody into the parlor. Story time. Where's Carmine and Maddelena?" Just as I asked I saw them off in a far corner of the yard by the Krauses' side. As I got closer to them I saw that Carmine had his strongbox of gadgets—magnets, magnifying glasses, and compasses.

"I can set your hair on fire with this," Carmine said, shining the glass on Maddelena's hair.

"Carmine! Cut that out!" I yelled, pulling his hand with the glass down. I sent Maddelena inside.

"Carmine, what the hell were you doing!?"

"I'm telling you said a bad word, Lucy."

"I said...Don't sass me, young man!"

He looked up at me, his thick black-rimmed glasses sliding down his too-small nose.

"I'm trapping heat and light. What do you think I'm doing?"

"Well, if I catch you doing it again on someone's hair I'll beat you to a bloody pulp, you hear me? And then I'll tell you-know-who and you'll be taken you-know-where."

He looked down sheepishly and muttered, "What's a bloody pope? A martyr or something, huh?" He stared at the long gangly contraption he had been assembling forever. It was made from old utensils and gadgets from our kitchen junk drawer and he had set it up on an old pastry board, so he could transport it without having to disassemble it.

"Carmine, what is this thing you're making?"

"Just be patient, you'll know someday," he said.

"Well hurry and finish up for now. Your father's waiting to tell a story."

"It's a music trap."

He had rigged grass, string, twisted scraps of paper to act as wicks for a flame sparked with his magnifying glass. The winds of fire would rock a little dollhouse-size metal pot of water. The water tumbled down into another basin. A ribbon of rope would pull on the knob of a bunsen burner. The burner would heat water until it turned to steam and the steam would activate the crude music box, one that Carmine had ripped out of the bottom of an old liqueur bottle. The song was the *The Anniversary Song*. Carmine called this invention his music trap. It rarely worked, but it absorbed untold quantities of his energy, time, and concentration. And perhaps someday he would perfect it.

"C'mon, Carmine," I said, "I don't know why you think that music is something you trap. Inside on the double. Or else."

"Rats," he muttered as he doused the flame that had just begun to kindle.

Dad said Mom and I could be excused from the parlor where he told the story of the *Men and Women of Agrigento* to everyone else. We could keep an eye on the pizza dough as it rose and listen to him from the kitchen while we prepared the supper.

The most beautiful villages to grow on the island of Sicily were in the mountains, a couple hundred miles from the the Conca d'Oro, the golden hills outside of Palermo, in the Province called Agrigento. There were two villages particularly stunning: San Giovanni-Gemini and Cammarata.

Leaven is so fragile, yet so necessary, my mother explained to me. Without it all chaos reigns. Proofing the yeast for our pizza that night was tricky, because a thunderstorm was brewing. On the one hand, the storm winds might make the yeast lazy, my mother said. On the other hand, the steamy air could make it *pazzo* and overactive. My mother tested the temperature of the proofing water on the inside of her wrist, where she tested the milk for babies' bottles. We added a little extra salt to the pile of flour to inhibit runaway growth, my mother said. Salt was good discipline for the yeast. Salt helped the yeast balance itself between death and life. But the most important ingredient was faith. If all else failed, she said, all we had to do was believe in the yeast and it would rise up, like Lazarus from the dead. As we waited in silence for the dissolved cake of yeast to bubble and foam, we fanned ourselves and wiped our sweat. And listened.

Here in these two villages, more so than in the rest of Sicily, life was rooted in the land, its seasons and cycles of hot and cold. The men, women, and children knew lives of splendid health. Their hearts beat in time with the earth's own heartbeat. For they ate what the land they stood upon offered. The earth pumped its very lifeblood through their veins and there was great fruitfulness for many, many years. Songs and prayers and wonderful stories and words of deep power fell from everybody's lips. And there was peace all around.

And everybody knew his and her place.

The yeast smelled like wine, so I knew it was growing and my faith was good. I said three aspirations to myself to Jesus and Mary for having said "hell" and losing my patience with Carmine. Mom chopped onions and fried them in olive oil, added the puree and seasonings, and stirred the pot with her long wooden spoon. The house smelled good even though it was like being inside a hot shower. I lined up the oil, oregano, and Parmigiano on the counter. Mom grated the mozzarella. The dough took only 45 minutes to double in volume and droop over the bowl like a roll of soft flesh, my mother's midriff after our last baby. I punched the dough down and kneaded it again. It took all my might and I perspired, but I loved watching the dough shrink and swell like magic and grow into food enough to feed us all.

The men bent over the land and tilled it with their hands. The scent of manure stuck in their nostrils through the day. They stomped the grape for its sweet juice and fermented it in oak barrels that they built. They pressed golden oil from the olive and used it for sustenance and healing. They brought farm to table and the family rejoiced in prayers that lasted a long moment through bowed heads each evening.

God was good.

The women toiled hard, too, between the gray stone walls. They peeled the pomodoro, the precious apple of gold. They strained its bitter seeds and mixed and pounded the pulp for hours in the sun until it was a rich blood-red paste. They took the ground wheat, the staff of life, mixed it with water and leavening and kneaded the dough with all their might. They raised the bread to heaven, blessed it with a few sacramental drops of olive oil. The women made sure the bread always remained right-side up. Upside-down bread was sacrilegious.

The men pinched the cheeks of the children to make sure they were well fed. The women said rosary every day.

When they were aged and nearer to death they bowed before the altars at every corner and bend in the village. They pressed their palms together over their chests, shook them at heaven, and asked God for a little more, for the little ones.

Mom and I broke the dough in ten rounds and set them aside. We oiled the pans, ten of them, 15x18 inches, and stacked them up. I watched my mother stretch and pull the rounds of dough toward the four corners of the pan. I tried to do likewise, but Mom never broke the dough. I made holes and she had to show me how to patch them. I filled one pan to every three of hers. And hers were smooth and perfect.

"Get the *cuppinu*, Lucy," she said, "and ladle the sauce over the pies." While I did this, she sprinkled the Parmigiano and the mozzarella, crumbled the oregano, and sprinkled the olive oil.

We were like the women of the Province of Agrigento. We knew our place. I was in charge of baking the pizzas and taking care of my brothers and sisters.

When the pies were cooked with their fat, thick crust, I cut them with Mom's shears. Everyone brought chairs back into the kitchen, squeezed around our table, and we bowed our heads and said prayers. At last we ate. I cut two slices of pizza into little strips for Maria and Teresa. I removed the crust from Nonnie's pizza altogether. Maria sat on my lap and Teresa sat in the high chair.

There was a brief period of calm as we ate and just as we were done a wind blew through the kitchen. We had two pies left over, enough for next morning's breakfast. As my mother and father were trying to get out the door, Nonnie helped me clean.

To get out the door or even to the next room, my mother had always to negotiate a maze of questions, baby feedings, bathing, and diaper changes. She had learned to meet her needs in the margins of others' lives. She nursed Teresa, put her breast away, then handed the baby to me. She took a quick shower. Standing in her slip in the torpor of the summer heat she remarked to Rena, "You're buttoned all wrong. Come here." She unbuttoned and re-buttoned Rena's pajama tops to her bottoms. She took out half her rollers and Maddelena came by. A safety pin slid from my mother's mouth. She secured a big fold in Maddelena's second-hand pajama bottoms at the waist so they would stay up. She removed the rest of her rollers, then found a moment to be alone with herself in the bathroom mirror. But Frankie called to her. "Ma, I can't get the TV to work." He sat six inches from the black and white scramble of horizontal lines on the screen. Brushing her hair out, she yelled back, "Frankie, it hasn't worked for two weeks and every night for two weeks one of you has sat in front of it and played with the buttons and knobs."

"That's because all week the Hunchback has been on *Million Dollar Movie* and all we can do is listen to the words. Can't see the Quasimoto."

"I gotta call a repair man," she replied through lips held taut to apply her red lipstick. She dunked a dirty diaper in and out of the toilet with one hand, opening the diaper pail with the other.

"When?" pressed Frankie, making the now-vertical lines go even crazier.

"When your father draws his next paycheck."

"That's what you say about everything."

She washed her hands and let Frankie, as she did everyone else, have the last word.

She called to me, "Lucy, come fix the back of my hair and spray it—it'll never keep in this humidity."

As I fixed her pageboy, our bathroom light flickered off and on quickly and hot flashes of lightning spilled in through the window. We could hear distant rumbles and rolls and the wind wildly rustling the top of the mulberry tree right outside our back door.

My mother whispered to my face in the mirror, "Wait until we're gone to phone your boyfriend." My father strolled by, fixing his tie knot. "Five minutes if you use the phone," he said raising five outspread fingers. "That's my orders. Don't forget it." My father could not understand talking to someone whose face and hands were hidden from his sight.

"Yes, Dad," I answered. "I'll try," I said to myself.

At last my father and mother were dressed in black and all ready to walk out the door. They moved from room to room, making sure they kissed all nine of us, because every good-bye could be a person's last. Dana had just come over to help me babysit. They hugged and kissed her, too, and told her to help herself to anything in the refrigerator. Make her eat, they told me.

Mario came out of his room and my father told him not to play his music too loud after 10 p.m. or Mrs. Lear would complain to the cops.

They found Nonnie settled down in her room.

" 'Ssa bbenedica," they said to her.

"Santi," she replied as she rocked in her chair.

My father lined up all nine of us and reminded the younger kids that Mario and I were in charge. He wanted no reports of squabbles.

"Yes, Dad," they all answered.

My father was the salt that disciplined the yeast. As soon as he was gone, Vinnie put some old, scratchy 45s on the Hi-Fi. Frankie volunteered to feed Dana. He brought out a tray of still-warm pizza. He dug the screwdriver into the refrigerator door, then let the door swing back and bang into the kitchen cabinets. He pulled out cheese, roasted peppers, olives, leftover tomato salad, and meatballs.

"No meat!" I screamed at him, "Dana observes Friday fast with us."

He started to fix himself a sandwich as if he hadn't just eaten. "Frankie, you little *porchetta*, you ate more pizza than anyone else!"

"I'm hungry again," he told me, dipping his cheese between a folded slice of sesame covered bread into the oil and vinegar of the tomato salad. He was dripping all over the floor.

Carmine opened a piece of Bazooka bubble gum and chewed fast and hard. He read the comic to Frankie and Rena between big chews. He filled a glass with scalding hot tap water and stood on the counter top to bring down the sugar bowl. When he was done chewing, he put the gum in the hot water, then rolled it in the sugar and passed the gum to Frankie, who chewed it until the sugar was gone, repeated the procedure and passed it to Rena. Rena passed it to Maddelena next and then it went back to Carmine. Vinnie asked to be included on the next round.

I should have scolded them for the mess they were making, but I was on the phone with Joe, counting the minutes between small talk. I wanted him to come over and join the party. He wanted to know if we could have a room to ourselves.

The doorbell rang. Mario, wearing his pink high roll shirt, tapered black pants, and spit-shined black shoes, ran down from his room again to open the front door for Barry, Jack, and Tony. His slide ruler was still in his hand, beating his thigh. He only put down his slide ruler to play piano, the old black upright that his godfather, Johnny Biondi, gave us. Johnny was a bachelor musician who traveled around the U.S. and the world in a bus with other musicians.

Twelve minutes had passed. Joe said he wouldn't come over unless we could be alone. I told him it would be easier to thread a needle behind my back in the dark.

Dana held Teresa, her teething spittle softening a crust of pizza to a shapeless mass all over Dana's shoulder. "Maria, you're making a mess," she said, patting her affectionately. "That one's Teresa!" I said, covering the phone. Vinnie walked around on stilts in the parlor, where he knew he was not supposed to go, entertaining whoever walked by.

I spotted a couple of pomegranates in a bowl on top of the refrigerator and all the commotion made me think I should eat something, too. I held the phone between my head and shoulder and tore into a deep wine-colored one. The color indicated the sweetness of the nectar, my father said. Carmine, who was waiting for the bubble gum to come his way again, started in on the other pomegranate. Suddenly everybody wanted a Chinese apple, so we passed them around, each grabbing a packet of the ruby seeds. I tore my quadrant and handed the fruit's tattered coat to my brothers and sisters.

I told Joe my time was up, and I hung up. And I stood there with everyone else, crushing seeds against the roof of my mouth, relishing the sweet-tart nectar slithering down my gullet. Juicy red pulp squirts and dribbles decorated Maria's and Teresa's faces. Dislodged rubies lay on the floor or clung to kitchen cabinets or to children's cheeks. Carmine shot his seeds from his mouth like pellets, machine-gun style at Frankie.

"Look at this mess! *Madonna*,'" I screamed. I was about to grab Carmine by the collar when a bolt of deafening music shot through the house like an electrical current. Even Nonnie jumped out of her old withered skin.

"*Chi ffù?!*" I heard her shaky voice, shrill and pushed to its limit, and then her shuffling black shoes moving toward the bedroom door. Her unbraided head appeared from the dark. The jolt was from the cellar. Mario and his band had been setting up their instruments. Barry had hooked his electric bass guitar up to the amplifier and plucked a few runaway chords.

"*Va beni, non ti prioccupari, Nonnie, pensa a saluti.*" I told her not to worry about anything but her own health. I only said that because I had heard my mother say it to her often. My comfort, the music, was about to drown out my torment, the chaos over which I had no control.

Jack hit a roll on his drums, Tony blew the dust out of his sax, and Mario ran up and down the keys. They warmed up on *Sunday Kind of Love* and then *Splish Splash*, and *Sincerely*. They all sang. They played a honky tonk number. Dana gave Teresa to Carmine and showed Rena and Maddelena how to dance the jitterbug. Vinnie came down off his stilts and danced with her, too. We all tried to get Carmine to dance with Dana, but he was as stiff as a pastry board.

As the night wore on the two youngest, Maria and Teresa, started to get whiney. We couldn't get them to sleep. So I brought all the kids down the cellar and asked Mario if we could do *Blue Moon*.

"It'll help me get the two babies to sleep, Mario," I said.

We went over the arrangement. On cue, Vinnie, Carmine, and Frankie would sing "Blue, blue, blue, blue moon" or the "dip de dip de dip de dip." Maddelena, Rena, Maria, and Teresa, whom I held, would do the "bom-boms." Dana and I sang the "rama-dama ding dongs." Mario sang low, Tony sang middle, and Barry sang high.

We practiced parts, then Mario said, "A one and a two and a three, hit it!" A few seconds into the first try Mario stopped and said, "Whoa, wait a minute."

"What's wrong?" I asked.

"Who's saying 'new moon?'" asked Mario.

"Not me," said Frankie, "Must've been Carmine or Vinnie."

"Wasn't me," said Carmine, glaring at Frankie.

"Not me," said Vinnie.

"OK, again from the top," said Mario.

This time we sang a few more bars and Mario stopped again and yelled, "Vinnie!"

"What?" said Vinnie.

"It's you! I heard you! It's BLUE, not NEW. BLUE, BLUE, BLUE, for crying out loud! OK, again from the top."

"E-nunciate," said Frankie.

This time we all got it right. We all sang our parts right on time, even little Teresa got her bom-boms right. Nonnie came halfway down the cellar steps, sat down, and listened to us, a feeble smile igniting her wrinkled face. Just as we were about to go a second round, a fuse blew in the cellar and the lights and amp went out. We continued to sing in the dark with no accompaniment. I wish I could say that the evening ended on that harmonious note. But life is not a Million Dollar Movie, as my mother would say. I had two crying babies to coax to sleep with bottled milk. And a mess from ceiling to floor to clean up before my parents returned home.

Mario, Barry, Tony, and Jack took a break and made sandwiches. Nonnie sat in the chair in her room again. Maddelena and Rena slipped under her long skirt and tickled her ankles as they often did, until she cackled at them and they ran away giggling. I needed help, but I didn't want to bother Mario—his music was his number one passion. I asked my younger brothers to help me.

"Carmine," I implored, "please put Maria or Teresa in the crib. Vinnie, please rock the other one....I'll let you stay up until Mom and Dad get home if you get her to sleep."

We asked Mario if we could borrow some of his 45s to lull the babies.

"OK," he said, "Just don't get one fingerprint on them and watch how you handle them." He brought out the case, which he kept hidden. He spun the lock combination and flipped open the lid. Vinnie and I chose the records from a list and Mario slipped them out of their sleeves carefully and placed them on the Hi-Fi stacker. Vinnie and I agreed on 14 songs and the exact order in which we wanted them played. We started with *Stagger Lee* by Lloyd Price and *Blue Moon* by the Marcels and wound down with numbers like *Daddy's Home* by Shep and the Limelites, *Hushabye* by the Mystics, and *Gloria* by the Passions.

Dana and I began to clean up the pomegranate seeds in the kitchen. I was consoled when I heard Maria's soft coos as she dropped onto Vinnie's shoulder. Carmine tried to quiet Teresa down. He laid her in the crib and fixed the mobile that he had made for her so that she could hit it with her hands. Her night light was broken, so Carmine placed a table lamp with no shade near the crib. The light from below cast huge shadows on the ceiling.

Dana and I found pomegranate seeds everywhere, as well as oil and vinegar, stray crusts of pizza, and bubble gum stuck to the table. Frankie started to tease Rena, Rena punched him and ran away. Frankie chased her upstairs, downstairs, and into the bathroom. Rena slammed the door shut just as Frankie was kicking it. His foot went right through the door. The bedlam reached its crescendo with Vinnie screaming at the top of his lungs for help. He was outdone only by Nonnie who was also screaming in a hoarse voice that the baby was burning, the baby was burning!

My mother was fond of the Blessed Trinity and of the Rule of Three. We should have foreseen that one hole meant two more were not far behind. The hole in the bathroom door was number one. The hole in the Hi-Fi was number two—Vinnie had been rocking away to the music and had fallen over backwards, the post of the rocker going right through the cloth cover over the speaker and the needle skipping across *Gloria*. Mario would make us pay for that!

The hole in the mattress was number three. When Carmine had backed silently out of Teresa's room, he'd tripped over the wire and pulled the lamp right under the crib's mattress. The bare bulb began to burn the rubber. Carmine, Dana, and I set Vinnie upright in the rocker, Maria sleeping soundly through the whole thing. We smelled the smoke and understood what Nonnie was saying. Mario was already grabbing Teresa from her burning bed.

A thick mantle of bluish smoke rose up to the room's ceiling. Teresa was still hitting her mobile when Mario picked her up. The smoke was not yet low enough to reach her. But the thick cloud curled quickly out from the gaping black hole on the underside of the mattress.

"Poor baby, who tried to set you on fire!" We passed her out of the room. Then Mario, Dana, and I picked up the mattress and quickly heaved it through the window into the backyard. The rain would smother any more fire. We ran out back to make sure it was far enough away from the house. We all stood there silently, watching the mattress. As a bolt of lightning lit up the yard, I saw the rain dance on the burned spot. The smell was foul, worse than the stench of the plastic and chemical factories on Linden Avenue.

I sat in my mother's rocker with Teresa sleeping in my arms. Dread began to fill me. I went over in my head how to explain the holes to my parents. It had gotten too late and stormy for Barry, Tony, and Jack to leave. They fell asleep on the parlor floor, where it was cooler. I stepped over them and put Teresa in my parents' bed. I climbed the stairs to my bedroom and listened for my parents' return. I thought I heard them. My father said to my mother, "Let's buy a fan."

"Next time you draw a check," replied my mother. They were stepping over sleeping bodies, hundreds of them, all over the bedroom floors and furniture. Some of the bodies were not Donitellas. It didn't faze them. I jumped up and told them to beware of the holes. They told me not to worry, so long as the babies were still alive and kicking. They pinched their cheeks. They kept stepping over bodies, kissing the ones they knew.

Then I saw the shadows.

I lay my head on my pillow. As the shadows danced and teased me, I said my prayers. And then my part in the song rose to my lips and as peace came I wondered, Was it me or St. Lucy in the darkness, humming my part in *Blue Moon*?

Vinnie (1960)

One day after many ages of perfect contentment, a volcano in the southeast corner of Sicily, where the Greeks and Phoenicians had settled, began to rumble. The island shook and quivered as deep in the Earth, steam and molten rock churned and longed to escape.

Rocks rolled, people fell.

The huge eruption came and the pent-up heat spewed angrily from Earth's bowels. And something changed. The people of the island were never the same again. It was as if something that had been asleep for eons had been awakened and brought to the surface. Something stirred deep in everybody. They couldn't put their finger on it. The peasants never felt satisfaction again with their simple lives. Discontent had reared its head in the Garden of Paradise. Civilization had begun to advance in leaps and bounds elsewhere in the world and even on the boot, the Land of Italy.

The island of Sicily, once the crossroads of the world, began to sense its isolation and its life-giving fruits were no longer enough for many people. And they began to leave their land. Still, some thought that life had always been a mixed blessing like the fico d'India, the prickly pear that covered the hillsides. Its rose blush color was beautiful, its juice ran like sweet, purple sugo. But it could send torturous prickling stickers under the skin and give a mouthful of seeds so that its sweet flesh could not be savored.

Despite the unrest haunting many Sicilians there were those who still lived in close harmony with the warm Earth they and their ancestors had turned, furrowed, and plotted over millennia. A few retained the old spirit and were not plagued by gnawing discontent. They still thought no place else on Earth offered a better life. Yes, maybe life could be easier, but certainly not better.

One of these was Gaetano, the old villager in Cammarata in the Province of Agrigento who seemed to have been around forever, who carried his load on his back happily every day and whose rich

Gregorian-like chant filled the dry summer air as he labored under the hammering sun.

"What fools!" he would say to himself, "to think there is a life better than this, where the sun floods the land, kisses the seed that swells with fruit for our bodily and spiritual benefit." Some laughed at his burst of poetry, and others, like the young Mario Anthony Donitella, admired him greatly.

Grabbing two fistfuls of his horse's manure, Gaetano raised them to heaven and shouted, "When I die, I want to be buried in this land. I want to be eaten by the worms of Sicily so the sun can turn me into the food my posterity eats. Amen."

His wife made him wash his hands before blessing the bread at dinner that evening. For all his grandstanding in the fields of his beloved land, Gaetano could not stop his paesani from leaving to pursue what they called the good life. But he could commiserate with his young friend, Mario Anthony Donitella, your grandfather.

"The big things are like volcanoes, they have to happen. It's the little things that annoy me, because they amount to a heap of nothing." I felt a deep sense of relief when I heard my father say these words the Saturday morning after I had fallen backwards into the new Hi-Fi. My father always said this when big things happened and it meant I wouldn't hear the crack of his belt. Falling backwards was as unstoppable as a volcanic eruption.

I was just helping Lucy, rocking my little sister Maria to sleep. There we were. I felt like Mario's metronome. Rocking and ticking. I'm no wise guy like Frankie, but I knew Maria was sound asleep by the middle of *Gloria*. I just couldn't stop rocking. It was the only way to break the rhythm. Knock over the rocker. Holy Jesus, I don't mean to take the Lord's name in vain for nothing, but I was mortified because Dana was there. I was thinking of her as I went down. Ah, it was a little thing. But my butt started to hurt when I saw the hole in the Hi-Fi. Sheesh, the holes in the bathroom door and the baby's mattress were minor in comparison. All I could think of was how many of my father's paychecks had gone to buy that Hi-Fi, so that we could all play our music. Music made up for all the vacations we never got to take, 'cause listening to music was like taking a trip for us. Kinda like my father's stories.

I was awake all night listening for an explosion. I heard my parents return and climb the stairs to Lucy's room, but their voices were soft. Like they were still at a wake. I didn't know what it meant. Next thing I hear Lucy humming all night.

God, why did I have to be the one to wreck it? What a *Giufà*! Well, at least I got to hear all the records on the stack. Before the rocker went out of control, so to speak, I was dreaming again that Dana and I would go on American Bandstand and win the dance contest. Heck, I mean we could dance better than those small town couples we saw every night. On the days our television worked. When I'm a little older Dana will forget Mario and find me more interesting. Don't get me wrong, I love my big brother, Mario, number one son, who will do good by all us younger kids. But he's never paid that girl the attention due her. Dana taught me some hip jitterbug moves that she picked up in New York City. I came up with some fast ones of my own. Pretty darn cool, Dana said. My parents used to be the best dancers before they had us kids, so I thought they'd be proud of me if I won the contest on American Bandstand. They didn't say it, but I could tell they didn't seem to expect me to amount to much else. Just wait til I'm 15 and can take the train to Philly. I'll convince Dana to go with me.

I was the first one up Saturday morning, because I was worried about the Hi-Fi. I was already restricted for the summer. How could I forget to be home on time for supper? *Giufà*. What more could happen?

Barry, Jack, and Tony were sound asleep in their chinos on the red carpet in the parlor. Lucy must've thrown the white sheets over them. Frankie and Rena were sprawled on a blanket. Everyone had a shine. The door and windows were wide open, so air could come through the screens. But the air was still and it was wet and gray outside. The only sound was Barry's breathing, like a low whistle.

I decided to perk the coffee and let it fill the kitchen. I didn't like when you heard more creaks than voices in this house. Noise I was used to and it worried me to hear the wood and brick move and warp. Like it was just another kid waiting its turn to speak up, to be patted on the head. I watched the glass bubble on top of the aluminum coffee pot. As soon as I saw the first perk I turned down the heat. Be extra careful, Vinnie, for today. If you didn't catch it right the pot would boil over, grinds and all, killing the flame. And ol' Grandpa Donitella would have to show up from the dead, I knew about that.

I didn't want to take any chances of messing up again. I went out back to examine the black hole in the mattress. Even though it rained all night it was still smoldering. It was like an internal wound that would take forever to heal, like my father's war wound from the South Pacific, the one that he told us kids should have killed him. Luckily, the laminated photo of my mother in his back pocket deflected the bullet. I saw that the creek was swishing by, brimming with rain. It was on its way to the Rahway River where Frankie, and I caught the tadpole. I would miss fishing the rest of the summer. A brainstorm hit. I found an empty milk bottle on the back porch. I scribbled a note in crayon on a paper bag:

If you find this tadpole, take care of him until

He has legs and no more gills

His name is Og

He's half turtle, and half frog

I liked to write little verses. I heard my Grandpa Donitella was good with words. Maybe I did this one thing better than Mario. Maybe my father would notice one day.

I glanced at Dana's bedroom and thought of yelling in how I loved the Mickey Rooney/Judy Garland step. I took Og out of the slimy red bucket, put him in the milk bottle with the note, and placed the bottle carefully in the water so it didn't sink. I was sorry I had taken the creature in the first place. I watched him float away, hoping the bottle didn't get stuck where the creek widened as it rounded a bend along River Road. A deadend street there across the river had this one dilapidated, peeling red house in the oak trees. Old Lady Kooze lived in it. Old Lady Kooze was related to Old Lady Lear, the kids on Creek Street said. Sisters, no doubt. Old Lady Kooze was so loony she ate nothing but caterpillars, worms, frogs, tadpoles, and kids. Kids had disappeared forever down her street. I seen her at the window when I ran down River Road. She gave me the creeps.

The tadpole reminded me of the beating at the wall. I couldn't bear another beating so soon. It wasn't for myself I worried. It was my father. I overheard him tell my mother how it hurt him more than it hurt us kids when he beat us. "You don't know how I bleed," he had said, "You don't know." I found it unbearable that my father felt worse than I did.

I sank my teeth into a bursting-ripe tomato from the garden and it bled juice and seeds down my arm. I pulled some weeds for my mother from the plot, which was soaked and flattened down with rainwater.

Back inside the coffee was just about to boil over. The aroma aroused everyone. Nonnie moved down the hall and others were shaking sand out of their eyes. Maddelena came down from her room and curled up on the sofa with a blanket and book. Teresa and Maria brought out toys, games, decks of cards. Carmine clomped downstairs on my stilts with a magnifying glass sticking out of his mouth. Kenny, Eddy, little Pauly, John-John, and Kathleen from down the block walked through the front door and waited to be invited to eat something.

My father, Mario, and Mario's three friends sat around the kitchen table drinking coffee. Mario had his slide ruler in one hand and moved it around on the table as he talked. Dana came by in her housecoat, a flowered kerchief around her hair in rollers. I poured her some coffee, but she filled her own coffee mug and yawned. The little kids, including the half-dozen neighbors, trickled into the kitchen to be near the adults. Teresa sat on my father's lap. Frankie asked my mother for a bowl of coffee and milk and Maria chimed in, "Me, too, me too!"

"Not too much coffee, you kids," my father said, sounding pretty happy. "You know what happened to my brother!"

"I forgot, tell us again, Dad!" begged Frankie.

That kid, he was lying, he always asked for too many explanations.

"Once upon a time I had a brother," said my father. "His name was Joe. But Joe loved his coffee. He drank and drank so much cof-

53

fee. He began to get so thin, and then before you could say Toscanini Goobachof, he had vanished into thin air. Poof! No more Joe."

"And to this day," said Mario, "his restless spirit is still floating around the pier down Elizabeth Port slurping up the last drops of coffee left in the bottom of coffee cups. Right Dad?"

"That's right, you kids," said Dad, taking a sip of his own coffee.

"Is that true, Dad?" asked Frankie. "C'mon, Dad, did you really have a brother? Mom, did he?"

"It's the honest-to-God truth, Frankie," said Mario, "You weren't even born, but I remember him. Uncle Joey, we used to call him. Until he disappeared."

Frankie turned his head to look at my father, Mario swung his arm around and tapped Frankie on the shoulder. Frankie turned to see who tapped him. "You feel something, Frankie?" asked Mario. "Maybe it's Uncle Joe's spirit telling you he's here."

"Mario!"

Dana was cracking up, so I chimed in.

"I remember him, too," I said to Frankie.

"Vinnie, if you're lying your tongue will turn black."

"Is it black?" I stuck it out.

"You just drink too much coffee and you'll find out if it's true," said Carmine. "That's the only proof."

"Hon, how about some *sosizza* for these boys?" asked my father.

"Coming up. Lucy, can you feed the baby while I make the sausage and *zeppuli*?"

Oh boy, I loved when there was leftover pizza dough and my mother made doughnuts. She poured the oil in the pot and heated it. She tested it with one dime-size piece of dough. When it sizzled she dropped in handfuls of dough. They sizzled and exploded into doughnuts. She put them on paper bags to drain, then sprinkled them with cinnamon and sugar. They disappeared piping hot.

"Tell your friends not to be so shy. C'mon. Eat all you like. Just sit at the table. No eating in the parlor," my father said.

The neighborhood kids gathered around as soon as they saw my father meant what he said. They didn't have to talk to him, just eat. Their parents never invited crowds into their homes.

"I guess you SilkTones were not too loud last night," my father said to the guys. Then he mumbled something in Sicilian to my mother, which meant "that pigheaded hag next door would have called the cops if they were." Nothing bothered my father worse than creepy old women. But he felt good because he had seen his people in Peterstown. He and my mother gave us a good report on the food at Lou's wife's house—nice pastaciutta, rolls, good cold cuts from Nocera's, sliced thin the way they liked, and Italian cookies and pastry from Bella Palermo.

And then my father said, "Poor Lou... Ah, for crying out loud, though, I guess the big things have to happen, it's the little things drive me nuts."

That was my cue. I knew it meant none of us had to worry about the mattress, bathroom door, or Hi-Fi. I felt so good I was about to ask my father if he wanted to see the new step Dana and I worked out last night. But my father was telling Barry, Jack, and Tony how glad he was that they all liked playing music. He himself used to play the French horn in his day when they had much better music.

"You'll never have the likes of Tommy Dorsey, Benny Goodman, the Mills Brothers, Duke Ellington, Frank Sinatra, Fletcher Henderson. I could go on and on. But this rock and roll stuff, I don't know. I encourage my son to play but he's got to have something to fall back on. He'll be a doctor or something great. He takes after me and his grandfather on my side. His grandfather wrote beautiful poetry. He could do anything."

I tried to remember the little verse I had just sent down the creek.

"Gee, Mr. D., you'll have to come hear us play some time," said Barry.

"Your music won't last. Mark my words. When it's been around as long as my music has, you come and tell me about it."

Dana came into the kitchen with her coffee. I got up to give her my seat, but she squeezed onto the bench next to Mario.

"Mr. D., now tell the truth," said Tony, "Didn't your father say the same thing to you?"

"Oh yes..." my mother started to answer as she threw out the used coffee grounds from the first pot of coffee, which had disappeared into mugs with broken handles, melmac tea cups, bowls.

"I'll answer for myself, thank you," my father said sharply. My mother was silenced.

"My father and I didn't see eye to eye over everything, but now I know he was right about most things. You'll see when you get to be my age, you'll feel the same way."

My mother made a sound like she wanted to comment but held her tongue. She put a tray of last night's cold pizza on the table for everyone to pick on between stacks of hot doughnuts. It disappeared instantly. The kids from down the street got a piece, too, and my mother said something to my father in Sicilian. Then, as John-John grabbed the last slice of pizza, my father said, "Malidizzioni!"

John-John looked stunned.

"What's that mean, Mr. D?" asked Jack.

"I don't know, nobody does," he answered, "just something we always said when the last piece of bread was gone."

Everyone crowded around the cloverleaf table. The noise level in the kitchen picked up. Old Lady Lear couldn't call the cops though, it was too early. I noticed how the table changed shape. Mr. Newman, my friend's father, did a good job building it. Mr. Newman called it a pear shape. My mother called it the shape of the Blessed Trinity. After Father Anthony came for dinner one Friday night and blessed it, she said it was to be treated like an altar. Food only on it.

My mother stood in her housecoat sipping her first cup of coffee while no kids cried for her attention, no arms reached out for her. She peered out at the muggy drizzle spitting and sizzling on the mattress.

"Mrs. Lear's imagination is no doubt running wild," she said softly.

"Who cares?" my father said loudly. *"Minni futtu* I always say."

Minni futtu was his expression for "I don't give a damn." The long-playing version meant "I don't give a damn what the world thinks about Vincent Donitella. Let the ham and eggers go pound salt."

"This is how a true Sicilian feels, *minni futtu*," my father turned and explained to Mario's friends. "I have to teach my sons the right way, the Sicilian way, because aside from my name and my stories that's all I can leave them. When they find a wife, they have to make a Donitella out of her, like I did to my wife. Of course, I would never tell my kids who or when to marry. But maybe their wives will have a little Italian blood or better yet a little Sicilian blood like my wife. My wife knows me. She sticks by her husband right or wrong. To be a man in the family means to have the final word on everything. My sons have to carry on my name. That's why I may be harder on my sons."

"My sons, my sons," said my mother, "What about your daughters?" I was wondering the same.

"Yeah, what about your daughters?" asked Lucy. She was spooning Gerber's baby food into Teresa's mouth. Teresa sat in the high chair, spitting out half of the orange stuff.

"My daughters?" he asked, like he forgot he had five of them.

"My daughters, they're beautiful. What more can a father say?" He picked up Maria and sat her on his lap.

Jack, Barry, and Tony laughed, but my father wasn't trying to be funny.

"Mrs. D." said Jack, "You make the best coffee and pizza in the world. I don't drink much at home, because my mother only makes instant coffee. She can't cook either."

"Everybody says that," smiled Vincent. "My wife! My wife is the best. She can do anything. I keep her on a pedestal. She comes before everything else. She takes good care of me. She has connections with the Blessed Virgin and with God himself. She has dreams like you wouldn't believe. She is psychic. When she dreams about you, you better listen up."

My father dunked some leftover pizza crust into his coffee and swallowed it in one bite. "Up there with God...she's up there with God, my wife," he was almost wailing, swallowing as if he had a lump in his throat. I watched Dana. Her eyes widened when she heard him say this. Maybe I'd talk about her like that someday.

My mother just ignored him and yelled, "Someone turn that loaf of bread over on its right side. It's upside down again! That's a sacrilege!" Nonnie grabbed the bread and raised it to her lips, her rosary beads still wrapped in her hands. She turned it right-side up and said, "*Talé. Va beni.*"

"She keeps things sacred," my father finished.

I ran and got my father his morning newspaper, the *Newark Star Ledger*, from the front porch. I knew this would make him happy.

"Excuse me a minute," he said as he scanned the news. I knew what he was looking for. He wrote the *Ledger* and the *Elizabeth Daily Journal* and told them to publish a story about his grandfather and one about my mother's father. My father's grandfather had been one of only 2,000 Garibaldini, men who fought with Garibaldi to unite Italy.

"People don't realize how many Sicilians fought with Garibaldi," my father went on. "There's a conspiracy to keep Italians from getting their due in American history. But even Jefferson wanted Philip Mazzei to be recognized for his contribution as a statesman. And there was Francis Vigo. He helped Clark in the Northwest. Salvatore Catalano, a distant relative of ours, helped the U.S. Navy raid Barbary pirates in Tripoli in 1804 and was given an award for bravery. Vespucci, Verrazzano, attempts are made all the time to discredit these guys. It's a crime." He flexed the newspaper hard.

When I heard the tone in my father's voice change, I yelled at myself for bringing in the paper. Everyone got silent. My father said he would write the stories himself.

"Me and a few of my friends from the Knights of Columbus." He said he had a former classmate who was half Italian and who worked as a reporter on the *Daily Journal*. My father would ask him to get the stories into print by next July 4. The Italian heroes who needed recognition included Louis Cesnola, a Civil War hero, William Paca, a signer of the Declaration of Independence, Father Eusebio Chino, a founder of Arizona, Sister Blandina, a missionary nun in the Wild West, Henry de Tonti, the Italian father of Arkansas, and so many more. "All you read are the denigrating stories, about the mobsters and the womanizers, I'm telling you boys, Judas Priest..."

Then he went on about how it really bothered him that the French got all the credit for the Statue of Liberty when the statue's architect had Italian roots..

I noticed that Dana had taken out her rollers. Later, when we were alone I would say, "Hey Dana, your hair looks dynamite!" It was too quiet now.

My mother said, "Vincent, why don't you tell the kids a story before you go to work."

He invited Jack, Barry, and Tony to listen to a story before he left. Mario raised his eyebrows and I saw the boys' eyes roll sideways toward him. Mario hesitated a second, then spoke.

"You guys, this is a rare honor. Please stay." Mario rolled his eyes so my father couldn't see and I saw Jack kick Mario and clear his throat.

But they stayed. So did Dana.

My father cleared his throat.

Your grandfather, Mario Anthony Donitella, was born in the mountain village outside of Palermo called Cammarata, in the month of July, a moonchild. His family had come from people who lived in Cammarata for ages. Being born under the strong influence of the moon, Mario had two distinct sides to him. There were those who said it was the blood of light and dark peoples in him, refusing to mix.

He could be very sociable and outgoing and devil-may-care. And then he could be dark and brooding. A genius, some said. His father had died shortly after his birth. So his uncles and the old villagers took care of making a man out of him. Mario impressed the old villagers who admired his silver speech, for he could speak beautifully.

Because he admired his elder countryman Gaetano's use of words so much, Mario secretly wrote poetry. He was romantic and had fantastic dreams. Though he knew he was just a peasant as far back as there were records, he felt a great sense of power. He knew in his Sicilian blood he was destined for some kind of greatness. He did not fret that life was hard. His skin was dark and his pale blue eyes always surprised people. From them came light, as piercing as a glint of sun. People with things to hide could not look him in the eyes for long.

One night some men from a neighboring village invited Mario to dinner. They said they wanted to talk to him about some work. They prepared food such as he had never eaten, but had heard was eaten in the north of his country. There was the sweet white meat of lobster, veal cutlets with lemon and capers, fine-grained bread and wine that tasted like ambrosia. Mario was wary of these men. They urged him to drink more and more wine. But he restrained himself. They offered him the finest cheeses and salamis and pastramis to take home to his mother. He accepted these at first. By the end of the evening, however, it was clear that these were dishonest men who wanted to hurt the peasants in neighboring villages by stealing from them in the name of the law. Mario stood up halfway through the meal and said he was no longer hungry and was leaving.

The men explained, "We are like one big family, Mario. Stay." Another promised, "You and your family will be taken care of for life." The men tried to keep him, but he was strong.

"You are un disgraziatu and I will never dishonor my father's name and his father's name. Go pound salt, you ham and eggers," he said, in Sicilian, of course. He gave them back the salami and cheese and pastrami with a final gesture. Once outside their door he spat on their threshold and then never looked back.

He should have known better than to trust these stinking men. He had been warned about these types by Gaetano. Gaetano told how this group of men had originally been heroic and worthy of the Pope's blessing, how they had done many good things for the Sicilian peasants who had always been stepped upon. But then greed *took hold of them. This happens. They became their own opposite. Now they were ruining Sicily and it was best to watch out for them.*

It was a full-moon evening and the road was well-lit. Mario decided to climb the mountain in Cammarata to a path he knew well since he was very small. There was a beautiful wild olive tree in full bloom, with small white blossoms, spreading its limbs near a spot where he would sit. It was Grandpa's spot. He went there to be alone and meditate, to listen to all the poems and songs in his head that one day he would write down.

The night was clear. He could see almost to the Temples of Agrigento, the relics of his land's past. The full moon gave his muse great energy. The radiant silver light shone down, right on his spot. Normally he couldn't see a thing, but this evening he had the most wonderful long shadow. Grandpa heard a poem in his head:

The stars peer between trees

Weeping dusty tears upon me…

…it started. It was so beautiful he cried…

My father sat still a moment. I knew what I saw in my father. That sadness. But he continued:

The next morning Mario felt a strange restlessness. He had always been so content with his village life in Cammarata, poor as he and his family were. He had watched many of his cumpari *leave his village and the surrounding ones for this place called l'America. Until this morning, he thought they were all foolish. He was of the same mind as his good friend and mentor, Gaetano, also called by some the village imbecile.*

Mario dressed and went to the corner stoop where he knew he would find Gaetano, resting with his cane against the yellow stucco of his home. For Gaetano was too old and infirm to go into the fields and work any longer. Gaetano felt Mario's presence long before the youth reached him. He raised an eyebrow and one eyelid and stared at the boy.

"Chi si dici, giovanottu?" he asked automatically. "What gives?"

"O, nenti….Mi piacissi nanticchia d'anisette. Haiu acitu,"
Some annisette for his heartburn he wanted.

Gaetano fetched some of the licorice-flavored liqueur and asked again what was wrong. He knew there was something, for he knew Mario from birth. But he could wait, he had patience now. By and by Mario began.

"Perhaps there is something to this place they call l'America," *he spoke slowly, "Perhaps…"*

Gaetano stiffened and sat up straight and said more with the look on his face than a thousand words could have said. Something had happened up on the mountain.

Mario knew Gaetano and he knew when he felt betrayed or was disappointed. They did not need a lot of words between them these days. Gaetano was disappointed but he understood.

"So, you have been struck by the thunderbolt, too," *he said with sadness and resignation. He had been about to lash out as he had in his younger days, when he had very little tolerance for opinions or ideas other than his own. But he was wise now and he knew when surrender was called for. He caressed Mario's shiny brown hair with his toughened brown hand and said that whatever Mario decided, he would have his blessing. Even if it broke his heart, he added to himself.*

Mario understood. They embraced and held each other tightly without words for a good long time. Mario ran home to see his mother and tell her they should prepare to find a better life like all the others. She felt they had nothing to lose and even though her son was only a teenager, she knew he was wise beyond his years.

The night before they left their land, so sweet and pure, Mario climbed the mountain of Cammarata, but had trouble finding his spot. Finally, he saw the wild olive tree had been struck by lightning the night before. He could not believe his eyes. For two seconds his heart stopped beating. Then he sat on the ground and wept.

I saw that terrible sadness again. So I jumped to my father's aid.

"Dad, how about if I finish the story so you can get to the stand?"

"G' head, Vinnie, you know how it goes," he said, looking down.

So I said the words quickly, because I knew Fletcher and Hampton were waiting at the stand to be relieved:

When Mario Anthony Donitella arrived in America, he bought a horse and wagon to help him sell hay, oats, and coal. But after several years of being u Carbunaru, he sold his horse and wagon. He learned to read blueprints and helped the American construction workers build. He learned to pour asphalt and pave streets. He worked so very hard just to make ends meet and to help out his other relatives who followed him and with whom he lived in Peterstown. All the time he felt his acida' his itch to do something really great.

But first he had to have a wife. He looked and looked and no one struck his fancy. But then he saw her. It was 1915. He was walking through Peterstown on the corner near Third and Kristyne. He saw the young woman with hair as black as ebony. She was hanging out fresh laundry. She had clothespins in her mouth and she still looked beautiful. He thought she looked half like an angel, half like a gypsy.

"Who are those gypsies?" he asked Mateo, a friend.

"They're the Conforti from Castronovo. They just got off the boat."

Mario was glad he had waited. For this was none other than Lucia Conforti, a vision to his hard-working eyes. At last he knew joy. They were married on the Holy Feast of the Lamb, in 1917. They had a special holy bread shaped like a lamb with eggs in it at the feast. Everybody in Peterstown celebrated that Mario had at last found himself a wife.

"Ok, that's enough!" My father interrupted. "I'll finish the rest."

Your Grandfather Mario Anthony Donitella worked very hard all his life in America. He struggled to give his children a good life.

Then one day he had to struggle no more. It was a winter day in December, eight days before the winter solstice and the very feast of Santa Lucia. Mario was feeling different than usual. He actually started to feel a deep peace for no apparent reason, late one evening after another long day of work. Suddenly he thought he was back in Cammarata, which he had not seen for over 30 years. He could smell the lemon blossoms and the manure-laden fields. The pure mountain air seemed to fill the room. He could hear the sweet chant of Gaetano, his old friend. He could hear the clomp clomp of animal hooves. He ran to the window and glanced through the curtains outside. The night was peaceful and white with new fallen snow.

Then Mario sat in a rocking chair and gently rocked and for the first time since he landed in America, he did nothing but think. He felt like a young boy again with the time to dawdle between chores in the fields of Cammarata. A song came into his head and his heart swelled with joy. He felt a flutter. The song grew and took shape and the words passed through his head. He was astounded, for it had been so many years since his youth and the time when he had dreamed of being a poet. His muse had risen from her sleep.

But his heart could not bear the burst of joy and the tune just carried his soul away. Just before his heart burst, he lay on his bed and asked his wife for some water. She went to fetch it and did not hear him say, "I want to go home." And so he went.

When Mario woke up he was in his favorite spot on the mountain of Cammarata. It was like he had never left. He saw Gaetano there and other villagers who had passed over.

Suddenly my father turned to me and said, "Vinnie, I want you to come work the stand with me today." No joke, my heart stopped for two seconds. Leave Dana alone with Mario again? But I jumped when my father gave orders. I glanced at Dana in her red and white silk housecoat with white bunny slippers and waved good-bye, but she didn't see me.

We were silent in the car on the way to the stand on North Broad Street. Then my father spoke.

"We'll drive the long way around through Peterstown. My guys'll watch the stand for me."

My father drove around in circles, passing his stand on Broad several times. I got worried. It was the same exact thing that had happened to me in the rocker! Like a spell!

"Dad!" I said abruptly, "How about if I tell you the story again, one more time?"

The very suggestion seemed to work and my father parked the car. Whew.

"Don't worry Vinnie, you make your grandfather proud wherever he is."

By the time we reached the stand, my father was crying and welcomed the chance to keep busy. Hampton and Fletcher, seeing he was emotional, said they had to run. My father paid them and they left.

"Thanks for helping out, Vinnie," my father said, "I mean with the story. You'll turn out OK. A little clumsy because of that music you like to dance to. But you're a good listener. Don't worry about the Hi-Fi. We'll get another one. Those things happen."

I didn't say anything. I was glad I could remember how the story went. Bet Mario didn't have that good a memory. But I was glad I was the one to help my father feel better. It was something I was best at. But it was not enough to stop my father's bleeding. Volcanoes had to blow, hearts had to burst, and only God knew why the big things had to happen.

My father grabbed a handful of water from the hose and washed his face. He blessed himself and kissed his silver cross and scapular. I did the same and watched as my father turned with his usual cheerfulness to greet his first customer of the day.

Nonnie (1960)

I was in my rocker when the man I called *il caro mio* appeared to me. It was almost exactly 10 years since my dear husband Pasquale died and visited me time to time in dreams. He came, telling me about his dream again, the one he had over and over. But this time he was the one telling me, *Wake up! Wake up!* It is not time yet. When I awoke I saw Saint Lucy waving her cloaked arms and I realized I been dreamin'.

Fire burned rings around my life, never touching me. Long ago I left the hotseat Sicily. I knew fire was through with me, but I could not say so much for my children and their children. I wondered sometimes if my brother Dominic's soul come to rest in one of my great grandchildren, perhaps in Franco—I saw that same fire in my brother's eyes. But I never said a word what ran through my head when I saw his foot go through the bathroom door.

My memory of the island flared up when I smelled the smoke and saw flame. Mario and Lucy came to help me. But my Pasquale came, too, the man who took me from the village of my youth. I knew he was waiting patiently for me to cross over, back to the mountainous heart of the island. The island I never dreamed I'd leave for this place called *l'America*. When I was a young girl in those mountains it was like going to the stars, to go to America!

But now as I sat in my room and waited for death, it was those mountains that seemed so far away, so untouchable, impossible like a dream. Those peaks and valleys called me like from a place in a fairytale. I would never see such majesty again, never see the clouds resting on the mountain's shoulders like a shawl, never hear its wind calling like a scared soul.

Or would I? For how little I understood, I knew that something waited still on the ancient mountain.

The end of our life is closest to the beginning, I thought, as I listened without understanding to the music of my children's children. The music of my own memory was at times faint as a whisper, at times a vibration that went so deep I felt timeless. When the vibration stirred me, I was sad I would leave this world before I ever spoke my stories from the time I left the mountain.

Even the candlelight and Saint Lucy seemed to dance with the kids' music. The shadows flickered across my face. They were soothing like a feather tickle. The rocking was fine. Help me say prayers in the morning, mid-day, and evening. I looked forward to evening, to the dark.

My grandson-in-law, Vincent, he tells stories. But he adds a lot of salt to the dough. He takes out the bitterness, he makes it all lighter. He made a sweet song out of pain, sorrow, want, and the death of children. I knew all of these firsthand. The salt was OK. At least he remembered some things for me.

It pained me there was so much I couldn't tell these children, my own flesh and blood. These children and I have only a few words to share. *Veni ca. Mancia.* Come here and eat, they understood. They speak to me like the child. And those rascals! Maddelena and Nazarena! They crawl like animals under my chair and stick their little hands under my long dress and tickle my ankles. My ankles looked foreign and strange even to me now. They didn't belong to this land. They got thickened by steep hills far away and so old. Here everything is so flat and new. And made of wood. Not something less vulnerable to fire like stone.

I liked living with my grandchildren and great-grandchildren —I came for a brief stay six years ago and never left. I never asked why. Maybe everybody just forgot my visit was supposed to be brief. I knew they had a lot more important things on their minds. The one thing that bothered me was that my granddaughter, Magdalena, made *biscotti* all year long. There was no longer respect for the seasons. In Sicily we counted the days and seasons, the holidays and holy days, by the *quaresimali, ciambelli, pignoli, cucciddati*. The time of year in the hazelnuts, almonds, or pine nuts we picked and dried. They told us which *biscotti* were made when. *Cucciddati* were my favorite and I used to look forward to Christmas to make them. Now, here in America they made them all year round!

The black wooden beads—my dear Pasquale's—I roll between my fingers are not all Hail Marys. "Forgive me, *Matri mia!* " I beg,

"But sometimes I feel the *cucciddati* dough between my fingers and I mark time remembering. I, Maridona Coniglio, who have been honored with your holy name, I ask you to forgive and understand this indulgence."

I said so many Hail Marys, between so many Joyful, Sorrowful, and Glorious Mysteries and Our Fathers. I sang *Salve Regina* and *Ave Maria* with my mother, sisters, and aunts in San Giovanni-Gemini. I sat with the village women in their chairs, facing the village wall, our backs to the men. Such modesty and humility don't exist here in America, I saw that right away.

Before I had thick old lady feet in heavy black shoes, I had beautiful ankles and long black hair. Not this face like an almond meat. I sat humble and waited for a husband. In America you would not think that a girl facing a white stone wall all day, sewing, stitching, peeling, would find a man. But Pasquale asked my parents for my hand before he had ever seen my face. He took my hand when I was young and beautiful. I knew of the tragedy of his first wife and that I would have to nurse his spirit. But he was strong for a man who was cursed so. He made me promise never to talk about his terrible loss. Never.

For the sixty-five years we were together, I honored this vow. But his dream mind was not so obedient to his wishes. How many times did he wake up screaming, in such searing pain! And I would have to comfort him and say over and over, "Pasquale, in dream time, fire warms, but does not burn!" I'd soothe his anguish, his guilt. I never mentioned his first wife, Estella. Pregnant with their first child, she was lapped up by the searing flame of an oven. The same oven that gave them bread and roasted peppers had sent a tongue of fire to swallow Estella and the baby. Pasquale mourned his tragedy for a year and never talked to anyone about it. From Pasquale I learned how it is far better to remember all at once, not in stingy, little moments throughout one's whole life.

And then there came my own terrible loss. Another kind of fire. But by then I knew. *Ma quannu si cunta è nenti*—Who speaks his troubles already sets himself free—not on fire. I told my brother's story many times, until the flag-draped coffin ceased to appear in my dreams.

It happened because Dominic my dear brother was not meant to come to America. He should have stayed in our village with our *cumpari*, I thought over and over after his death. Back home he was a rascal of sorts, a *rumpiscatuli* like my great grandson, Franco. He was so attached to that parched, brown land. He had a little plot that a rich landowner lent him and it kept him too busy to listen to the Devil. He could have finished out a long life there. Perhaps not plentiful, but long and satisfactory.

I saw the change occur on the boat. The voyage was tough and the crowds, like we never saw before, made him so nervous. We slept with the steering wheels, below waterline. So little light or fresh air. The stench of vomit was awful. For Dominic this wretchedness was America. He should have gone back after passing inspection. But he slipped away fast.

Dominic's fear of the *malocchiu* grew and grew. He believed there was the Evil Eye, a spell on our house at 714 Kristyne Street from the moment he saw it. He took a room in a boarding house a few blocks away on McGee Avenue. He would try to visit me, but he wouldn't let so much as his big toe cross the line where he imagined the Evil Eye dwelled. He stood below my window and called my name from behind the hedges until I appeared. I'd run downstairs, open the door and beckon him inside, always I hoped this will be the time and he would forget his nonsense. But he'd always hold his fingers to make *i corna*, cross himself, and shake like he was bit by a *scurpiuni*.

"You come here, Maridona," he begged, a grown man on the verge of tears. He would not even sit on the porch. I tried to tell him it was all in his head. Fire on the brain. But he would not listen. So I gave in. I brought two chairs and some leftover macaroni, wine, or a sausage and pepper sandwich. We sat in the street, the neighbors probably thinking we were both *pazzi*.

"This house, Maridona, is dangerous. There are houses like yours everywhere here, where devils live. It's so evil. I don't want to go up in flames like..."

"*Statti zittu!*" I would have to hush him before Pasquale heard him. He would shake and cry like a baby though he was a man of 22 years. When he calmed down a little, he'd let me lead him down the alley next to my house to where he could see over the hedges into the garden. He would recite to me what he saw like he was reciting poetry to break his spell: *"Avemu pipi, pomadoru, milanzani, zucchini, cucuzzi...va beni..."* Sometimes he'd repeat to me what he saw three and four times, *"pipi, pumadoru, milanzani, zucchini, cucuzzi..."* Like he was memorizing.

This chanting seemed to calm Dominic down. He would smile a little and say, "This is a good sign, Maridona. If God is letting things grow from the earth here, it is a good sign." He kissed his *cornu* and crossed himself. Sometimes he even took an eggplant or pepper or tomato back home with him.

I took heart when Dominic took it upon himself to become an American after a few years. In June of 1918 he became a naturalized citizen. He immediately joined the Navy and in September was sent to Panama to work on the canal. A couple months later, I received a letter from a Joseph Tellone in Dominic's Machine Gun Company, 33rd Infantry. Dominic could not write, so he asked Mr. Tellone to send a few words on his behalf to me. Mr. Tellone wrote: *"Dominic has been in this Co. since Aug. 1918. He has an excellent character, always on the job and one of the best and hardest workers in the Co. He does not speak English well, but understands better than most people think and surprises his superiors by fulfilling his duties when told in English. Having been his superior while I was a corporal in the M.G. Co. I could notice it better than anyone else. Dominic sends his love to you and Pasquale and thanks for the early Christmas gift. I can verify that Dominic is in very good health, for at meal time I have a hard time of keeping up with him and I'm a pretty good eater. P.S. Being Italian naturally I could not but think of his interest and personal welfare.*

My son read the letter to me, translating it into Italian. I was overjoyed and made Franco read it to me and Pasquale three times. I tried to imagine this Mr. Tellone, this friend of Dominic's, hoping one day to meet him.

During the next year I received two brief letters from Dominic. Neither message was possible to decipher, but I appreciated the effort. Then, on December 28, 1919, three days after Christmas, I opened a piece of tissue-thin correspondence. My son showed me at the top it was marked *Dispatch, Navy Department, Office of Navigation, Washington, D.C.* He read it two times: FOLLOWING MESSAGE RECEIVED FROM GOVERNMENT HOSPITAL PANAMA QUOTE REGRET TO ADVISE THAT YOUR BROTHER DOMINIC DIED HERE YESTERDAY ADVISE IF YOU WISH BODY SHIPPED GOVERNMENT EXPENSE GIVE NAME AND ADDRESS UNDERTAKER LETTER FOLLOWING PERIOD SIGNED KENNEDY UNQUOTE SEND YOUR REPLY TO NAVY DEPARTMENT BUREAU OF NAVIGATION WASHINGTON, D C.

Dominic shot a bullet of fire into his head, probably right where his fear of the *Malocchiu* lived. This was a very sad day for me, because I knew that Dominic would have left his hard head alone if he never took his feet off his native soil. The biggest tragedy was that he died so far from his own blood.

I accepted his death, God's will be done. Dominic, my little brother, came back to me in a box draped with a flag of stars and stripes. I could not bury him in the Church but I could bury him as an American!

"We began to dig his grave the day we left San Giovanni," I told Pasquale.

But I didn't curse America. In Agrigento there were times when my father went into the mountains and scrounged for wild squash shoots, finocchio, and some snails. In Agrigento I buried nine babies right after baptizing them. God let me keep three, Franco, Anna, and Giovanna. Here in America, everyone got a better deal.

"But what's the use to complain?" I asked myself. Life is not complex anymore. Here God has taken his great rolling pin and flattened out the bumps of life and the land. He did not paint with so many colors. There is much more black, white, and gray here in America.

I am nearly out of time. Even my deepest prayers sound stale. I twirl my beads, I recall the hills of Sicily, the pink blossoms of almond trees in spring, the perfume air, the drying almonds for making *cuccidati* at Christmas. This was how my mother, my aunts, and I made *cucciddati*:

Hail Mary Full of Grace

We start with a fine, soft grain, white flour, *cucitta*, the one that cost so dear,

The Lord is with Thee

We knead the flour well with salt, butter, hen's eggs, and a handful of sugar.

Blessed art Thou among Women

Meanwhile, we soak the figs and dates in Marsala. We add vanilla, too.

And Blessed is the Fruit of Thy Womb, Jesus.

We toast the almonds until the kitchen smell like heaven. And then we chop them.

Holy Mary Mother of God

We mix the nuts and fruit into a thick, rich, dark paste. We roll the dough on the board blessed by Father Antonio.

Pray for us Sinners

We cut full moons out of the dough and spoon in some filling. Then we roll up the dough like a crescent moon. We make slits with a sharp knife in the outer edge.

Now and at the hour of our Death

We bless the cookies and bake them until golden brown like the fields in summer.

Amen.

Vincent (1963)

The lemons, the limes, the carrots, the celery, the lettuce. Artichokes, cardoons, dandelions, escarole, spinach, chard, broccoli rabe. Fennel in winter. In fall, the cranberries, in spring the damn blueberries, in summer the cherries and watermelon, Chinese apples. Stack 'em up, take 'em down. Sell 'em before they rot. The whole damn thing, it goes on and on in vicious circles. It never ends. Seasons turn. A seed is planted. A plant is seeded. Another child appears at my table. Another mouth to feed.

And all I really wanted was not to be piss poor but to be a priest. My father had to stop me. He said I could never be still enough for the contemplative life.

I do my best to make ends meet. A pool for summertime. Who needs shoes. Who needs books, tuition. Thank God they all have their health. Father Murphy wants something for the church coffer. He didn't exactly say it, but I could tell the way he looks at me during the sermons. I put my damn finger in one hole and three more would appear in my life. The bathroom door, the Hi-Fi, the baby's mattress. For three years these holes have been staring at me like the eyes of a dead man waiting for me to do something decent with his corpse.

I may be just a lousy fruit and vegetable vendor, but I do the job well and I make honest money. I keep my wife and kids fed and clothed. I'm proud, I'm honest, maybe too honest! I know I don't command the respect my father Mario Anthony Donitella told me I deserved.

"Who's better than us?" he always said. Especially after a day of hearing Dago, Wop, Ginny, Greaseball. I thought they were terms of affection until I heard him talking to my mother.

I still go along with the endless jokes and jibes—how many really in jest? "C'mon Vinnie, 'fess up," they tease, "your stand is really a front." Fess up? If anything I pay extra taxes just to prove otherwise. I declare everything, keep good records. How many offers have I turned down? If the walls at Spirito's pizzeria only had ears. I could have been a driver during Prohibition, they wanted to cut me in. If my father hadn't been proud and made me the same way, I'd have been on Easy Street the rest of my life.

But aren't all Sicilians one way or another connected, they always ask? They say I can't feed 12 mouths on what I make selling the lousy produce. So, what if I get the spot rent-free? My buddy Ralph Giordano in Linden owns the land. I don't ask questions. Like when the bootleggers from Newark asked to store some barrels of flour in my father's barn. My father looked the other way and never asked any questions. My father only asked that they tell him nothing. I do the same.

Sometimes the most important thing is that one hand wash the other. Like when my father got the insurance money for Lenny Spinello for losing his eyesight. My father believed Lenny had gone blind even though the doctors couldn't find anything wrong. My father, like any honest man, believed Lenny. Then one day as my father was delivering the check to Lenny's home, as he did for all his clients in Peterstown, he walked in and noticed Lenny reading the newspaper at the kitchen table. My father walked right past Lenny into the dining room and hugged Lenny's wife and asked her, "Anna, where's your husband today? I'm sorry I can't wait around for him." He gave the check to Anna and left.

To hell with the questions and the little things. *Minni futtu!*

I could have gone to college or taken the civil service exam and worked at a regular steady job for the government, but I wanted to answer to as few higher-ups as possible. I could have taken the easy way out. I'm no dummy, nor was my father. Did he take the easy way? He never sat on his behind and let the American government take care of him. Not from the day he stepped off the boat and put his foot on American soil. He worked his balls off. Hay, oats, coal. He sold them all. He bought the horse and buggy with his life savings. The people in Peterstown knew him as *u Carburaru* when he delivered the coal. He learned English on his own. He sold insurance to Italians in Peterstown. He turned down a job as supervisor at the Prudential because that Irishman Burns told him, "There's no room for your kind up here." But he made ends meet and took care of 16 cousins, aunts, and uncles.

God forbid one of my sons or daughters should disgrace me. My father would turn in his grave. I'd have to kill them. Or at least beat the living daylights out of them. Teach them a lesson. I don't know any other way. But, it kills me. It hurts me more than it hurts them when I have to take them to the wall. They don't see that. They never know how I bleed inside. They don't know why I go to my bedroom afterward. They don't hear me cry. I don't cry for myself. I can't let them disgrace me. I can't let my father down. I have to train them the best way I know how.

I should have been a priest. I wouldn't have this Monday night restlessness. My father died on Monday night. So did Lou Cataline. Maybe being a priest would have put an end to all my wild impulses. My kids don't know about that. Only God knows. I had a wild youth. I rebelled against my father and my mother because for a while I thought they were ignorant immigrants. OK, I admit it. Sometimes, when my father asked, "Who's better than us?" I answered under my breath, "Just about everybody." I paid for that.

I was a smart son of a bitch. When I was nine years old he began toughening me up. My mother was sent away with woman problems. She had started bearing children when she was fifteen and she took sick after my youngest sister was born. My father drove her to the hospital in Marlboro where she had to stay for several months. This made me angry. I had all my cousins, aunts, and uncles living with us, but I wanted my mother home and I blamed my father for letting her stay there. I stayed away from home a few nights and made him angry.

He didn't beat me up then because I got a cold and an infected boil on my leg. A neighbor came by and put a slice of potato on the boil and bandaged it. The boil went away, but the cold didn't get better. It developed into pneumonia. I heard my father talking to my older sister, Marialia, about calling Doctor Palmieri. My father said they would try my Godmother Katie Furillo first. My fever soared higher and higher and I felt no pain, just burning up and missing my mother. When I told my father I missed Mama, he told me not to whine over trifles. I would take his place someday. But only if I knew how to be a man.

77

I saw Aunt Katie peek through my bedroom door. She was a huge, big-bosomed woman with rolls and rolls of flesh; she breathed through her mouth because she couldn't close it. "Mama!" I called. Aunt Katie came in with Marialia and my father. She had a box in her sausage-like hands and I knew what was in there. I began to scream and kick even though I was weak. My sister and my father made me turn over on my stomach and take off my shirt. Aunt Katie kept saying over and over, "*Sta tranquillu, Vicenzu, chistu ccà ti fa beni pû malu sangu...Videmu...*" I heard her open the box. I could feel her hot breath on my back and the cold, slimy leeches sucking my *malu sangu*, my bad blood. It felt like dozens of them crawling all over me. I kicked and screamed for my mother while my father and sister held me down.

After the leeches took the poisons, I recovered and my father took a bunch of us to see my mother in the hospital. We piled into the old Nash sedan—cousins, aunts, uncles—all 16 of us. The car stalled on the hill leading up to the hospital in Marlboro. We got out laughing and pushed it to the top. We had to sneak everyone in, two at a time, because my mother was only allowed four visitors. One person would go back down the elevator with a pass and bring up two more past the head nurse.

Mama scolded me for being too skinny, for not eating. It made me so happy. The next Sunday I thought we would go see her again, but my father said she was too tired. I didn't believe him. He sent me to the corner store for a pack of Camels. It began to rain hard and I started jumping puddles and forgot about the time. I climbed the wrought iron fence by the park on Second Avenue and found some real big puddles. I was splashing around in the concrete pool there, soaked to the bone when I looked up and saw my father's face. He beat me right there on the spot. I deserved it. I deserved all the beatings he ever gave me after that.

Except for one. I was in grammar school at Thomas Jefferson. I was sitting in front of my cousin, Andy. Andy tapped me on the shoulder and when I turned around he blew tobacco in my face. I reacted instantly and punched Andy. He bellowed. The teacher took me, not Andy, to the principal, who called my father. My father took off his belt and beat me right there in the principal's office, without ever asking for an explanation. He never gave me a chance to explain that for once I was not guilty. Just that one time he could have spared me. I never forgot that. From that day I vowed never to beat my kids without giving them a chance to explain whether they deserved it or not.

When I told my father I wanted to be a priest I thought he would be the happiest man. He wasn't. He said he had but one son to give the world and that was me. If he had another son who would marry and carry on the name, I would have had his blessing. My five sisters didn't count because women can't carry the name. I gave his name to four sons and he wasn't even around to see them, to see that I made something of myself after all.

After years of hanging with the Baghdad Beauties down the Port, I found and married Mary Magdalena. But only after I'd tried everything. I even thought about playing French horn with Johnny in the traveling band. I'd have been too wild for the music life, though. I needed a wife, someone to tame me down.

And I found her in 1938. Frankie, Johnny, and I had driven into the City. We were heading uptown to the Apollo Theater. Johnny had a brand new Cadillac. We had stopped in front of Radio City Music Hall to watch the pretty broads come out. When Johnny turned the key in the ignition, nothing happened. The car wouldn't start. So three of us got out, all dressed in our suits, top coats, and fedoras. Frankie and I start pushing the Cadillac in the middle of crowds coming from Radio City. It's a cold, clear winter night. All of a sudden Johnny turns the key and the car starts. He pulls away, laughing his head off.

He drove around the block, leaving us there like *gavon'*. We were discussing revenge when I heard my name. I turned around and saw it was my sister Angela with six other girls. They were at Radio City Music Hall. It was Angela's girls' club, the Nickelettes, and it was their yearly night in the City.

I wouldn't have even noticed Magdalena. But she was the only quiet and shy one. The others all yacked away, too *chiacchiaruni* for me. I liked quiet women. But Frankie and Johnny didn't care. They both met their wives that night, too. Of course, none of us knew it at the time.

Angela, my sister, had always been good luck. For Frankie and Johnny it was probably just the right eye contact, smelling the perfume, or seeing the right amount of leg maybe. For me it was the Sicilian thunderbolt, a kind of spiritual experience. Her dark eyes had a sacred gleam. She was sexy and didn't seem to know it. We didn't say much. Just exchanged long hellos as Angela introduced us. We held each other's gaze a long, long time. The noise of the traffic died down and it was as if the sky opened for just us two and the angels played a concerto. I knew right away. We both knew. The traffic noise returned then and Johnny came back and picked up us fellows. The boys teased me for having stars in my eyes as we headed up to the burlesque show at the Apollo Theater. But I played it tough and pretended she looked like just another dame.

The comedian was great that night. We laughed hard at his burlesque show, *Tobacco Road*. He took his pecker out and peed on stage. They had the bare-breasted girls, too. It was Georgia Southern, the redhead, who took it all off. But she wasn't as good as Gypsy Rose Lee. Gypsy never went all the way, though. They had the strong arm men there that night. They thought Johnny was making a pass at one of the usherettes. The men picked Johnny up by the arms to throw him out on his ear. But the usherette said she knew him. He was only saying hello. That Johnny could get us in more trouble. The bouncers took us to our seat. Later we flirted with some colored girls who were very pretty.

I had to corner Angela that week to find out what I needed to know about Magdalena. I couldn't just come out and ask Angela if she was stained or not. I didn't want to bother with another stained woman. I'd had enough of those. I needed a Madonna, someone pure, now that I had matured. Angela was no dummy. She gave me my answer. "Magdalena's my best friend, she hasn't dated very much at all, and she's too good for the likes of you." That was all I needed to know.

I needed a woman who was too good for me. I had found her.

Now, here I was, driving home after putting in 12 hours at the stand and thinking about how I had met my wife 25 years earlier. I decided to take a detour to the Port where I used to drink, smoke cigarettes, and hang out with Johnny, Frankie, and the Baghdad Beauties. We never laid a hand on any of the Beauties. We looked up to them, because they were older than us. Some of the girls actually got out of the business, settled down, and got married, I heard.

I stared out at the water and smoked a cigarette. The pier, which always looked as if it was moving away, was a soothing spot for me. I felt for a moment that it was really moving, carrying me away from all I'd buried myself in, away from the heap, the rat race. Those were the days, before I got married and still had my freedom. But I hadn't known what to do with it. The Manhattan skyline sparkled like distant diamonds. The story of my life—the diamonds always within sight, an arm's length away.

I decided to stop at the Villa Roma and have a drink with Frankie. As I drove through Peterstown, I noticed how neat the houses were. Much neater than the garbage heap that the rest of Elizabeth had become with its housing projects. The place has gone to pot. I should never have taken my family away from Peterstown. But I had wanted to get away from the monotony of the Italian neighborhood, where all they talked about was whoever wasn't present. They all had the same thoughts, same aspirations, same language, same expressions. They were a bunch of immigrants with silly, naive ideas. I wanted to hear an original thought for a change. If my father had lived, maybe it would have been different.

My father had tried to beat the restless streak right out of me. And now my wife was trying to beat out the pride. Maybe my pride was a thin cover-up for contempt, like she said. But who was she to tell me?

There were more of my kind there in Peterstown. My people! We should have stayed. But the Anglo Americans were starting to eat our peppers, zucchini, and eggplant, our Italian vegetables. I decided to branch out from the Peterstown market to pick up some of the slack out in another area, where more than just Italians came by. Then Ralph offered me the lot for free. Ralph is a good guy.

I also wanted a house for my kids on a nice, safe street. The *mullingians* were moving in too close—not that I had anything against them, "Scratch a Sicilian and find an African," they used to say in Peterstown—but not next door to me.

I was also tired of having my wife's mother as a landlord. She was a bitch with a capital B, but I didn't blame her, I blamed her husband who should have put her in her place. A woman needs a man to tell her to keep her mouth shut. She raised the rent every time my wife got pregnant.

I found Frankie tending bar at Villa Roma just as I had hoped. Frankie and I could still talk. He was a *cumpari* to my son, Frankie. We had grown up together, cut our teeth on the same grit, shit, and dirty air. His people came from the same province, Agrigento, as mine. I had a couple shots of bourbon with Frankie and we talked for a while about the good old days, like we always did, and where our gang had all gone. Who died, who never married, who was still running around, who was still tied to his mama's apron strings. I started to feel better.

Frankie didn't ask the wrong questions, like why did I have so many kids, how was I going to feed them and put them through school. He asked about Magdalena. I told him she was fine. She was great. I never said a word against my wife. She was the perfect Sicilian wife, I told him, and what more could a bum like me ask for? We laughed. And then as we talked and Frankie listened, I felt warm all over and decided to tell him the story about how I married her.

I saw her for the second time on the Field of Dreams in Warinanco Park. There were great big silver birds soaring against a sky of royal blue. They dipped down along the green. There were sparks and fireworks. She appeared to me, a vision in billowing bloomers of soft, blue cotton, her long legs entwined modestly. In my heart I knew already. I took her to the christening of my nephew Michael for our first date. She was a young woman, still a child but in high-heeled shoes and silk stockings, pink hat, and gloves. Her lips were unpainted but as ruby red as the juice that bleeds from the pomegranate.

A wise old woman, my Godmother Katie Furillo, came to me and said, "Vinnie, go with her. She'll make something of you."

I took her to the Regent Theatre on Broad Street to see Gone with the Wind. I took her for egg creams, uptown Manhattan once. I took her dancing. We danced beautifully, Magdalena and I. The peabody, lindy hop, the jitterbug, the Suzy Q, and the truckin. We always moved in perfect harmony, especially when we danced to my favorite song, Stardust Melody.

But it was one night when I told her the moon was a piece of green cheese and she believed me, that I knew for sure. That was the final test. She passed it.

The day I came home to tell my father, who loved Magdalena from the beginning, that I was going to marry her and pass on his name to many sons, he died. Five minutes before I got there. Angels called and he had to go.

But a greater task remained for us. We had to ask Magdalena's mother. Her mother had never approved of any men before me. No one was good enough for her daughter, but I had the balls to stand up to her. One night at dusk I went to the pier to be alone and think. I passed a dead man on my way to the edge of the water. A man had hanged himself. It was the Pole, the stupid bum. His eyes and tongue bulged out hideously from his head. This death did not distract me. I ignored the fool who probably killed himself over a woman.

The lights were coming up across the water in the City.

I prayed and prayed. My father appeared to me and told me not to worry about Magdalena's parents, Gemma and Franco Coniglio. He would help me.

"Do exactly as I say," my father said to me. "Go to Nocera's in Peterstown and ask Gianfranco the owner for a block of the oldest Parmigiano he has. Take it with you when you go to dinner at the Coniglios this Sunday..."

"But, Pop," I interrupted, "I'm not going to dinner there. They haven't even let me set foot in the house yet!"

"Shutup and listen to me," my father responded quickly. "Don't think I can't deck you still or take off my belt. You just do exactly as I tell you. Now, at the dinner you must insist three times that they use your cheese on the macaroni."

"But Pop!" I cried in desperation as my father's spirit grew thinner and vanished and all I could see again was the sparkle of the Manhattan skyline. Mannaggia! Damn it!

So I went to Nocera's and asked for the oldest Parmagiano. Gianfranco winked at me and said, "Aspetta, Vinnie, one moment." He disappeared into the black hole that was the opening to his world on the other side of the storefront. He was gone 10 minutes. He returned with the chunk of cheese wrapped in paper and as he handed it to me, he said, "No charge, Vinnie, curaggiu!"

I noticed that even through the paper and the bag, the cheese smelled to high heavens. I could hardly stand it. What was my father trying to do to me? I wondered. Perhaps it was the Prince of Darkness himself I had seen in my father's flesh and bones!

Sure enough an invitation to have Sunday dinner with Magdalena and her parents, Franco and Gemma, arrived. I put on my Sunday best, my blue gabardine suit. I spit polished my shoes. I slicked back my hair. I looked sharp, real guapo! I put the cheese in a double bag. It took every ounce of faith to trust my father's scheme. I sneaked out the back door so my sisters, cousins, and my mother wouldn't ask any questions.

I made my way over to Kristyne Street and rang the doorbell. As I waited, big drops of water fell on me. The sky was clear except for the huge cloud of black smoke belching from the refineries. I looked up and saw it was wet laundry dripping on me. Then Gemma slid open the window on the second floor and stuck her head out to see who was there. She slammed the window shut. She returned in less than a minute, opened the window and threw something out at me. A skeleton key missed my head by a hair's breadth. She slammed the window shut again.

I stuck the key in the door, opened it, and climbed the two flights of stairs. Franco was slowly backing out of the door that led to the attic. In his hand, he had a jug of reddish-brown liquid, the wine he had made.

"Veni ca," was all they said to me. Come here.

Magdalena was brought from her bedroom. Everybody sniffed the air and wrinkled their noses. I extended the bag and said, "Please take this, the finest aged Parmagiano."

"Franco," ordered Gemma, "Take it." Franco held it at an arm's length and put it on the counter.

We sat down and Franco and I put on white linen bibs to protect our white shirts from splashes of red. Franco said the prayers. Then he began to grate the cheese for the pasta. I was so busy staring into Magdalena's dark eyes I almost forgot my father's orders. I felt a nudge on my shoulder. I looked around. I saw no one.

"Please, use the finest cheese I brought," I suddenly blurted out.

"Heh?" asked Franco, as he continued to grate.

"You really should try the Parmigiano."

"Shut up and eat," said Gemma.

Franco made a loud sucking noise as he aspirated his macaronis.

"I insist that you save your cheese and try this one," I said for a third time.

I was just following my father's orders.

"Franco, use his cheese," ordered Gemma. And this time Franco picked it up and began to grate it with the mouli grater, slowly, over the steaming mound of spaghetti. And as he did, the cheese became a soft nugget of pure gold. Franco and Gemma could not take their eyes off the glittering flakes falling upon the macaroni. They sparkled and gave off a shimmering light that filled the room. Franco and Gemma saw nothing else. And my future wife and I went to the front room and danced to the Stardust Melody. *A full moon sent a shaft of silver light through the window and it followed us wherever we danced.*

I knew my father was nearby and that he rejoiced for me. He had sold hay, oats, and coals and paved streets in one life. In the next he helped me, his only son. I think my father stole into Franco and Gemma's kitchen then and snitched a cannoli to mark the occasion. There was one missing and Gemma later blamed me for its disappearance.

But Gemma and Franco consented to our marriage, in spite of themselves. We exchanged vows in the Church of Saint Anthony of Padua. An angel came and sang the Ave Maria *in Latin.*

After the ceremony we went to the Knights of Columbus hall and had a grand reception. We ate ravioli and meatballs. We had lots of fancy wedding cookies from Bella Palermo. My father watched over us and while everybody danced the tarantella he stole another cannoli. It was the last one. Angela had been going to take it, but she turned her back for a minute. We all blamed Gemma Coniglio for the missing cannoli.

I had one more shot of bourbon with Frankie, then left. I stopped to say a prayer over at St. Anthony's, where we were married in 1940, where I had been an altar boy, where I christened all my kids, where I confessed all my small and grievous offenses in the cedar boxes against the wall.

I stopped at each of the Sorrowful Mysteries in stained glass. To hell with the Joyful and Glorious ones. I preferred the Sorrowful: The Agony in the Garden, The Scourging at the Pillar, the Crowning with Thorns, the Carrying of the Cross, the Crucifixion. My kind of suffering.

Then I lit some candles. One to Saint Jude, one to Saint Anthony, one to the Sacred Heart. I bowed to the Blessed Virgin Mary and told her I would let my wife speak to her and intercede for us. Women should talk to women. Besides, she may not have wanted to listen to a bum such as myself. I felt good there in that big barn of a church. It was dark and quiet and smelled sharp of incense and old women. Two of them in black knelt in a pew. I liked this church much better than the Sacred Heart, better than the Holy Rosary, or Saint Michael's. The Irish kept us in the basements of those. But here they left my kind alone.

"Damn Irish couldn't understand how we could get work done, go to church on Sunday, raise our kids, and still have time to make a barrel of wine." I must have thought out loud, because one of the old women turned around and said, *"Zitti!"*

I genuflected, crossed myself, and left, driving past the two-family home where all my sisters and my mother still lived on South Park. Something stopped me from going in for a quick visit. Then I remembered another Monday night death many years ago—Philip Lieber, my oldest sister Marialia's fiancé. I wasn't sure she didn't still hold me responsible. I was sorry I felt the way I did, but he had deserved to die.

It was on a Sunday, years ago, after 12 o'clock mass, that Magdalena and I had taken the five youngest kids to see my mother. My sisters and some of their husbands, some of the aunts and uncles were sitting down to macaroni. Marialia's fiance, Philip, was there. Perhaps he thought he was being funny, but he wasn't. He said, "You only come around when it's time to eat."

That hurt my pride real bad, but no one came to my defense. I was humiliated by this creep. My wife was mortified, too. After all, we never went empty handed anywhere. I always brought something little, some cardoons, broccoli rabe, some Chinese apples, which my mother loved. I wanted my kids to see their grandmother. I never liked that bum. I knew he was no good, rotten to the core, the half-baked Kraut.

But what hurt the most was that I knew the insult would not have happened if my father had been alive. My father Mario Anthony Donitella would have seen that I got the respect I deserved as his only son.

I took my wife and kids out of there immediately. Months later I had the opportunity to punch Philip out in front of his girlfriend, my sister, on South Park. This time he made the wrong crack against the wrong person. He asked Magdalena if she was pregnant again. She told him she wasn't and he said, "Well, Vincent could fix that."

I could not believe my ears. This time I didn't have to hesitate. I socked him across the kisser. Hard. He was bleeding. My sister tried to stop me.

"He's been drinking, Vinnie. He didn't meant it!" she screamed, keeping to his defense, which pissed me off even more.

"I don't care, that's no excuse to abuse my wife," I said as I pulled him up off the ground by the shirt and said, "This time you were lucky." I pushed him away. A month later he was dead of a heart attack at age 33. He was no good for my sister or anyone. Nobody insulted my wife and got away with it.

Philip's bloody face was still on my mind when I got home and threw the tomatoes, *cucuzza*, and eggplant. The peaches were spared because I had already put them down on the counter. It was the part about the pride that got me going, not the drinking this time.

It was all I had left sometimes, I thought, and my own wife wanted to deny me that. She wanted me to let some damn Irish nun one-up me.

I had swallowed my pride when we first moved to Rahway and I went to enroll my younger kids at St. Mary's. It was too bad my kids couldn't go to St. Anthony's with the Italians in Peterstown and that the only Catholic school in Rahway was run by the Order of Preachers, the Dominicans, most of them damn Irish. I had considered sending them to public school with the *mullingians*, but I swallowed my pride and talked to Father Murphy and the principal Sister Helen Marie about paying the tuition in installments. I even told them, "You can slap my kids around if they get out of line and disrespectful. But don't teach them about where they came from. That's my job."

"How many drinks?" Magdalena asked without even looking at me when I got in.

"Since when do you greet me this way? What are you turning *'miricanu'*?" She knew I didn't want to hear anything until I got my kiss and my hug.

Sister Helen Marie had gone around to the classrooms to hand out the report cards that day. She had sent my son Carmine home. Not because he was too smart or mouthing off, or God knows I'd have crowned him one. She sent him home because of his hair. The note said, "Couldn't you do something about his hair? He looks like the wild man from Borneo. We'd like him to look neat in his uniform like everyone else." Signed, Sister Mary Helen Marie, O.P., St. Mary's Principal. Of course she didn't have the balls to write out the rest of her message. She told Carmine to ask my wife, "How come the Donitella boys have the curly hair and the girls have straight hair? It would look so much better the other way around." Couldn't Magdalena get Toni perms for the girls, cut the boys' hair? The parish would pay for everything if his parents couldn't afford it.

"What the hell business of hers is what I could afford or not?" I asked.

"Why don't we just let them pay, I don't want the kids to stand out. Don't be so proud, Vincent."

I didn't say a word at first, so help me God. I bit my tongue until the blood dripped down the corner of my mouth.

Then she said, "You don't have to be so proud all the time. You only have to be caring. The kids only need..." She never finished because the smashed vegetables got her to pay attention to the fact that I was not in the same ballpark.

"I never asked for hand-outs," I hissed.

"Maybe she's just trying to find a way to show the parish's gratefulness for the 50 pounds of sausage and 200 cannoli we made for the annual parish dinner," she said. It made me livid that she would try to defend the gall of that nun.

"My name is Vincent Joseph Donitella."

"I know what your name is, now what should I tell Sister—"

"I said, MY NAME IS VINCENT JOSEPH DONITELLA!"

"Why don't you yell it a little louder so the one next door and all the neighbors on the block will hear it?"

"DON'T YOU TELL ME WHAT TO DO AND NOT DO!"

"OK. Would you like your dinner now?"

"WHO DOES SOME LOUSY STINKING IRISH NUN THINK SHE IS ASKING WHAT I CAN AND CAN'T AFFORD!"

"She didn't mean..."

"DON'T TELL ME WHAT SHE MEANT. I TAKE CARE OF MY KIDS. NOBODY GIVES A LOUSY DAMN..." I was running out of words to put to the tune of my anger, it was so deafening. So I said calmly, "You are my wife and you are never to say a word against me or what I think." And then I found that we had a lot of other unfinished business. My sisters and Philip and her mother...I had to tell her that she was acting just like her mother, Gemma Coniglio, who liked to argue with every little thing I said.

"My mother, my mother...How about your mother, your family?" she threw in. "How they treat you, the only son? Why don't you pick on them instead of my mother for a change?"

"With your mother I'll never have enough class," I said. "Her and her *alt'Italia* ideas. Makes me disgusted. Her and her lawyers and her doctors in her family. You could have married one and she'd still find something to complain about. Your poor father!"

"My poor father? Why do you have to drag my parents into this? This is about you and your damn pride, your hard headed..." She stopped as if she had run out of steam mid-sentence.

"That's enough about my pride!" I shouted. I heard the doors open and close and the kids run and hide.

I heard her grandmother close the windows on the side of the house where Mrs. Lear lived. From the hall, I could see Mrs. Lear's silhouette across the alley way, a shadow exploding in the half dark, another ball-busting woman. Then I saw the hole in the bathroom door and the one in the Hi-Fi and each was just one more little thing to eat at my insides.

My wife gave up arguing and bent down to pick up the mashed vegetables. The eggplant was bruised beyond recognition, its black and blue skin burst open, like a shameless *buttana*. The *cucuzza* was shorn in two at the weak point in its scrawny neck. How fragile the thin skins that held things in place.

She put them in the sink and ran water over them and just stood there leaning over the sink and the running water for a very long time.

I never meant to come home to these scenes. I thought that driving around for a while would have helped. I sat down to read the newspaper in the parlor and got annoyed again. My wife, her grandmother, and every last one of my kids knew my rule about the newspaper. Nobody was to read it before I had looked at it. If they touched it, they were to fold it back exactly as it was.

I stood at the bottom of the stairs and called my sons to the landing, "Mario, Vinnie, Carmine, and Frankie!" They came filing out of their bedroom good and fast and stood at the top of the stairs. "I want to know which one of you four read my newspaper."

"I did, Dad," Carmine answered.

"Have you forgotten my rule about my newspaper? Is your memory that short?"

"No."

"No, what?"

"No, Dad."

"Mario and Vinnie, go back to your room. Carmine, I want you and Frankie to recite the poem I taught you last week."

"Which one, Dad?"

"What do you mean, which one, you don't remember?"

"You taught us two, *Trees* and *Abou Ben Adhem*," said Frankie.

I still had a bad taste in my mouth about the goddam intellectuals over at Rutgers, who fought having the plaza in New Brunswick named after Kilmer, because they said he didn't use good grammar.

"Make it *Abou*," I ordered them. "And make it snappy. I'm waiting."

They stumbled over every last line until I had to get angry and shake up their memories with a threat before it came back to them. Finally they got through it:

Abou Ben Adhem (may his tribe increase!)
Awoke one night from a deep dream of peace,
And saw, within the moonlight in his room,
Making it rich, and like a lily in bloom,
An angel writing in a book of gold:
Exceeding peace had made Ben Adhem bold,
And to the presence in the room he said,
"What writest thou?"—The vision rais'd its head,
And with a look made of all sweet accord,
Answer'd, "The names of those who love the Lord."
"And is mine one?" said Abou. "Nay, not so,"
Replied the Angel. Abou spoke more low,
But cheer'ly still; and said, "I pray thee then,
"Write me as one that loves his fellow men."
The Angel wrote, and vanished. The next night
It came again with a great wakening light,
And showe'd the names whom love of God had bless'd
And lo! Ben Adhem's name led all the rest.

When they were done, I said, "You forgot something." It took them a while to remember, but they remembered the author's name. I made them recite it a second and third time until they remembered to say the title, the author and all the words of *Abou Ben Adhem* by James Leigh Hunt. And then I sent them to bed.

After reading the paper for a while, I felt like writing a poem for my wife. She was sweeping the floor because her grandmother would not come out of her bedroom when I was angry. I had her respect at least. My wife swept and swept for a very long time. I could hear the broom sweeping up dirt and debris that couldn't possibly be there any more.

"Hon, what're you doing?" I asked her as I finished the poem.

She didn't answer me. I let her get away with ignoring me. I started to get annoyed again because she wouldn't stop the sweeping noise.

"Come join me," I ordered her.

"I have to finish cleaning the kitchen first," she said in a far-away voice.

I went to the bedroom to write down the little ditty I composed for her, then to the kitchen to get her something. When I returned she was sitting very still in her oak rocker. She was staring into space. I handed her the poem and she read it silently, then let it drop onto her lap. She rocked gently and didn't say a word. That was OK. I knew she loved me even if I was a bastard at times. I put the Mills Brothers on the shabby Hi-Fi—*You Always Hurt the One You Love*.

"Here, Beaut," I said, calling her by the nickname I had given her while I was overseas writing to her when she was pregnant with our first son. "Here, have a glass of your father's red wine and some of the peaches from Angelo. I peeled and sliced them just the way you like them. I got all the fuzz off for you. Put some in the wine. I don't want any right now. I've got a bit of *àcitu*. Here's to our precious love. You can't take that away from us. We got some great love between us. You're worth every drop of my blood, sweat, and tears. Here, take this, don't ignore me."

She took my gift and slipped three slices of peaches into the wine goblet. She said nothing, just sipped the wine and I knew she was feeling better, too.

"I'm going to take you and the kids down the shore in two weeks when school's over," I said.

"With what? Our good looks? We just promised half of your next three paychecks to St. Benedict's. We may have to mortgage the house if another boy goes."

"We can stay with my *cumpari*, Johnny, at his shore house. He'll be in town then. I'll bring him a bunch of crates of good stuff. The artichokes will be here then. We'll have some from California. We'll make *sosizza*. We'll bring some *biscotti*. He'll take the kids crabbing in Barneget Bay. We'll have plenty, don't worry. Don't we always have enough?"

"Sure," she said.

"You're awfully quiet, Beaut. It's OK to talk to me now. Tell me how you feel."

"I'm very tired and I don't want to argue anymore."

"Nothing to argue about. I'm the man of this house and you are my wife," I said firmly, raising my voice slightly so she got my message.

"Your pregnant wife," she said just like that, telling me she was carrying our tenth child. Perhaps I should have gone back to the Port and jumped off the pier with cement shoes on both feet. But I felt great. I knew everything was going to be all right.

"Hallelujah!" I shouted. "I'll join you in the wine, hell with the *àcitu*. It's about time you got pregnant again. Teresa's going to be three soon. About time. Here's to number ten. May it be another son. Five sons oughta round things out real nice! You feel OK, Hon? Huh?"

"I feel fine. Why don't you go to bed and I'll be in soon. I want to finish the peaches and wine."

I kissed her a good long good night and lay down in bed exhausted. I heard her rock, then get up and put other records on the Hi-Fi. I forgot to ask her how she liked my poem. I would ask her when she came to bed if I was still awake, if I was still alive. After all, it was a Monday night.

93

Magdalena (1963)

I couldn't swallow the peaches without the wine. I became so accustomed to the sweet with the sour, it all tasted more naturally that way. Since I was a little girl, I drank my father's wine with its big sour taste along with the nectar-sweet peaches that came as a sapling-tree from his village in Sicily.

It was late when I sent my husband to bed. It was the only way I could finish a thought. When I had a turn to rock in the chair, rhythms wound their way through my head. But not my own. "Even the rocks, even the wind sang…" I could not stop the words from sounding in my head, like a litany, like an aspiration we said in church to soften our mortal suffering, to distract us from our naturally wretched selves.

This was my weakness. I'd start to speak, start to say the truth that had crouched in my chest so long it was like steam longing to escape into clear space, burning like a very bad case of *àcitu*. But then I'd back down when I saw the blood. My strength was spent tending to the little things, so my husband wouldn't get bruised. I had nothing left for the big things.

Rocking and raising my feet was just a way to let the swelling, the numbness go somewhere else in my body for a change. Every time I put my feet up and saw them, I would think the only reason they kept moving was because they had come so far already. From Peterstown, from my parents' home, from dancing on big floors in Harlem, from singing and sewing with the Nickelettes! From my intention to have just four children.

Those feet didn't look so lumpy and misshapen after the fourth child. Nor was my body so numb and stretched out like pizza dough then. I thought when our fourth child was three years and I didn't get pregnant again, Mother Mary had smiled down on my own song, my own thoughts. But then the gypsy, Carmela, the devout Catholic one we used to see at the Peterstown market, read my tea leaves. She moved her hands around my belly and said she felt a light radiating from me. More children in there. Carmela said all our children, except for one, would dwell near great bodies of water. She said one would have the calling—enter the spiritual life. She said I would cry an ocean of tears before I stopped crying and finished my mortal life peacefully. She said other things would happen, too, before I could rest.

Even as she spoke I was pregnant with the fifth child.

I never minded having the children. Carrying children was easier than most people thought. After a while they slipped right out, as if they were coming through me, not from me, each one bringing another chapter to the story of the Donitellas. Now number 10 was on its way.

My mother was bitterly happy for me because she had struggled and suffered so much just to have the three of us, me and my two brothers. She too had known the bitter with the sweet. But she had lost so many babies it left her hard inside and out. Her womb had betrayed her in the worst way. So she wanted to hold on to the only other stability she knew, the money that she and Pop had made in America as tailors and landowners.

She had her own childhood snatched away by tragic events. When my mother, Gemma Leonforte, was just six years old, her mother took sick with a disease that affected her mind and then her body. She died quickly. My mother's father was a wine and cheese merchant in the mountain village of San Giovanni-Gemini, but he began to go senile soon after his wife died. My mother had to wash him and stand on a pedestal by his bedside to feed him. Her two brothers already took the boat to America.

My mother took care of her father until she was 15. Then he lost his mind completely and began to run naked through the village. She was so ashamed. Finally her father died and her brothers, who had begun to reap the riches of America, sent for her. They married her to Franco Coniglio, my father. They met him at one of their factory jobs. My mother liked to talk only about her high falutin' memories—her father the wine and cheese merchant, her uncles, the doctor and lawyer—never about her shame. But my father's mother told me everything when I was old enough. I thought that having as many grandchildren as she has would ease my mother's disappointment, just as I thought that my being a Madonna would ease my husband's sadness.

No, I didn't mind the children. It was trying to be the Immaculate Conception that was so hard. Trying to pretend that I had no dark spots on my soul gave me the most agony. Vincent called me his Madonna like it was a blessing, not a curse. He had too many troublesome women in his life before me, he said. I thought I could be the perfect wife. He put me on a pedestal. But after a while I wanted to get down.

I wanted to speak my piece once in a while. I wanted to forget my place from time to time. I wanted to go to Paris, not down the shore. When I saw the bruised and battered vegetables on the floor I saw myself inside out and I knew I was no longer going to keep my mouth shut. I opened my mouth and fell from grace.

I saw the children slip into their rooms, Mario, my oldest son, slamming his door shut with his slide ruler. I saw my Lucy take care of the small ones. She put Maria and Teresa to bed. She pulled Maddelena and Rena upstairs in their bedroom. Vinnie, Carmine, and Frankie locked themselves down the cellar until the worst was over, then slipped up into their room. My grandmother slipped into her chair to pray the rosary.

I saw Mrs. Lear's shadow, too. To hell with the neighbors for once. I saw the blood in my husband's eye. But I still said what I had to say about his pride. I had to tell him that his pride was running his, mine, and the kids' life like a religion. And if it was really pride why did it sound so much more like something else? This sort of pride was like a bruise on a good piece of fruit—you best cut it out before it poisons the whole piece of fruit and every piece of fruit near it. He was more thin-skinned than he liked to believe or to show the world. I saw the blood in his eye, on his lips. After his father died he had gone to one war and come back ever ready to commit another. If it wasn't his sisters, it was me or my mother. And I was tired of being the grimacing Madonna.

In the beginning the song in my head was my own, not a song of Vincent's that echoed through my overtired mind, until my ears started to throb. It was a Perry Como song, *Don't Let the Stars Get in Your Eyes*. If only I listened. Just to hum a few bars of it brought a calm feeling.

But in the beginning my husband was a different man. When he told the stories to the children I still caught glimpses of that younger man. I saw my younger, thinner self, too, before my body was scarred by so many babies. I always thought that in the fullness of time, when all my children were grown and on their way, when Carmela's prophecy was fulfilled, maybe we would have a few years of life left to hum our songs together, to enjoy a polished dance floor once again. Perhaps that day would return. But even the rocks, even the wind would have to learn to sing, I thought as I rocked.

My husband and I didn't have the same story of when we first met. He said it was in New York City in front of Radio City. I recalled no such meeting. He said he also saw me at Warinanco Park for the big Air Force show. I vaguely remember his being there. The first time I saw him was at the Nickelettes' meeting at his house, because his sister Angela was my best friend for years.

The Nickelettes were once the beginning and the end for me. We started as a sewing club, seven of us, high school friends in Peterstown. We all attended Battin High School. We all had parents from the other side. We would see each other in the halls and exchange our secret look and hop. We called ourselves the Nickelettes because every other week we paid a nickle for dues. I had been best friends with Vincent's sister, Angela, long before I met Vincent. Angela had always wanted to introduce us to each other during the time when, as Angela said, "He was still running around with every vamp that flirted with him."

But my parents were strict about dating and the only way I could get out of the house was for the Nickelettes. My father had to drive me and pick me up. We met Fridays after school at one of our homes, most often at Angela Donitella's. We saved our nickles and held raffles, and soon we were able to get out of Peterstown, away from all our nosy people there. We bought tickets to go to see the Rockettes or to a play. I loved going places with my girlfriends and I had always thought that after high school we would go to sophisticated, wonderful places like Paris together. I would get to use my

French. I would buy an ounce of expensive perfume! But it was not to be.

We sold tickets for the raffles to our neighbors all around Peterstown. The prize was always a special crocheted scarf, if we had finished one, or a chenille bedspread that we bought at Woolworth's. We bought spools of nice thread from the seamstress on Second Avenue at the Saturday Peterstown Market. We crocheted the finest stitches—single, double, triple—in chevrons, rosettes, and wheels. We made doilies, tablecloths, and shawls. We had all learned from our Italian mothers and grandmothers.

I remember our first meeting in 1935 at Angela's house. We put all our names in a hat and each of us picked one, a secret pal, who we'd send birthday and Christmas gifts, trinkets, anonymously for a year or two. I picked Agnes.

We made little round puffy things from brightly colored calico. We gathered the fabric with a drawstring thread and put them around jars of canned tomatoes like little nightcaps. We were so proud of our creations, we sold them door to door to the wives in Peterstown, just three cents apiece.

We began to bring cakes, cookies, and wonderful treats from Bella Palermo Bakery to our meetings, if we had a few extra pennies. Or we would bake some goodies.

I remember the meeting where I finally met Vincent. My father drove me to Angela's in our red and white 1934 DeSoto. I asked him to stop at Bella Palermo on North Broad. I knew that Jenny the owner would give us the broken *biscotti*—the pignoli, chocolate, *cucciddati, quaresimali*, and the almond ones—all for a penny, if we were not with my mother. My mother could never get a good enough deal in America. Everything was so much cheaper in the old country. She drove people *pazzi* with her constant complaining, "too dear."

At Angela's house, Mr. Donitella was saying good night to the young children. Even though they were younger, these children—Mrs. Donitella's younger brothers and sisters—were aunts and uncles to Angela and Vincent.

"*Dio ti benedica,*" Mario Donitella said to each child before sending them upstairs.

"*Santu*," each child answered. "Did you bring us a surprise?" one asked.

"*Dumani sira*," he said with a twinkle in his eye, but they knew he was playing, so he said, "Which pocket?" Mario Donitella brought them candy and little trinkets. That night the surprise was torrone noughat candy from Italy. Then I heard them say their prayers together, kneeling at bedside, just as Vincent would do with our children later. They blessed everyone by name—in the house and all the relatives still in Sicily.

Mario Donitella no longer sold hay, oats, and coal when I met him. He helped support all 16 who lived in his small house. He ran a deli business for a while with a soda and beer delivery route. Then he got a white collar job selling insurance. He sold to the Italians in Peterstown for 25 cents a month. He first came to my front door when I was little. I never dreamed that someday I would be best friends with his daughter and marry his only son.

He had brought home some insurance policies to work on that evening with his oldest daughter Marialia. So the Nickelettes moved to the back porch so we wouldn't disturb them with our loud laughter and singing. We started our meeting as we did all meetings by singing *Siràcusa*, a song that people who belonged to the St. Lucy Society sang. If you came from Cammarata or San Giovanni-Gemini you were automatically a member of the Society, but anyone who revered St. Lucy could join.

After singing, our voices all warmed up, we took care of business first. We were saving for the next outing to New York City. We had to sell more tickets to our families and friends. The prize this time was the best ever, an extra large crocheted tablecloth, with the finest, most intricate stitchery. We had all taken turns working on this one, using stitches from the old country.

"Girls," said Agnes, our treasurer for the year, "I want you to know that we are still five dollars from the total needed to see Lena at the Helen Hayes. Get the lead out and sell those raffle tickets."

"Is that busfare, dinner, and all?" asked Rosie.

"You bet," said Agnes. "Dinner at Mama Leone's again."

We all clapped and whistled and Lucia Donitella stuck her head out on the porch and said, "*Zitti*."

"OK, Mama," we all whispered. We all called her Mama.

Someone always told a story as we sewed to help pass the time. It was Francesca's turn that night. She decided to tell "The Ghost of Warinanco Park," one she had told many times before, but which we all liked.

Francesca, our club president, was the best storyteller. This one was about Giuseppina, or Giussi, with her "thick flowing crown of black ringlets and her rosy red lips and nice hips." The story could go on for as long as was necessary to pass the time. But it ended tragically when Giussi's lover, Amadeo, announced to her he would not marry her. He didn't tell her it was because he had found out from his friends that she was not a virgin. She despaired and went to the big oak tree in Warinanco to hang herself in her wedding gown. Meanwhile Amadeo found out that his friends were only fooling him and ran to find Giussi just as "her body was swinging from the branch with the last flutter of life leaving her body." The story always ended, "In the silver light of the full moon, to this day you can still see the ghost in her wedding dress, flying around the old oak tree, calling in a shrill voice, 'Aaa-maaa-deee-ooo! Aaa—maaa-deee-ooo...'"

Well that particular evening we were all very quiet. You could hear the insects outside and the sound of nimble fingers and thimbles pushing needles through cloth. When Francesca uttered this last line, her voice sounded as if it came from outside the screens of the porch. For a moment a chill went through all of us as we looked up. Then there came the laughter. It was Vincent and his friends, Johnny and Frankie, calling Aaa—maaa-deee-ooo outside.

Francesca got very indignant and yelled at him. "Vincent, you no good, lousy...you son of...you were eavesdropping?"

"Who, us?" said Johnny. "We didn't hear a word."

"Not a word," said Frankie.

"But why don't we go down to the old oak tree in Warinanco?" asked Vincent, busting up laughing. Francesca threw her pin cushion at him and the guys all laughed. We all did.

"You guys can stay five minutes, Vincent, then out!" said Angela. "This is girls only." Angela said this more for Francesca's benefit than anyone else's.

"Second the motion," said Francesca, who still wore saddle shoes and baggy pants, pigtails. She was never interested in boys like we were. She worked part-time as a salesgirl and took care of her mother and grandmother who spoke no English. She thought the rest of us worried too much about hair, clothes, fingernails. Angela, who wanted to study to be a beautician, made us all beautiful. But Francesca would never let Angela near her. "How will you ever find a man to put a big rock on your third finger?" asked Angela. Francesca would scoff at her. She wanted to go to college to be a teacher. The rest of us just wanted to go down the Port to shop like the Jewish girls with all their good taste and their eye for bargains at the warehouses and at Levy's and Daffy Dan's. Francesca never had time to go with us.

Vincent came over and sat by me and said, "You seem like a fine seamstress."

"Thank you," I said, keeping my eyes on my stitching. I didn't have anything to say to him then.

"What are you making there?" he asked.

"A scarf," I said.

"A scarf?" he said. "For what?"

"For a dresser."

That was it. Our first conversation. Nothing to make a Million Dollar Movie about. I went into the kitchen to help Mama get the coffee, cake, and cookies served. The kitchen smelled of freshly fried garlic and cooking tomatoes. She was leaning over the sink straining peeled tomatoes from her garden. With the wooden cone she worked the pulp through the cone-shaped colander. The muscles and veins in her forearm bulged out. She wore a calico apron that the Nickelettes had given her. After a few turns of the straining cone she'd take her index finger and wipe down the juice that had collected on the outside of the colander into the pot. Mama had a bunch of tomato seeds ready to sprout and plant in her garden out back. Her English was never as good as her husband's, so we spoke half in Sicilian, half in English. I asked her how she made her *sugo*, maybe with the thought in the back of my head that one day I'd cook for Vincent.

"First, don't burn the garlic in the olive oil like some do. Aaagghh!" She spit some air from her throat. "Leave a bitter taste, if you burn. I use some plum tomato, some puree, some paste. I show, *aspetta...*" She went into her pantry and returned with canned paste. "Always strain the seeds. Or, otherwise the *sugo* go bitter, too. Best you cook a nice long time, maybe three hour. I put a little sugar, a salt, a pepper, *accussì.*" She cupped the palm of her hand to show how much. "*Ma*, sometime, I no putta salt. I crush *l'anciova*, the anchovie, *accussì*, with a fork, *capisci*? Vincent and his father like-a that way."

I didn't say anything about the sugar, but I thought, "*Chi schifu!*" How awful!

She had *carduni* soaking in the salt water and I asked her what she intended to do with them. "Vincent love this, too," she said. "I soak away the bitter with the salt. Then I just dip in egg, in bread crumb with some oregano, *basilicò, maggioriana,* fry in olive oil. That's all. Everybody eat-a cold next day." I didn't ask where she picked her *carduni*. My mother and father never told anyone where they picked theirs. You didn't ask that kind of thing of someone you didn't know too well.

A few days after that meeting Vincent called me for a date. I was surprised because I didn't think I'd made much of an impression. He took me to see *Gone with the Wind* on a Saturday afternoon. Then that evening, around 10 p.m., I was braiding my grandmother's hair, coiling it around her head so she could sleep. We were in my bedroom on the second floor, with my window to the alleyway open. Suddenly, I heard a few strains of *Stardust Melody*. I knew that Hoagy Carmichael was Vincent's favorite composer and that was his favorite song. I knew it had to be Vincent because I recognized the French horn.

My mother, who was about to get into bed, came running into my room, opened my window all the way and shook both her fists, cursing at the top of her lungs, "*Figghiu di buttana, vaffannapuli, cretinu!*" She turned to me and asked, "You know this lousy bum? You tell him I call the cops!"

The music stopped and I heard the footsteps running away. I kept braiding my grandmother's hair. "Oh, Ma, it's just some kid playing a joke."

"Don't tell me no lie!"

My brother Pete looked in and saw me smiling to myself. He wagged his finger and laughed.

"Ma, don't worry, you worry too much about everything," he yelled to her. She would listen to her son. I lit a votive candle in front of St. Lucy's picture in my grandmother's sitting room and I said an Act of Contrition for my little white lie. I lit another one in front of the enamel altar, the one with Christ's body being removed from its sepulchre and tended to by his mother, Mary Magdalen, and the women. This one was important. It was so that one day my mother would accept Vincent.

But my mother never trusted Vincent. She never said so outright, just things like, "Honey, you gotta marry a good man, who work hard like your father, who make a good living," or "He's not like his father." Or she reminded me about my two uncles, Tonino and Arturo, a doctor and lawyer, who came to America, made a lot of money working in a factory in Newark, and then returned to live like lords in Sicily.

My mother kept in touch with her cousins in San Giovanni-Gemini. From the other side, they sent her burlap bags filled with almonds and dried figs from their trees. They wrote long letters about their births, weddings, deaths, and life there in the old country. My mother always wrapped a one-dollar bill inside her letters to them so that they would know how well she was doing here. She and my father owned three apartment houses in Peterstown. But here in America, they acted like paupers.

Vincent didn't have enough education, money, or status for her, but worst of all he never had enough humility. But he had passion—you could tell he wanted to suck the sweetness from life. This was what really attracted me to him at first.

Who else would have found a way to change cheese to gold, to convince my mother to let me marry him? Who else would have waited with Mother Cabrini all night for me to show?

When the Nickelettes finally had enough money to see Lena Horne in New York, we got our tickets for a Saturday night. We would eat at Mama Leone's first. I would sleep at Angela's house that evening because it would be a late night. Angela agreed to come with me to the shrine of Mother Frances Cabrini in New York to leave a bouquet of roses. Mother Cabrini was one of my favorite patrons. We were supposed to go to the shrine before dinner, but we were so late, we decided to go after dinner and the show. When we arrived, I was saying a silent prayer in front of Mother Cabrini when a figure came out of the shadows. I almost jumped out of my skin—it was Vincent. He said Mother Cabrini was one of his favorite patrons and he always paid her a visit late on Saturday nights. Later Angela told me he had been waiting there for hours, knowing we were coming. Johnny Biondi was with him.

They asked us to go dancing with them up in Harlem. We took the subway uptown to the Savoy. I had never been to a place like the Savoy. It was on the second floor. Benny Goodman and Duke Ellington were playing that evening, such great entertainers. The stage ran the length of the building. Vincent paid a half dollar for each of us to get in. It was magnificent inside that dance hall!

Lenny, a colored friend of Vincent's, took us to a table. The women on stage, with shiny copper and mocha skin and purple lips, were beautiful in the tropical blue light. We sat at a small round table. I remember in the middle of the table was a small lamp with a velvet shade the color of over-ripe persimmons. It had cream-colored fringe. I was playing with the fringe on the shade and Angela remarked how my nail polish, which she had chosen for me, matched the persimmon color. Vincent took my hand gently and said my nails were a prettier shade. I blushed and as usual didn't know what to say.

But just then the drums and cymbals crashed. The music began. Vincent pulled me onto the dance floor. It was our first time, but we moved in perfect harmony dancing to the swing along with the best of the colored dancers. We did the peabody, lindy hop, truckin, Suzy-Q, and when we did our own steps, everybody cleared away and made a circle around us like they hadn't seen anything like it before. We were grace itself. The floor fell away, the music moved through us, and we were a smooth and elegant wave of harmony. Not like later.

When we could dance no more, we drove in Johnny's Cadillac along the Harlem River on the East Side, all the way to Throg's Neck and the Whitestone Bridge. We took the Lincoln Tunnel back to Peterstown in time to drive to the end of Trumbo Street in the Port, stand on the pier and watch the morning gild New York City.

We got home long after sunrise. Angela and I slipped into her home separately from Vincent.

After that, Vincent and I saw each other regularly. The first thing he ordered me to do, once it was clear I was in love with him, was to stop wearing make-up. He said he hated showy women. It made them look hard. He liked his women soft and feminine, women who looked natural. He said I had beautiful Sicilian eyes and skin like the women who just got off the boat. One day after we had dated a few years he wanted me to see what he meant. So he invited me to accompany him to Ellis Island where he had some family business to tend to. That turned out to be a happy day for me but a most tragic day for the Donitella family.

Mario Donitella's cousin Alfonso Tuzzalini and his family had arrived a couple days earlier from Cammarata, Sicily. They were all detained because of Alfonso. He had passed the physical test. A buttonhook tool was used to turn back all their eyelids to make sure they did not have trachoma, a contagious disease. But Alfonso was being held on literacy grounds. He appealed to a Board of Special Inquiry.

Vincent appointed himself legal counsel for Alfonso and told me we were still fighting a turn-of-the-century personal vendetta of Henry Cabot Lodge and the likes of him, who wanted to keep out Italians, Russians, Poles, Hungarians, and other immigrants who didn't speak English. Vincent had helped other new arrivals from Sicily get working papers and pass inspection.

My mother had been able to purchase second class passage from Sicily and bypass Ellis Island. But my father and other relatives, both of Vincent's parents and all our people had come through its doors. Vincent's mother and aunt had spent 40 days and 40 nights on Ellis Island, quarantined because of their seasickness, not knowing if they'd be let in or not. Then, immigration laws had changed.

Many still came, though fewer than during the Great Depression of the early '30s.

It was a bitter, cold gray winter day in December when I accompanied Vincent to Ellis. The gulls squawked and scraped the dingy waters of the Hudson as we ferried across from Liberty Park in Jersey City. The Statue of Liberty was a ghostly silhouette in the thick mist and as we neared the immigration station it seemed haunted itself with so few immigrants coming down the steps of its Great Hall—not like in the old days. Its main red brick and limestone building with its four copper-domed turrets must have sent a message to all those foreigners seeking refuge here once, that this was going to be one Hell of a country.

Before I knew it, our little footsteps were echoing down the Great Hall with its tall arched windows, bronze and glass chandeliers. The vaulted ceiling gleamed with the dove-tailed terra cotta tiles laid by the Guastavinos, Italian immigrant masons.

I thought of my father and of my grandmother and my other Sicilian-born relations getting their first glimpse of this place. Having seen nothing fancier than the gray stone walls of their medieval villages in the mountains, they must have thought they'd skipped over a few centuries.

It took forever to walk from the back of the Great Hall to the front where the Tuzzalinis and the immigration officer awaited us. As we walked, my arm through Vincent's, he turned to me and proposed. He said it so *sottovoce*, at first, I didn't understand. "Magdalena, would you marry me?" When I didn't answer right away he said, "I don't like to repeat myself, but I will this once. Would you marry me?"

"Yes," I said, *sottovoce* also, because I was beginning to get embarrassed, "Of course, I'll be your wife." What was I going to say, NO, right there? Later we learned the Hall was a whispering gallery and everybody heard every word no matter how low you spoke.

We kissed. The officer cleared his throat. We greeted Alfonso and his wife and two sons. There was a big pile of baskets and baggage nearby that looked like it just slid off their backs.

"*Comu stati?*"

"Tutti bene, tutti bene!" They all answered.

When we were all done hugging each other, the officer showed Vincent the literacy test and Vincent was allowed to explain it to Alfonso in Sicilian. The test looked like a child's puzzle. There were 24 moons with eyes, nose, mouth. The moons were placed six on each of four rows. Alfonso had to find and point to the four moons that were looking to the left, the two that were looking up and the three that were looking right. He had 15 seconds and he had to begin at the upper right hand corner and proceed along each line, left to right.

The officer was very nice, but he got a little impatient when Vincent took so long to explain the quiz. At last Alfonso began. He took a little longer than 15 seconds because he confused the English words for left and right a couple times. But the officer seemed eager to be done with this, and he allowed the extra time. He gave Alfonso some columns of numbers to add up. Alfonso made one mistake only and finally the officer said with no great joy in his voice, "Welcome to America." We completed the paperwork and left to celebrate, the snow beginning to fall. We had prepared only for a success.

The Nickelettes had prepared the food for a big party at the Sons of Italy hall in Peterstown. Little did I know we'd have another reason, our engagement, to celebrate. We had made fennel sausage, meatballs, antipasto, bread, trays of lasagne, cookies, cannoli, baba rhum. We got wheels of provolone, paper thin slices of prosciutto, olives, pepperoni. It was December 13, the feast day of Saint Lucy, so someone made *la cuccia* with the wheat, ceci, honey, milk, and cinnamon. We got a band together—accordion, fiddle, and piano—all the *paisani* from Cammarata and San Giovanni-Gemini to sing and dance.

It was a grand party. We drank homemade anisette to keep warm. My mother came over and sang *Santa Lucia, Torna a Sorrento*. We all sang *Siracusa*. Vincent played his French horn with the band. We all danced the tarantella for a long time. Vincent's parents were to show up late, because his father usually worked overtime. He said in a little while we'd run over to his house to get them and tell them about us before we announced our engagement publicly.

First he wanted to give a little speech welcoming Alfonso and his family. *"Ai miei cugini,"* he toasted with a few words in Sicilian first. Then he said how lucky America was to have so many Italian immigrants coming to her shores. "No other ethnic group alone has done more for this great country and the Sicilians in particular. Italians as a whole have contributed more to the arts, culture, and science of the world. Even today as I speak, the Anglos are starting to eat our foods. They eat our macaroni, they come to Spiritos in droves and eat our pizza pie. They put our meatballs and spaghetti in a can. They're starting to catch on to our vegetables. Soon they'll be eating our eggplant and our broccoli rabe. Mark my words." When Vincent spoke like this, it didn't matter if people agreed with him or not, they listened.

His pride egging him on, Vincent quoted an 1896 speech by Senator Lodge, in which he derided Italian immigrants for lowering the standard of living by taking wages lower than any American ever would consider. It was just 43 years ago that the Senator had predicted that the illiteracy test would show what a disgrace the whole lot of Italians, Russians, Poles, Hungarians, Greeks, and Asiatics were.

Before he could finish, I saw Angela squeezing frantically through the crowd, with such a look on her face, I knew it was not good. She whispered something in Vincent's ear. He told the *paisani* to continue to celebrate and calmly stepped down off the platform. He told me to grab my coat. "It's my father, taken ill or something," he said. The three of us ran like the dickens to his house, through the bitter snow.

Inside it was quiet. Vincent's sisters, Marialia, Rosalia, Santa, and Antoinette, who ordinarily could melt the ears off a brass monkey, were sitting on a couch, their heads lowered or buried in handkerchiefs.

"Chi cosa?" he asked. Marialia had rosary beads in her hands but was very still. We went to Mario's bedroom, where Dr. Palmieri and Mama were at his side. Father Anthony was there, and so was Vincent's godmother, Katie. They had been praying low, their lips moving fast. We all knew. But Vincent hoped.

"He's still with us, right. Doc?"

"He was a great man, your father, Vincent, did a lot for us Italians...I'm sorry..."

"What do you mean *was*?"

"I'm sorry, Vincent. It may have been a blood clot that burst. His pulse just stopped minutes ago, I tried to revive him. Looks like a blood clot. He felt no pain."

"Aunt Katie, the leeches, did you bring them? What about the glass with a candle, try something..."

"*No*, Vinnie, *è troppu tardi.. non pozzu...*" and with that Katie let out a blood curdling wail and Mama cried, too, and I heard Vincent's sisters start in and we were all weeping, one louder than the other.

"He asked for you, Vinnie," said Doctor Palmieri, "he called your name over and over before...we lost him...I'm sorry."

This made Vincent feel worse, that he had missed his father's final request. But as Vincent wept, he spoke to his father as if he were listening, telling him that he had made something of himself, that we were engaged, and that he would pass his name on. Who knows? Maybe Mario was still there, his spirit maybe. He came to us both later in dreams—to save Vincent's life, to tell him how to change cheese to gold, to bless our children, his grandchildren. Who knows...

Still, not making peace with his father was the great tragedy of my husband's life. Later we learned how close we were. That lousy Senator Lodge had the last laugh. While Vincent was quoting the dead Senator, his father was slipping away. Mario Donitella would have been so happy that his son was marrying a full-blooded Sicilian. Vincent never forgave himself for not being able to tell him that.

A few months later he joined the Army and we continued our engagement. We married in 1941. Our first son, Mario Anthony, was born while Vincent was overseas in the South Pacific. Vincent didn't see Mario until he was 15 months old.

By the end of the War all the Nickelettes, except for Francesca, had married and begun families. Angela got a man to put a big rock on her finger, just as she said she would. Francesca became a teacher and took care of her mother and grandmother. We only met once a year maybe. And when we met, we were all too tired to sew. We ate cakes and cookies, drank coffee and watched our bodies thicken all over. We played Bridge or Pinochle. We still had good laughs together. We kept up our secret pals, guarding our anonymity over the years. I never knew who mine was but she sent me those nice oil paintings, from Woolworth's, of Montmartre, the still-lifes of fruit and flowers, rainy Paris scenes with all the people who have no face, or the Toulouse-Lautrec ones with the bold colors. I hung them around the house even though they were torture sometimes. My secret pal only meant to send me hope.

I had finished the peaches and wine and completed my thoughts for the evening when I read his poem:

For Beaut
The radiant smile upon your lovely face
Fills my heart with joy pain can't erase
Your lilting laughter, as warming as the sun
Can brighten a day with clouds begun
My dark-haired beauty, eyes raven as the night
Let us not waste words on another silly fight

I wondered what to make of this. I wondered other things.

And then he broke my reverie as always with his wailing. He always called so loud, like a hurt child, from deep in his sleep. "MAGDALENA! DON'T LEAVE!"

As he turned and tossed, not even his fears waking him, I wondered, Where did he think I would go?

Frankie (1963)

I was out to disgrace the family name. Everybody said so. My father said, my mother said. Even Mario said.

"Francorino, you know how he is, you must be trying to raise his hackles, straighten up, kid," said my big brother.

That summer I almost missed going down the shore. I was trying too hard to disgrace my father's name. But I could do it so well. Better than Mario and Carmine with their outstanding intelligence quotients. Better than Vinnie the best dancer. Better than my sisters. At this one thing I could be better than average.

I had been restricted to my backyard on Creek Street because of my wizenheimer behavior in the back of my seventh grade classroom at St. Mary's. Patrick Torre slipped me a piece of chalk during Sister Martina's Geography lesson.

"I dare you, Frankie," Patrick whispered, "write something."

I rose to the occasion without a moment's hesitation. On the floor between our two desks, I wrote, "PRUNE IS THE FRUIT OF THE LOOM." Hell, Sister Martina knew everyone called her Prunie. Her face was a mass of wrinkles and puckers bulging like a piece of dried fruit from her too-tight black and white habit. But Torre blew it. He burst out laughing.

"Brash!" Sister Martina said very low, her lips puckering and unpuckering as if she had no control over them. "Just so brash!"

I got sent down to Sr. Helen Marie's office. The principal said nothing. Hot breath just blew from Our Lady of the Perpetually Round Mouth. Her bosoms heave-hoed and her bushy eyebrows came together as one.

I tried to explain to my father that Patrick had dared me. My father cut me no slack. My father said I better learn the difference between being a chicken and taking an unpopular stand. I went to the wall, which would help me learn more quickly. In my role as a disgrace I went more and more to the wall. This time my father said,

"Perhaps, I'm not doing my job. Perhaps I ought to send you to re-form school where you'll eat bread and water."

But there was little chance of doing disgraceful things down the shore. Because down the shore the only rules to break were far too big for even me to mess with. There the tides ruled, high and low ones every day. And there was sunrise and sunset back and forth across the beach and boardwalk, the bay, rocks, and jetties, come Hell or high water.

The map of my memory is dominated by sand and water. Every summer we went down the shore for five days. We went to Lavalette where my father's best friend, Johnny Biondi, lived, godfather to Mario.

Down the shore meant not having to close windows to cut off the disgraceful sound of hot words. It meant breathing in salt mist, drinking in too much sunshine, swallowing too much saltwater, catching too much sand in our bathing suits. It meant space—the big wide open. Not the closed, tight, cramped, inland quarters of Creek Street. My father left his fruit and vegetable business behind to his colored friends for a few days and was happy. My father told stories and sang on the way to and from Lavalette. My mother never had an unfinished sentence. My parents never had words. They parked on the beach all day long. They sipped Johnny's martinis with olives each evening under Johnny's gazebo, met Johnny's latest girlfriend. They cooked big suppers, which Johnny called "dinners," and they invited strangers they met on the beach to eat with us at night.

Me and my brothers slept outside in Johnny's big, fancy back-yard with its peach and cherry trees under the stars. I would stay awake all night just listening to the endless surf, a block away, listening for the slightest change in the crashing on shore. I could tell when the tide was coming in and when it was going out just by the sound.

Down the shore we had freedom. As far as I was concerned, Creek Street when we left it each summer, could vanish from the face of the earth. One summer it almost did.

Before we left for the shore, Carmine and I had to get our hair cut. My father took us to his cousin's barber shop in Peterstown. Carmine the barber was also a *cumpari*, being my brother Carmine's godfather. He was round as the dome on St. Mary's with a low voice which I imagined was so low because it was held down by rolls of fat. His breath came like waves hitting the shore. Bald Carmine probably became a barber so he could touch hair.

Padrino Carmine's shop was on Kristyne Street in a dark red brick building with an apartment above it. His store smelled sweet and perfumy like Mario's musician friends. Rows of colored tonics in tapered bottles with sprinkle tops reminded me of the soda syrups at the Italian cafe at the other end of Peterstown. Carmine kept his combs in a big vial of mint-green liquid. Carmine made each of us two boys sit, one at a time, in a big padded chair. He tied a cloth around our necks and turned us to face the mirror that covered a whole wall. He talked the whole time and forgot sometimes he was cutting our hair. Old Carmine's hands were in the air speaking to my father half the time. The scissors disappeared into the fat folds of his right hand. The barber pulled and pushed my head around. I only knew Carmine was cutting my hair because I saw a carpet of black wavy hair grow on the floor.

Padrino Carmine spoke...*cattivu*...and snipped. He spoke... *malasurtatu...accussì...un pettu ca non finisci mai*...and pushed my head and snipped...He shouted, *MALA FEMMINA!...accussì* and cut....*la biddoccula...beccu curnutu. Un piccatu...*

Here's what I got: A man, a nice man with a big heart... who lived above his shop... had an awful thing happen to him... a shame. His wife, a young and beautiful woman with a nice chest... cheated on him and her husband's heart was broken. But he didn't throw her out and kill the other man like he should have for making him grow horns. Like would have been done in Sicily. She was an evil woman, but he was worse for taking her back.

But what could you do? My father and the barber complained. They were '*miricani*'.

Carmine sighed. "Want some *ciambella*, boys, eh? My wife, she make some, *aspetta*." He returned with a round tin and my brother Carmine and I each took two spongy cookies.

"I'm sorry I no have coffee for to dunk," he said. I was, too.

"*Mala Femmina..*" Big Carmine repeated to my father as he watched in the mirror and cut my brother's hair. He finished and then pulled two bottles from the liquor cabinet which was next to a cabinet with the bottles of tonic. He poured some brandy into a shot glass and gave one to my father. He poured us boys a small amount into whisky glasses.

"*A saluti,*" we all raised our glasses.

I thought of it first. My father was out of earshot. I couldn't stop myself. I raised my open palm, quickly swiping the back of Carmine's new haircut and whispered, "Swats! Got ya first!" Carmine was studying the hydraulic chair and was taken by surprise, but he turned to swat. I had already dodged. My father turned and said sternly, "Do I need to settle a squabble, boys?" and we both answered, "No, Dad."

"Too bad he didn't slip and cut your ear off," Carmine whispered. "I'll get you later."

"Suffer!'

My father pulled a roll of money from his back pocket to pay Carmine. Carmine's voice boomed around the barbershop as he insisted he could not accept the money of his *cumpari*. My father said he would never come here again if Carmine didn't accept payment. They argued back and forth in English, in Sicilian, in English, raising arms and pushing the hand with the money this way and that. Finally Carmine threw most of the money in his cash drawer, except for a few bills. He turned to Carmine and said "Here, you my godson, I can give a something." He stuffed the money in Carmine's shorts pocket and we heard our father say, "*Ma, chi cazzu!*" which we decided meant "ballbuster." My brother thanked his godfather, who turned to us again and said, "I tell your father he is *caputostu*. You know what is *caputostu*? You don't be like your father or you gonna be hard head. That's what is."

My father laughed and said, "My sons! My sons! They all take after me. I raised them right. They respect me for being a hard head."

I knocked my head with my fist and said, "That's right, I'm gonna be a hard head, too, when I grow up, just like my Dad." My father and Big Carmine laughed, but my brother sneered.

My father said we had to go to the Peterstown Saturday market on Second Avenue. He said he wanted to pick up a few things, but I knew my father just wanted to talk to his people.

"How come this area is called Peterstown?" I asked my father. "Does it belong to a man named Peter? If it's part of Elizabeth, how come there's a town inside of a town?"

Carmine smirked. He never asked questions like me. He just studied all the time. Everybody said I asked too many. But my father was in a good mood and laughed.

"This section of Elizabeth was named for a German man Peter Somebody who came here in the 1700s."

"How come Germans don't live here now, Dad?

"*How come, how come*," Carmine mocked.

"Because Frankie, our people—your grandmothers and grandfathers came here from Italy and made the place Italian. The Germans, the Irish, the Jews, the Poles, and all the others left and moved to other neighborhoods. They left Peterstown to the Italians.

"Will the Italians leave Peterstown to someone else?"

"Parts of it are already taken over by the Cubans and Puerto Ricans. But some parts will always remain Italian. It's changing but I'll tell you how it used to be years ago when your Grandfather Donitella first came."

My father parked and took us to sit in the Second Avenue Park, where mothers and grandmothers played with their children. We sat in front of a round concrete pool that was filled with a foot of water and children splashing.

My father said, "Your grandfather found me splashing around in that pool once in the rain and gave me a good beating."

But Carmine and I already knew that story. My father wanted to tell us another one.

Once upon a time the streets of Peterstown, New Jersey, were paved with gold. The people from all over the world came and walked down these streets just so they could say that there was gold at their heels. By the time the Sicilians began to arrive here in Peterstown all the gold had been worn away, picked at and gouged away by the previous peoples. But that was OK, for the Sicilians were very resourceful, having bloodlines from all four corners of the globe. All they needed to live well was earth, water, and air. Although at first they found this a gray, dingy place, the Sicilians planted their seeds and turned everything into a garden of plenty. They planted colorful geraniums, marigolds, azaleas, pansies, petunias, and tulips. They brought peach and cherry trees. Everyone had a backyard strip of good earth and because the Sicilians brought sunshine and a lighthearted disposition to replace the gold, the land gave them all they wanted for. It put forth onto their tables peppers of red and green, of hot and sweet, milanzani, cucuzzi, zucchini, scarola, chard, tomatoes for sugo. And here, just as in the homeland, they took the best of each of the seasons, be it grain, grape, olive, or fruit.

When your grandfather, Mario Anthony Donitella, sailed from Sicily in 1907 with his widowed mother, they first landed at Ellis Island. After passing inspection, they took the ferryboat across the river and boarded the Jersey Central railroad in Hoboken. They took the train all the way to Peterstown because they knew paesani here who had a boarding house where they could stay until they could make their way.

By the time they reached Peterstown the Sicilians and other Italians had set up almost everything they needed to live well, worship well, and die well. The Church of Saint Anthony of Padua was erected to guide them from cradle to coffin. The Funeral Parlor of Cardoni prepared the body when the soul had departed it, for its final farewell to friends, relatives, and paisani.

And there was all the good life to savor in between birth and death: From Saraceno's bakery, which still makes the best bread. From Bella Palermo, which makes the best cannoli. Nocera's grocery store sold the best salami, pepperoni, prosciutto, capocollu, sausage, provolone, mozzarella, ricotta. Even the 'merican' came to Peterstown for the figs, dates, almonds that your grandmothers used to make cucciddati. The fish man Cuzzo cast his nets and *brought back the calamari, scungili, the baccalà, scampi, clams, and oysters. In the open marketplace the farmers sold what they grew. The old wives still come through in spring with their aprons filled with* carduni *and walk down the street, chanting "Carduni, carduni, buy this* carduni, *don't be* un tuzzuni." *In winter they brought the finocchio and sweet anise.*

Others brought their wares. There were stands that sold special utensils, strainers to separate the bitter seed from the sweet tomato pulp, mouli graters, and colanders for the macaroni and big pots to boil lots of water for the ravioli.

The Italians all helped each other create life here as much as possible with the good things they had left behind in order to come to America and make this a better place.

To keep their morale, in their halls and in the streets they had feasts and they danced the tarantella. Even though the streets here were no longer paved in gold, they were clean and well swept daily by the old women. They have always been the cleanest streets in all of Elizabethtown. In summer they sparkled, and everybody always sat outside on the porch or on the stoop and shared their stories of their lives. Women nursed their babies on the porch. Men played murra *and card games like* scopa. *They drank homemade wine or anisette.*

They reminisced a little about the old country and someone would always say, "Ah la Bella Sicilia, we will never have it again..."

And someone always answered with the question, "Will we ever have America?" Silence and sighs always followed the question as their eyes darted up and down the clean streets of Peterstown.

Before my father was even done with his story we had started walking and soon were at the edge of the open market. Now I could ask my question, "Dad, what's a tootsoon and goddune?"

"*Tuzzuni*, Frankie, I'll tell you when you get a little older. As for *carduni* or *cardoni*, as they say in proper Italian, it's a thistle, like the artichokes we eat, only wild. Only Italians know where to

119

find them in the fields of weeds, but they keep their place of harvesting secret."

We entered the thick of the market and I felt swallowed by the streams of people towering over me, pressing against each other, grabbing the fruits and vegetables like they were going out of style.

I tried to stay close to my father. I listened to all the voices like they had no bodies talking over my head. I was amazed by the hands spread with wrinkled peppers, or beans still in the pod, or plump tomatoes, the voice and the hand both saying, "Buy mine, buy mine."

The trucks were packing up as it neared noon. I watched the water gush from the fire hydrants into the gutter carrying the fruit wrappers and rotten fruit down the sewer.

I noticed an open shop selling brassieres and girdles and a woman, short and fat, like my Grandma Coniglio, holding a girdle with dangling garters up to her front. I called Carmine over and we both began to giggle until my father came and pushed us on. A man with a cart was on the corner selling Coney Island hot dogs and my father said we could have one for lunch. I ordered mine with the works—sauerkraut, relish, mustard, onions, and lots of Tabasco sauce—like my father's.

"We can't leave without paying respects to Carmela," said my father. "Carmela will show you what a *carduni* is, Frankie." Carmela, the gypsy who told my parents what the future held, was brown and wrinkled from head to foot. Her greying brown hair was thick and whirled around her head and tucked under a flowered kerchief. Coral and bright gold earrings dangled from her ears.

"*Chistu ccà è Francu, e chistu ccà è Carmine.*" My father introduced us to her and she wrapped her old, bony hands, one around each of ours. Her lined face with its bright blue eyes was sad and beautiful. She worked outdoors on her farm in south Jersey. She let go of our hands and returned to peeling her weeds.

I took an interest in Carmela's *carduni*, a dull blue-green flat stalk, like celery covered in fur and with points. Carmela squeezed a small paring knife in her left hand. Holding her thumb angled against the knife's blade, she pulled tough strings from the back of the stalks.

She saw me staring and said, "Nerves. I take away the nerves or otherwise, too firm."

I watched as the nerves curled up into little ringlets like gift-box ribbon that my mother curled with a scissor blade. Every now and then Carmela pushed the curly nerves into the gutter where they floated away with other rotten food down the sewer.

My father told Carmela that my mother was pregnant again and Carmela's face lit up like a candle in church. She said she already knew. "*Va beni*, Vinnie, *chi bedda cosa*! God bless!"

"God willing it'll be another son," said my father, "to even out the number."

Carmela bowed her head and blessed his wish, then looked at me, saying, "Franco, you too sweet. You eat more dandelion, some nice bitter green."

She looked at Carmine and said, "Carmine, you too deep down there in thought. You eat more *cassata, u tiramisù*."

My father laughed and said we wouldn't be getting *tiramisù* in the near future. In that case, Carmela said we should eat some Torrone. From under her table she pulled out two blue boxes of the nougat candy. I nudged Carmine as we each pulled out a foil-wrapped piece and said, "Carmine, look, you can't chew this candy, it's sandwiched between Holy Communion host." And it was. But we ate it anyway.

"Load 'em up, Francorino," my father kept saying each time he'd hand me a bag or box to pack into the car. At last we had a car big enough for all of us to fit in. The new station wagon, all black and shiny, was so cool even Mario rode in it when he was home from college for the summer.

Lucy asked me to go with her down the cellar to look for her summer dresses in storage. Lucy never went alone down the cellar. I stayed down there after she ran back upstairs. I passed the wall, where I found a deck of playing cards. I passed the piano, where I stopped to play both parts of *Heart and Soul*. I found my white bucks and my boat-neck shirt in the storage area. Then I couldn't resist peeking into the science laboratory that Mario had set up. I saw the trap door. The trap covered the sewage that ran under the street. When the two bathrooms in the house were overused the trap backed up and the waste came up into the house and the house had bad breath. I saw the water through the grate in the concrete floor.

In the lab I examined all the rows and shelves Mario had put up, lined with chemicals, weights, scales, flasks, vials, test tubes. There were bunsen burners and half-done experiments. Sometimes Mario let Carmine help him, but never me. The only window in the whole cellar was in the lab. The sun was shining through. I grabbed a flask of black and yellow crystals in the shadows and opened it. It made me sneeze. I put some of the crystals in a dish to examine them in the sun. I was about to turn on the bunsen burner when I heard footsteps. If Mario found me I'd be in hot water. I threw the crystals in the dish down the grate into the sewer and dashed out of the lab.

Lucy, Mario, and Vinnie were not going down the shore. They all volunteered to stay and take care of Nonnie. They were also having a party with Mario's band playing. Vinnie was going to the last Catholic Youth Organization dance of the year. He asked Dana to it.

I got back into the bucket brigade from the front door out to the car, passing bags of food, boxes of clothes, blankets, pillows, rubber tubes, and beach toys. Mario started us singing *Mademoiselle from Armentiers*.

"What if we get a flat?" I asked, but no one answered me.

We were on St. Georges Avenue about to get onto Route 35. I heard the hiss and felt the bumps. From the front seat I heard, *"Ma, porca buttana, vaffannapuli!"* Everyone had to get out of the car and unpack half of the boxes, bags, toys, and tubes, so my father could jack up the car. We formed another bucket brigade and sang just the Inky, Dinky, *Parlez-vous* part of *Mademoiselle from Armentiers*, over and over until my mother asked my father if he couldn't teach us kids another song.

We got going again, this time down Route 27, because my mother said she had dreamed about the number 35 and obviously it was unlucky.

We drove to the part of New Jersey where the houses thinned out. We rode down narrow backroads bordered by green, rolling farmland. We had to drive around a horse-drawn hayride that was moving too slow. An old man with a horsewhip couldn't make it go any faster. A few kids lay on a bed of hay in the back and stared at the black station wagon. I raised my five fingers to my nose and my mother saw me and slapped the back of my head.

We passed small white churches with high steeples. Each time I asked my mother if the church was Catholic, so that I'd know whether to cross myself. We passed farms with horses, cows, pigs, and goats. We drove down a long dirt driveway to our first stop, Angelo's farm. Angelo's chickens roamed around inside a fenced-in pen on one side while his pigs huddled over scraps in another.

Only my father got out of the car to talk to Angelo and after hugging and laughing, Angelo filled three crates with artichokes, corn on the cob, tomatoes from his vines, lettuce, some eggplant, peaches, and watermelon. I started to get restless in the car, so I said I had to go to the bathroom. So did everyone else.

We pulled in at Johnny's house just before dark. Johnny and his new girlfriend, Bertha, ran out to meet us.

Mario was lucky to be the firstborn, I thought. He got the best of everything, including godfathers. Johnny's house was like a castle. He lived in a beautiful white stucco house with archways and a golden dome that he had imported. Johnny admired the style of houses in a little town outside of Tunisia. All the other houses at the Jersey Shore were just plain old wood. Not Johnny's. Inside was a maze of rooms connected by one or two doorways. He had no wife and kids so he could blow his money however he wanted.

The brass knockers on his doors were all in the shape of a lady's bent leg. Johnny loved women, I heard my father say. Bertha was just his latest girlfriend. My father said Johnny would never marry. His wife was the sea and his mistress was his music.

Johnny had an orchard with peach, apple, and cherry trees, which a gardener took care of while he was traveling around the world. He had a rose garden that kids were not allowed to enter without an adult. He had hedges manicured and sculptured in the shape of animals—an elephant, giraffe, lion, and horse. He had a hothouse where he kept a few date-palm trees that he had shipped from Tunisia, and some exotic flowers from Hawaii.

Best of all, Johnny had a built-in swimming pool with a big patio around it, diving boards, and an outside bar with music. Inside he had his baby grand piano on a stage and fancy art on all the walls.

Johnny was cool. He never got older like my parents' married friends. He had black, wavy hair and he was trim. He dressed like a movie star. He wore silk robes and scarves around the house, soft leather shoes and no socks. He wore gold chains with the corno and the horn on them. He had a diamond watch and a big gold ring with a dozen diamonds in it. He smoked a pipe at night and I loved to watch him. The curls of cherry-scented smoke rose up from his mustache and his mouth. I knew I would be just like Johnny someday.

I couldn't wait to swim the next morning first thing. "Take Rena, Maddelena, Maria, and Teresa with you," my mother told me and Carmine. Rats, I thought, but didn't argue because my father was in earshot.

What I loved about the shore was the way things tumbled in the surf. And when the ocean had enough of them, the ocean spit them out. Down the shore the water was God.

I loved to walk along the shoreline, gathering the things that came to the surface—the mussel shells, the clamshells, the driftwood and colored glass, the scraps of seaweed. Even dead jellyfish, looking like a wet windowpane, were beautiful. I'd grab for sand crabs that were too fast for me, escaping down sandy hatches.

I longed to dive into the eye of the waves and collect some hidden treasures. I wanted to steal something from the ocean to see what things looked like before the ocean was through with them. There was always the moment when the water went slack, like the ocean would never roll again. If I could just toss my body down to the sandy bottom, where it was calm and dark under the foam, I could safely make a grab for something. But I retreated as the water arched and its turmoil formed again. I grabbed nothing but sand. You got to let the tides do their work. I retreated to collect what was available at shoreline.

At the beach I could see the Ferris wheel and the wild mouse in the distance at Seaside Heights, warped by the heat boiling up from the yellow sand.

I looked at Carmine, who had the same thought. Carmine got the girls digging a hole with the buckets and shovels and building a sand castle. I told them, "You girls play nice, we're just running back to the house to see what's taking the adults." Maddelena and Rena, now eight and nine, wanted to do everything us boys did. So I couldn't tell them where we were going.

Carmine and I started walking to Seaside Heights. It seemed to be maybe a mile away. We walked along the boardwalk until it ran out and then we walked in the street, but our feet started to burn on the black top. "Ooch, ouch, find white sidewalk!" screeched Carmine.

We were walking about a half hour when a Lincoln Continental pulled up alongside us and the driver stuck his head out and said, "And just what are you boys doing so far from the beach?" It was Johnny.

"We're just walking over to Seaside for a look-see," said Carmine, who couldn't think of a good lie.

"Seaside Heights? You know it's seven miles away?"

"It looks so close. How come we see the Ferris wheel so clearly?"

Johnny laughed and said, "Things are not always as close as they seem. You guys will tear the soles off your feet with no shoes or anything. Hop in and we'll go for a spin."

Johnny pushed something on the dashboard and the white leather roof went down and Carmine and I sat up on the back seat with the hot wind blowing us, waving to girls who waved at Johnny. He turned on the radio to WNEW and sang along with Tony Bennett singing *I left My Heart in San Francisco*. I asked Johnny to put on WABC so we could hear Cousin Brucie. The Chiffons were singing *He's So Fine*, and I sang along. Johnny said, "Those *mullingians*, even today, they can sing the best."

Johnny pulled over to a grocery store to buy some tobacco and phone home. He told Bertha to check on the girls at the beach, so we wouldn't get in trouble. Johnny knew my father would deck us. I heard Johnny say, "Thanks, Legs." He kissed the phone.

At the Seaside Heights Boardwalk Johnny bought us a strip of tickets so that we could go on all the rides, the wild mouse, Ferris wheel, bumper cars, Swiss bobs, round-up. We went through the funhouse and Carmine and I had a punch-and-run, got-you-last fight.

In the Penny Arcade we played skee ball. We dropped more coins than I seen in my life at the game booths. Carmine wanted to play one where you were given five round flat black disks. You dropped the disks from a few inches above a round red circle. You had to cover the entire red circle with the black disks to win a stuffed animal. Carmine tried five times and would have stayed there all day, gaping through his thick glasses, if Johnny didn't pull him away.

"C'mon, I know a better game," said Johnny. It was one of the game wheels where you had to put your nickel on the picture or number that comes up. I knew Carmine would prefer a game of skill to a game of chance, but Johnny insisted. Johnny knew the woman who spun the wheel and who shouted out the winning pictures or numbers. I saw him lean over the counter and whisper in her ear and hold her hand tight a long time. Carmine won a prize from the top shelf on the first try, a five-foot-high shaggy stuffed dog.

We were gone practically the whole day. When it got late, we drove back to Lavalette along Barneget Bay.

Johnny said, "I known your father since we were younger than you guys are, even before we were *cumpari*. Your father's the best. We used to work at the carnival together every summer, down on Trumbo Street in the Port. We smoked our first cigarette together there. Don't tell your father I told you, but we were only 12. We hung around the ladies of the night, the Baghdad Beauties, as every-one called them."

"Were they really from Baghdad, Johnny, the ladies of the night?" I asked.

"No, Hoboken, Birdbrain," said Carmine, "What do you think?"

"Shut up Carmine, you *cafuni*, I'm not talking to you."

126

"You don't even know what a *cafuni* is, so why are you calling me one."

"OK boys," said Johnny, "You don't want to ruin a perfectly good day now, do you?" He drove with his right hand, his left arm hanging over the open window. "The ladies, they were all-American girls from Short Hills, the rich town up north. Not really bad girls. Just no family to speak of. I don't know what became of them. They used to dress like Persian belly dancers at the carnival. That's where their name came from."

"I think my father misses those days sometimes, Johnny," I said, "Do you?"

"Yeah, I guess so. Those were the days, when we were young. Piss poor but young."

"Hey Johnny! Did you hear how my father scared off the Jehovah Witnesses?"

"No, but I have a feeling I'm going to very soon. Am I right?"

"It's a few months ago, right. I have to stay home from school because I have this little cold, well not really a bad cold. My father is sleeping late because he was working the late shift. My mother's cleaning house and the doorbell keeps on ringing every 15 minutes. First it's the Fuller Brush man. Then it's the Dugan man. He comes with his big iron crate of boxed cakes and cookies. The Dugan man really likes Mom, so he stays a pretty long time talking to her, about his kids, about her kids, where to buy shoes for them all real cheap."

"Frankie, you're just like Mom says. You could talk the ears off a brass monkey, the way you tell a story. Get to the point. Quick," said Carmine.

"Don't interrupt me again Carmine or I'll deck you." I felt courageous. "The Dugan man finally leaves—gives my Mom a pecan coffee cake for free 'cause he likes her and all...The doorbell rings again. This time I answer it. A man with blond hair, dressed in a dark suit and tie, is standing there carrying a book bag. I let him into the parlor and call my mother. I hear my Dad say, 'Judas Priest, now who is it?' My mother tries to get him to leave. He says he's come to talk to her about her salvation. She says she has very little time to think about it right now. He says, 'You have time for nothing else, Ma'am" and he pulls a Bible out of his bookbag and starts to

127

read. My mother whispers to me to go tell my father it's one of those Jehovahs and she can't get rid of him. I've never seen my father get out of bed so quickly, Johnny, so help me God. He runs into the parlor and sees this strange guy standing there reading a passage from the Bible. My mother's biting her hand saying, 'Vincent, just tell him to go! Don't start something! Just tell him to go!' My father says to her, 'Stay out of this.' The guy sees the look in my father's eyes. I swear, Johnny, it was the funniest thing to see him back out the door."

"Any more Jehovah's Witnesses coming to your door?"

"Oh man, Johnny! You oughta see them. They still come down Creek Street. They travel in partners. As soon as they get near 2724 Creek Street, they cross over."

"You exaggerate, Frankie," said Carmine, staring out at Barnegat Bay.

"Maybe," laughed Johnny, "But your father is still a character. Someday when you're older I'll tell you some more stories."

"Aw, c'mon John, tell us now," I begged.

"Nope. We gotta get you both back for dinner. Especially if we're going to go crabbing tomorrow nice and early."

Next morning, Johnny took Carmine and me out in the motorboat on Barnegat Bay to do some crabbing. Maddelena and Rena both asked to go but were told the trip wasn't for girls, just boys.

We packed raw chunks of fish meat and put them in the traps. We lowered the traps and waited for the crabs to crawl in. Then we hauled them up. We had to keep knocking the captured crabs down the sides of the buckets as they tried to crawl out.

We returned home around noon and walked to the ocean to find Bertha, my parents, and the four girls. The tide was coming in but I was ready for a swim and some body surfing. I got tossed and churned and my bathing suit fell to my feet once, but I got it back up under water and worked the sand and rocks out through the bottom. I stayed in until my lips turned blue and my mother ordered me out.

I laid on my back on the warm sand and dozed. I swam so long in the waves that I still felt as if I were rising and falling on water.

Something ragged at me. What had I done or forgot to do down the cellar before I left?

I was trying to remember what it was when there was a sudden explosion of water at my feet. A runaway wave woke me up with a shock.

When the tide began to move in, we went back to the house, where my mother was showing Bertha how to make artichokes. It struck me how Bertha's stiff reddish-blond hair fit her head like the overlapping leaves of an upturned artichoke. I couldn't believe that Bertha had never seen an artichoke before.

My mother explained patiently, "You trim the sticker ends with a sharp knife, not too much or you take the good meat. Then you make a mixture of bread crumbs—I use Colonna, it's a good brand. You add some grated Parmagiano, crumbled oregano, basil, marjoram, parsley, salt, pepper. You push the mix down between the leaves. Then you squeeze some lemon juice, some olive oil. I steam them in a little water for about 50 minutes. You try a leaf from the middle to see if it's done. You can eat them the next day too. They're good."

Bertha tried to follow my mother's instructions, but her long red fingernails kept getting in her way when she tried to push the bread crumbs down between the leaves. By the time Bertha had stuffed one, my mother and the girls had finished the others.

"OK, you boys, bring me those crabs you caught," said my father. I watched my father work over the big crab pot, adding spices, stirring with a big wooden spoon, and tasting the broth. The water was dark brown, almost black, smelling of newly mown lawn.

My father tasted the dark broth one last time and said, "The only thing missing is a little crushed fennel." He pulled a little vial out of his shirt pocket and sprinkled some powder into the broth.

"Him and his fennel," my mother murmured.

"Don't interfere with my cooking," my father scolded her. He started adding the crabs to the hot water and they went from dark sea-blue to bright red in minutes.

My mother said, "He thinks the fennel cures his *àcitu.*"

Bertha asked what was àcitu and Johnny explained, "It's a very bad case of indigestion. Vinnie got it overseas during the War. They used to mix all the food on one plate, salad and all. Can you imagine?"

"So how does fennel help?" asked Bertha. "I have some Brioschi in my purse if you like." But nobody answered Bertha. My mother yelled, "*Pastasciutta* is ready, everybody to the table."

As we sat down to eat, Johnny brought out nutcrackers for the crabs. His nutcrackers were brass in the shape of the bottom half of a lady. You had to put the crab claw between her thighs and squeeze. I thought Johnny said in Sicilian, "These are the only ballbusters I have."

After dinner we all went into Johnny's living room and Johnny played his piano. He played *Stardust Melody* and my parents danced. I knew what was coming next. My father was all warmed up and feeling good, so we would have to sing the family song.

My father had written the song when he found out that my mother was pregnant with Maria. We sang it to the tune of *MacNamara's Band*:

We are the Donitellas

You've heard so much about

People stop and stare at us

Whenever we go out

We're noted for our winning ways

And everything we do

Everybody likes us

We hope you like us too.

We waited to be told whether or not to sing the second verse. "G' head," said my father, "it's OK, Johnny's one of us."

So we sang:

We are the Donitellas

We're not so very neat

We never take a bath

And we never wash our feet

We're lower than the dirt of the earth

And all we drinks is booze
We are the Donitellas
And who the hell is yooze?

"Oh Vincent!" Bertha laughed, uncrossing and recrossing her legs and clapping her blood-nailed hands together like she had no feeling in her fingertips. Johnny clapped, too. Then we were sent to bed.

Carmine and I set up our army blankets and pillows in the orchard. Over the laughter and talking of adult voices I heard the rise and fall of the ocean as I fell asleep.

All of a sudden I heard my father call gently, "Francorino, Francorino..." I looked up and saw a shadow coming toward the orchard, saying, "You were in Mario's lab. You touched your brother's chemicals. You touched something that didn't belong to you. Where did I go wrong with you, Francorino? You're a disgrace. A disgrace to the family name of Mario Anthony Donitella." His voice sounded so odd. It was too calm. Like he was reading the newspaper.

I saw my father take off his belt slowly, through one loophole at a time. Then the belt moved by itself, like a snake, slipping out of his belt loops on its own. Standing just above me, he raised it over his head.

I threw off the blanket and began to run to the ocean. My father followed close behind me. The belt sliced through the air, making a sound like the ocean. "Franco, you're a disgrace. You'll never learn until I tear you limb from limb," my father said. I ran barefoot through the sand and then jumped into the water. I saw dozens of conch shells and chambered nautiluses floating around. Then I began kicking to get to the surface. I heard the sound of the belt again...

"Quit kicking and shut-up, Frankie!" Carmine yelled suddenly. I woke up and saw stars overhead. I heard the calm sound of the surf.

"Why were you yelling, Frank?" asked Carmine.

"I don't remember." I saw that the lights in Johnny's house were out. The adults had gone to bed. I rolled over and slept until sun-up. I ran to the ocean to jump waves and swim. Again I stayed in until my mother insisted I come out because I was blue and purple all over like a *mullingian*. Everyday until we left I stayed in the water until I was blue, collecting shells. Every evening we ate big dinners and invited people from the beach. Every night Carmine and I slept in the army blankets and I tried to remember what I had forgotten to do. I felt like *Giufà*, the simpleton. But for the life of me or him I couldn't remember.

Too soon we were staring at our packed station wagon. We all hugged Johnny and Legs good-bye. My father and Johnny hugged tight a long time and I thought my father would cry. "Don't be a stranger," he said.

Johnny put the cooler with the fresh, live crabs from that morning in the back seat. As we pulled away my father rolled down the window and said, "*Si bravu*, you're OK, *cumpari* even if you are half *Napulitanu*.

"Which half should I watch out for?" asked Bertha, but they were out of earshot, so no one yelled back. When we were a block away my mother spoke softly to my father. "Can you imagine! She was ready to feed us casseroles and canned soup every night! She had the Betty Crocker cookbook there all ready. *Chi schifu!*"

"Don't worry, Magdalena," my father said, "I know my *cumpari*. Maybe next summer he'll have a Sicilian."

When we were a few blocks from home, Rena leaned over the front seat to talk to my mother and I saw an opportunity. Quietly, I picked a live crab out of the cooler and carefully let its claw grab onto the backside of Rena's shorts. It hung there for a few seconds until her hand came back to investigate. The other claw grabbed her hand. Rena screamed at the top of her lungs and my mother screamed over her, "What! What is it? What's the matter?" My father pulled onto the shoulder of the road. We got the crab back into the cooler and set out again.

My mother said, "Frankie, keep an eye on the cooler. Damn thing must have pushed the lid up somehow, I don't know how…"

She was on the verge of figuring out what had really happened when we reached the corner of Creek Street. Something was wrong. Our street was blocked off by police cars. All we could see toward the middle of the block where our house was, were two fire trucks and clouds of smoke. We parked and walked through people crowding the sidewalk, staring at our house.

I started to remember. The flask of crystals. I had meant to return it to its shelf in the lab. I forgot to go back.

My mother, carrying Teresa, murmered *"Madonna"* and bit the back of her hand.

My father said nothing. The smoke seemed to muffle sound. Through clearings in it I could see Lucy, Mario, Dana, and Vinnie in a huddle. Lucy and Mario came running to greet us and explain the big, unnatural opening in the side of our house, the side where the lab had been. Its window was blown out. The kitchen, above the lab, was exposed. Streams of water pooled in the driveway and ran along the curb down Creek Street, where little kids jumped barefoot into puddles.

"Where's my grandmother?" my mother asked.

"Out back," said Lucy.

Lucy, Mario, and Nonnie were eating supper at the picnic table in the yard when they heard the explosion. At first they thought that the pharmaceuticals factory a few blocks over had had one of its summer explosions. Merck almost always exploded when it got this hot. But then Mario saw that the smoke and flames were too close. They were coming off the side of our house. Dana had already called the firemen.

Mario said the firemen had traced the explosion to the flask of gunpowder in his lab, which must have been ignited by the sun coming through the window. Mario said he didn't know how he ever left the gunpowder on the wrong shelf. He had always been careful to leave it on the dark side of the lab. He apologized over and over and my father said, "Don't worry, Mario, the big things have to happen."

Dana comforted my parents and offered to take the little girls to the candy store.

.

I followed at my father's heels as he talked with a fireman. Tell the truth and shame the devil, I thought over and over. "I was the one who moved the powder into the sun," I said under my breath. My mouth, dry as cotton, barely worked. I started again, "Dad, I want to tell you something." But my father ignored me and spoke with the fireman who was writing on a pad. I tried again. "I was the one who moved the gunpowder. I didn't know it was so explosive."

"Frankie," my father said impatiently, "what are you trying to say?"

"Dad, I want to make a confession." There, I said it loud and clear. I looked my father straight in the eye, disgrace that I was, and saw the change in his expression. I knew he understood, then. He knew what I meant. My father turned to face me fully and I could tell by his look it was coming. I would go straight to the wall right then and there. It was just my luck that the wall was on the side of the house that remained.

My father looked me in the eye and said: "Frankie. That's great, son. I'm proud of you. There's hope. You're a good boy. Now, just go and say an Act of Contrition. We'll take you to Confession this evening or tomorrow. Can you do that son? While I figure out what's what here and where we're going to live?"

My mouth wouldn't work anymore. I remembered my dream. Maybe I already paid for what I done.

Everybody stood around huddled in little conversations. Nonnie sat alone in a lawn chair saying the rosary, her lips moving with new life.

As I stared at the gaping hole, exposing the insides of our house, I thought, "Geeze, Francorino...maybe you should work hard at something other than being the family disgrace..."

I sat on a chair next to Nonnie. I said my Act of Contrition. To myself.

Carmine (1963)

One day a long time ago, Gianfranco Nocera woke up very early, before sunrise, before the birds even. He dressed in his work clothes and his white apron and went to open his grocery store on Third Avenue in Peterstown. When he arrived at the front door he took out his keys, but suddenly he looked down and scratched his head. He was staring at a box of olives that had been delivered to his store, dropped off during the night. The stamps showed pictures of his homeland, the Mountains of Agrigento in Sicilia, but there was no packing slip to say who sent it.

Now every Sicilian knows that the olive is the most fragile and precious of fruits. It is an ancient and sacred fruit, dating from well before the time of Christ. The olive yields the oil that is the very soul of Sicilian cooking. But the olive knows little life past the moment it is plucked from the branch of the tree. And if the olive touches the ground, it is tainted and lost forever—like a soul black with sin!

But for some reason this batch of olives not only survived the first day of picking, but even traveled a great distance. All the way from Sicilia. And these olives were unharmed, unbruised, unmarked by decay or blight as if they had just been picked.

"This is uncanny," thought Gianfranco, still scratching his head.

Gianfranco turned one fleshy specimen between his thumb and forefinger. It was just too impeccable. In the box, there were some green unripe olives, which could be pressed into a fine olio maschio—a manly oil— sharp and peppery. And there were some ripe black ones, which could be pressed into fruity, sweet—olio femmina—a nice round feminine oil.

Gianfranco had never seen such olives. They seemed to glow. They were firm and their flesh was thick and meaty. With no mark of deterioration anywhere, they looked like fine jewels. Even when Gianfranco jabbed his fingernail into the meat of one of these small globes, it did not darken. It did not rot as most olives would, but it repaired its wound right before his eyes!

Now, Gianfranco was a good church-going, God-fearing man. He was not a dishonest man and he would never sell anything to his paisan' in Peterstown that he himself would not eat. So he asked his wife, Mary, to cure a batch. It takes a good deal of salt to leach the bitterness from olives. Mary took the precious olives and soaked them in big vats of very salty brine. For lo and behold, when they were cured, those olives tasted nothing less than divine.

So it came to pass that Gianfranco saved these gems for his favorite customers, your grandmothers Lucia Donitella and Gemma Coniglio.

When Gemma Coniglio came by to pick up her groceries, Gianfranco told her about the wonderful olives. "You must try some, Gemma," he said. She complained that the price was too high, so Gianfranco gave her a few of each kind at a bargain price. When she brought them home and tasted some, she could not believe her own taste buds and even Gemma Coniglio knew that she had paid too little for this fruit. She ate one black olive and two green ones and it was not long after that she gave birth to her children, a girl, your mother, and the two boys, your Uncles Pete and Riccardo.

Gianfranco also sold a batch of the olives to Lucia Donitella who found them very sweet and heavenly. She ate two green ones and five black ones and soon after she bore two boys—me and your Uncle Joe who, as you know, vanished from drinking too much coffee—and five girls, your Aunts Angela, Marialia, Santa, Antoinette, and Rosalia.

And that's how all you kids came to be born. From Magic Olives! An Angel, Guardian of Green and Black Olives, came during the night for many years and delivered green or black olives to your mother, while she slept.

We all sat listening to my father's story in a garden that had grown out of the good blood between my Grandmother and my Grandfather Coniglio. My grandparents had exchanged marriage vows in this country only after it had been agreed that there was no bad blood between the Coniglios and the Leonfortes as far down the line as anyone could recall.

My grandparents had been very lucky in America. They owned three two-family apartment buildings in Peterstown and had money in the bank. But they continued to work too hard, my parents said. Their memory of poverty was too fresh.

When my father was done telling the *Story of the Magic Olives*, we could speak.

"Daddy, how come the Angel delivered mostly green olives first to Mommy?" asked Rena.

"Because the Angel wanted you girls to have lots of big brothers to protect you!"

"I don't need boys," said Maddelena, "Anything they can do, I could better, if you would let me."

"Your brains are smaller," I said. "Girls can't be scientists."

"I can too," she said, "I'm better at science than all the boys in my class. Mom can't girls be scientists?" she asked.

Our mother didn't answer.

"Maybe because boys take longer to mature," said Lucy.

"Yeah, that's why you came first, Carmine. Boys are immature imbeciles!" said Maddelena.

"Watch the language!" said my mother.

"Daddy, which color olive did Mommy eat this time? A green or black?

"We won't know Maria, until the Angel wants us to know," said my mother.

"But Mommy, don't you wake up when you hear the Angel coming now and peek at the color?" asked Rena.

"Enough questions for now," said my mother. "Go wash your hands for lunch. Maddelena/Rena take Maria/Teresa and help them wash. Lucy set the table. Mario/Vinnie, make sure enough chairs are around Grandma's dining room table. Frankie, lend a hand."

Frankie jabbed my ribs and whispered, "Didn't say nothing about no olives in that anatomy book you brought home!" I raised my opened hand to signal silence, but my father stared at me, so I scratched my head, like Gianfranco.

When my mother turned around to see who else was left without a task, she saw me and said quickly to my great joy, "Carmine, you go ask Grandpa if he wants you to get a jug of wine from his cellar."

She stopped short as big drops of water fell on my father's head. We all looked up. It wasn't raining. Normally the summer sky in Peterstown was as gray as the lead in my pencil. The soot from nearby oil refineries spewed into the air and clung to the mist and clouds that rolled in from the seashore. But this Saturday morning, the day after our house blew up, the air was crystal clear and the sky was a rare blue.

My father moved out of the way of the falling water and he and my mother spoke very quickly to each other in Sicilian. It was my grandmother's laundry.

"Why didn't she run it through the ringer first?" my father asked as Grandma leaned out the window of the second floor of her house, slinging wet sheets over the clothesline.

My mother said the ringer was broken. "She's baptizing you," she joked uneasily.

She was still on edge a bit. How would Grandma and my father get along with each other for the next few weeks? We all had to live here while our house was being repaired. My father mumbled something about just making sure Grandma's fennel plants didn't go to seed if it started getting hot because he was probably going to need a lot of antacid in the next few weeks. It was the same thing he said about Mrs. Lear.

Why did hard-headed women give him indigestion? I wondered.

"*Chi fai, Ma?*" Grandma didn't hear my mother. With a single thrust of her short arm, its upper fold of flab shaking, Grandma pushed the clothesline swiftly along its pulley. The screech it made was so high pitched it bored right through our ears.

I was happy to fetch the wine in the bin. The stalls in the cellar and the attic were some of the hidden places to explore at Grandma's and Grandpa's. Probing those places was like reading between the lines of my father's stories. Kids were expected to read between lines. Why else would my parents speak a foreign language?

My brother Frankie didn't understand this. Frankie didn't know how to look for answers in hidden places. If only he'd listen to the gaps between words. Listen and observe, he'd stop asking why I didn't flinch at the wall. I always had enough time between the order to go downstairs and the first crack of the belt to insert the catcher's mitt. Even a deck of cards in the right place helped. My father never saw me.

Dana could have Mario, Vinnie, and Frankie. She said I was a cool breeze. I wasn't trying to be. I just couldn't think of anything interesting to say to her or most girls. I couldn't dance with her like Frankie and Vinnie, because my feet lagged behind the counting in my head. I would never ask Frankie and Vinnie how they got around this problem. I would observe. Everything, even my father's stories, was light, sound, and motion that could be reduced to numbers, real and imaginary. You had to break things down to understand them. For example, those curves in the shells Frank gathered down the shore were nothing more than the mathematical Fibonacci Series. I studied and plotted a numerical series for the way Dana's torso, feet, and head moved in opposition to one another. Incontrovertible laws governed everything. You just had to remove yourself from the event.

I reached the second floor just as my grandmother hung the last sheet. The hall smelled, as always, of bleach and fresh air and garlic. I saw that the only way she could reach the line was by standing on a footstool that my grandfather had built for her. He had built footstools for her for every room, including the bathroom.

"Grandma, where's Grandpa? Mom told me to look in his bin for some wine for lunch," I panted.

"*Sì, sì*," she said. She was happy to have her grandchildren nearby again. She sang a few lines from *Torna a Sorrento*, one of her favorite opera songs, and closed the hall window.

"We have some nice homemade wine with lunch. Grandpa already down the cellar. Go look."

I found him, the deep purple wine sloshing in its clear jug dangling from his index finger as he climbed the stairs.

I noticed the way Grandma's singing bounced down the hall. I thought her songs were ripples of the sound that had escaped when the volcano my father told us about had erupted in *Sicilia* and rocks rolled and people fell. But sometimes at night Grandma would sit in her rocker and just hum. A strange music came from her after she had worked hard. It had no time or pulse. It was a chant with no beats or gaps. Just soft peaks falling into round valleys, without beginning or end.

Grandma and Grandpa, who got along like opposite charges, never just sat in the garden with us during my father's stories. They pulled at ripe vegetables that weighed heavy on the vine. Or they swept the stairs or the little stone path through the garden. Or they polished the garden trinkets—the elves, flamingoes, statues of Saints Lucy, Anthony, Joseph, and the Madonna.

They only sat still at night to stare and hum a while before bedtime. They didn't say the rosary like my mother and Nonnie. They were too tired from going up and down their stairs so many times. All day long as I played in the backyard, I listened to their footfalls moving them toward the next weed, the next pot on the stove, the next heap of laundry, the next crate of grapes. My grandmother's shoes might have been carved for her feet from a carpenter's black two-by-four blocks. No one else's feet echoed with more purpose on those linoleum-covered stairs.

We had lived in the apartment downstairs from my grandparents until six years ago when we moved to Creek Street in Rahway. My parents told my grandparents to move downstairs when we moved out so they wouldn't have to go up and down so much. But my grandfather said, "It's bad luck to live downstairs. People walk all over you." My parents thought they were foolish. My grandparents rented the downstairs flat to an Italian couple from Calabria. The man worked as a disc jockey for a local Italian radio station, was seldom home, and he paid his rent the day it was due.

"Mario and Lucy, I know you want to go see your friends and play music, but it would be nice if you'd sit down with us for lunch first," my father said, thinking of the gypsy's prophecy that there would come a time our family would be separated from each other. But then a time would come when we'd all be reunited.

"We didn't think we had a choice," said Lucy.

"What do you mean?" asked my father, "I don't tell you older ones what to do anymore, especially you. In a few months you'll have a new boss to answer to."

Lucy was engaged to marry Joe Kelley, her boyfriend of the last six years. They would marry in August when she turned 19. My father had almost called it off when someone had slipped him an inflammatory note at his produce stand. Enclosed with Lucy's betrothal announcement from the *Elizabeth Daily Journal*, it read, "I see your daughter at least had the good sense to marry an Irishman." But my father really liked Joe in spite of himself and now he was preoccupied with plans for a big wedding at the Villa Roma. My parents had such a long list of people to invite that Joe's family had to shorten theirs.

Everybody wondered who Mario would ask to the wedding. He had not yet found a wife, but my father reminded him he would have to one day pass on the family name. Mario was working hard at Brown in Rhode Island. Soon he'd go to medical school at Johns Hopkins in Baltimore. When he came home he worked a part-time summer job at the Esso refinery—and played his music. Perhaps he would switch from pre-med, he told me. Maybe to chemistry, which he loved. Maybe to physics, which I could help him with. Or even astronomy. Anything but music. I had helped Mario solve many calculus and trigonometry problems—without a slide ruler. But I would let him be the scientist because he was firstborn.

When we were finally all seated around the table for lunch, Grandpa poured us kids a little wine in the short water glasses. My mother unwrapped the meats and cheeses from the white store paper. My father said, "I hope Nocera's sliced everything thin, the way he knows I like it."

My grandmother said abruptly, "You never you mind. He slice thin because I tell him I like 'em that way."

My mother began to bless herself quickly and loudly, "In the name of the Father, Son, and Holy Ghost..." All the kids joined in, Mario bowed his head and said Grace, and Lucy extended prayers with some special intentions. Then she asked the little kids what they wanted on their sandwiches. Dad broke off a big hunk of sesame bread from Saraceno's and piled on some capocollo, prosciutto, provolone, and Swiss for his own sandwich. Everything was sliced thin the way we all liked our cold cuts.

When we were done eating there were crumbs everywhere. Lucy said, "I'll sweep up."

"No, let Nonnie do it," said my mother.

As they cleaned up, Grandma started cooking the *cucuzza* she had brought up from her garden and meatballs for that evening's supper. Since there were so many of us, we had to talk two meals ahead, my mother said. I watched Grandma's hands disappear into a big mountain of chopped meat smothered in bread crumbs, grated cheese, eggs, and herbs. She asked me to run down to her garden and grab another handful of fresh mint. I returned and dropped the leaves into her meat-covered hands. She rubbed her palms vigorously and the leaves fell in shreds upon the meat.

Maddelena and Rena were helping shape the meat. Maria reached up underneath Grandma, stuck her hand in the bowl, and popped a handful of meat into her mouth. Grandma yelled, "*Non mangiari chistu ccà!* You get worms!" She picked Maria up and squeezed her cheeks together over the sink until she spit it out.

My father came into the kitchen and said, "My wife adds crushed fennel seed to the *cuccuzza*, Ma."

Grandma looked over her shoulder and said, "*Chi pinsasti ca sugnu fissa?* What do you think—I'm stupid? Who you think taught my daughter how to cook?"

"I don't think you're stupid, Ma, I'm just telling you what I like. *Vaffannapuli...*" he trailed off and waved his hand as if to dismiss the topic. In her presence my father's own words lost some of their power. But he could never make peace with an old woman who sassed him.

"Your husband, Magdalena! I swear!" So much kinetic energy came from my grandmother, short as she was.

"Ma, let it go," said my mother, washing Maria's face and sticking a *biscotti* in Teresa's outstretched hand.

Frankie wanted to go talk to some girls down the street, but I talked him into playing hide-and-seek. We told Maddelena and Rena they could join us when they were through making meatballs, because we didn't have our friends Eddie and Kenny from Creek Street here. Vinnie went off to visit cousin Alfonso who lived in the neighborhood. We watched Mario and Lucy pull out of the driveway in the vintage Lincoln Continental that Mario's godfather had just given him for his twenty-first birthday. They would go where Mario could play his music with his friends. I could see neighbors come to every stoop and wave as if Mario were some celebrity pulling away in his shiny black car. Mario's godfather had pinstriped it in gold and inscribed his favorite quote on the rear: "Music is my mistress and she plays second fiddle to no one." It was a quote from Duke Ellington.

Hide-and-seek was the way to open doors in the cellar and attic and see what hid behind them. I could survey a room quickly for ideas to trap the music hidden in its contents.

In the cellar there were three stalls. I could only enter two of them. One contained the wine press and bottles and jugs of wine, some purple-black and some, so-called white wine, cloudy amber-colored. There were also giant tins of olive oil and mason jars of canned tomatoes. In the second stall was coal for the furnace. The third stall was always padlocked. Only Grandpa came and went through its door. He told me, "Kids can't go in there, because they would fall down drunk from the smell of fermenting wine." But why did he always go in and come out empty handed?

I snuck into the attic to hide while I waited for Maddelena, who was it, to find me. There I could examine dozens of objects. My grandparents never threw out anything. They stored all their dishes, housewares, cookware, and utensils from the old country as if they might move back there some day.

It was always dark and hot in the attic and smelled like cedar. There were two small windows, one at either end of the long railroad flat. Metal items lined a ledge along the stairs. I could see mouli cheese graters, nut choppers, pressure cookers, canning equipment, mortars and pestles, and scales. On the floor-to-ceiling shelves were ravioli dough cutters; knives for grapefruit, shellfish, steak; ladles; *cuppina*; wooden spoons; tongs; wine bottle openers; hand-painted salt and pepper shakers from Sicily; liqueur bottles in the shape of animals, and one in the shape of a little Italian country boy straddling an oak barrel. There were fancy demi-tasse cups and saucers, espresso coffee pots, Venetian glass and decanters, stem glasses, napkin holders, sugar bowls, strainers for tomatoes, pastry boards and rolling pins of different sizes.

I stared in concentration, my mind extracting from each mute item a way to move sound along a chain of objects.

Next to the shelves were mops and sets of brooms for different sweeping jobs. In one dark corner were an old typewriter and two old black trunks big enough for me to hide inside. Big enough for what secrets of Grandma's and Grandpa's to hide?

In one trunk were piles of old photographs, holy pictures from dead relatives' funerals, old letters written in indecipherable Sicilian script, parchment, and fountain pens. In the other trunk were an old wedding gown and veil, shawls, crocheted doilies, and more pictures, including a wedding photo of Grandma and Grandpa. In the photo they both had thick black hair, not gray like now. Grandpa's hair looked just like mine did before Sister Helen Marie made me cut it. Grandpa had on a dark suit and Grandma was wearing the gown in the trunk.

I opened the drawers of a dresser and found just more holy pictures of Jesus, Mary, and Joseph, of a saint—or was it Jesus?—who bore the Stigmata. I also found a Sick Hall. I slid the wooden crucifix from its base and found nestled inside it the candles and ointment for administering last rites of Extreme Unction to a dying person.

There were some screen windows and floor-length mirrors leaning against the slanting wall, making a little cubby. I pulled open a drawer and found a rippled crystal-glass doorknob. When I held it up to the window it was like a kaleidoscope, fracturing everything into multiple versions. I held it up to a cuckoo clock and watched the birdie go around and around.

I knew the attic had to have something to show me, but it was like an oven, and I got so hot that I snuck downstairs before anyone thought of looking for me. Maddelena was yelling, "Ollie, Ollie home-free!" Frankie had left the game to go talk to the girls. "He said to tell you he was going to find out if they have any olives," said Maddelena.

I couldn't play hide-and-seek without Frankie. So I went to watch my grandfather fix the old ringer washer machine. He let me hand him tools. This machine had an agitator for washing clothes and two cylinders for squeezing the water out of the washed clothes. My parents told him to buy a new automatic washer and dryer, but he said why should he, this one still worked fine. I was sure hand-pressing water from water-logged clothes reminded him of pressing juice from grapes.

"When your mother was a little girl her hand went right through this ringer, Carmine, and got all smashed," said Grandpa. "You know that?"

"Yes," I answered. I had heard that story many times. "And then Grandma rubbed it back together with olive oil, right? That's why Mom has no scars." Grandma had rubbed Maria's shoulder back into its socket and Vinnie's foot back into place when it got caught in the bicycle spokes, too.

"That's right," said Grandpa, tightening a bolt. "Don't need no doctors with your grandmother around. Doctors too dear for how little they know."

When he had fixed the machine, he said I could help him crush the grapes. He had built his own wine press in Sicily and brought it here. First we had to wash our hands and make sure everything stayed very clean. We poured the purple grapes from flat wooden crates into a basin that had a metal cylinder with long prongs and spikes at the bottom. Grandpa let me turn the crank of the cylinder and I watched the spikes remove the stems. The partially crushed grapes fell through the bottom into a deeper basin. The juice ran through the broken skins. Grandpa said there was good yeast on the skins that would turn the juice to wine in a few days.

As we turned the cylinder crank he spoke and I understood how different a man he was from my father. "We gonna have good wine this time. No vinegar. In Sicily the grain grow everywhere, in the mountain, by the sea, on flat land or on the hillside. But the grapevine is different. The vine is a fussy woman. She only bears fruit on the right ground. *E, sì,* she like a struggle, so some rock is good. But what she needs is lots of sun and some water trickling down her breast. In Sicily, we were so poor. But we always cultivate wine. The grain and the olive is important. But the wine is our blood, Carmine. Not just like in the Bible. We eat a little less bread is OK or even sacrifice a gallon of oil. But we always gotta have some wine with each meal."

He was silent through the remaining cranking and we blessed ourselves when we were done. We put labels marked *Cent'anni* on some bottles of wine already aging. Then we went on to the next step, crushing the grapes. Grandpa said we were making *vinu niuro,* red wine, so we would let the juice soak on the skins for a few days and get nice and dark. He showed me the oak barrels where we would season the wine in a few days and then the big glass jugs where the fermenting juice would go next. The jugs had special corks, fitted with tubing that let gases escape. My grandfather did not have as many words as my father. But he knew a lot about conductors and containers, how things worked. And about fussy women.

Over the weeks at my grandparents' house I thought of an experiment many times whenever my father and grandmother were in the same room. In his Lab on Creek Street Mario had put a sliver of copper wire into a flask of silver nitrate. Within a short time, we could see specks of shiny silver clinging to the copper at the bottom of the clear blue liquid. The copper was a catalyst, drawing the silver out of its liquid compound form into its solid state. Dad and Grandma seemed to draw something out of each other that we otherwise did not see.

Like the day Grandma took Maria and Teresa to Carmine's Barber Shop and had him cut their hair short. My mother had been out shopping. My father came home from work and was really annoyed. He didn't like short hair on girls or women, he said. She had taken a liberty she had no right to. Grandma said the girls' long hair was too much work for my mother, who had to brush out knots and braid it every day. He said it was his job to decide what was too much work for his wife.

Another time, Grandma gave me a quarter to run around the corner to Saraceno's for bread. When I returned my father saw her counting the change I had handed her, a few pennies. She asked me how much the bread cost. My father stepped in, waved his hands around, and said, "*Mannaggia*! What do you think, your own grandson's gonna cheat you? He's not one of your tenants."

She yelled back, "*Miserabili! Porca buttana, vaffannapuli.* You mind your own business! I swear one day..."

"That's my son, he's my business!"

"He's my grandson, *porca buttana*...!" She yelled louder. And my mother picked up Teresa who started to cry. Maria grabbed her leg. My mother shook her head from side to side, as if she were dancing to old familiar music.

Grandma received a little burlap bag of almonds, dried figs, and a letter from her cousin in Agrigento. The cousin told her about everybody, including Grandma's two uncles who were a doctor and a lawyer. She read the letter out loud and then wrote back to them immediately. She slipped a dollar bill inside the letter. She made comments all evening about how well off her family was in Sicily. Finally, my father said, "If they're so well off why don't you go back to them." Grandma shook her pudgy fist and didn't answer and my father continued to read his newspaper. Grandpa just smiled.

Except when Grandma and Dad filled the room with their yelling matches we never felt crowded at my grandparents'. We kids slept on the parlor or dining room floor or sofas. My mother and father slept on two lounge chairs pushed together on the screened porch in the front of the house. My mother was starting to need extra room for her belly, which was growing fast.

My grandmother liked having us kids around to cook for. She had big steaming bowls of milk and coffee ready for us each morning with bread to dunk in it. Sometimes in the afternoon she asked me to pronounce words for her in the *Elizabeth Daily Journal*. That was how my grandmother learned English. She also asked me to read her utility bill and her phone bills, and made me call the phone company to say they overcharged her.

My parents were happy about being near their people, who all lived within a 10-block radius. We would walk to market and run into friends, but mostly relatives. And I began to understand that our leaving Peterstown for Rahway was almost as major as my grandparents leaving Sicily, for America. Why had my parents moved so far away? When would they come home?

My father seemed to have less need to tell us stories while we stayed in Peterstown. I didn't miss them, the way I missed the stick ball game on Creek Street and the tree we climbed in Kenny's backyard or the chance to sneak away to Squire Island to fish and see what the older boys were up to. People spent a lot more time in the same spots here—hanging on stoops, talking in Sicilian, sweeping streets, bleaching steps, nursing babies. There was not even a Good Humor truck with its bells to break the monotony in Peterstown.

Each evening after work, my father would say Hon, why don't you bake some *ciambelli* for the boys tonight? Hon, why don't you bake some *quaresimali* for the boys tonight, or Hon, how about some fennel cookies or pine nut cookies tonight? The "boys" were my father's buddies from the VFW and the Knights of Columbus who were repairing the damage the Trinity had not spared on the house. The fire in the kitchen had left undamaged only our clover-leaf table. My mother said the Blessed Trinity had saved it, although Mr. Newman said he had made it out of fireproof material. The repairs wouldn't cost a cent, thank God, because the men all knew how to build, how to lay foundations, bricks, and paint. The men would accept food, but never money. One night Nonnie, who even seemed to be getting bored, insisted on baking *cucciddati* for the boys and my mother let her have reign of the kitchen.

"Donitellas, fall in line, single file!" yelled my father. Whoever was home at that moment—Vinnie, Frankie, Rena, Maddelena, Maria, Teresa, and I—all had to go shopping with my parents. My father went to the cellar to get bags.

"But Ma!" I begged, "Frankie and I were going to take the girls to the park." Frankie looked at me incredulous, but added, "Yeah, Ma, c'mon. Talk Dad out of making us go."

"Your father wants his kids with him," she said. "The owner of a farm in Union where Grandpa used to work offered him a bunch of rabbits and pheasants. We're having a big feast tomorrow, so we have to shop."

"Ma!" I said, "all we do is shop for food, put it away, take it out, cook it, eat it!"

"What's wrong with that?" she asked. "Your father's side and my two brothers and their families are all coming."

"Oh brother!" moaned Frankie. "That means we can't go to the park tomorrow either." He was thinking of those girls.

"If one of the aunts asks once 'What's the matter, cat got your tongue,' I'm going to....." I stopped short because my father returned with the shopping bags and said we had to go.

He wanted to see what the other farmers were selling at market. We had to stop and light a candle at St. Anthony's, where my parents had gotten married. We passed houses that were so close together, my father said that they used to be able to hear everyone's habits through the wall. Some were shingled or wooden, but most were stone or brick built by the Germans who had lived here before the Italians arrived, my father said. The Italians softened the hard lines with hedges, small lawns, gardens of flowers. Geraniums, tulips, roses, daffodils, coreopsis, petunias, and pansies were everywhere in pots, on porches, or climbing wooden trellises. Houses on corners with enough front yard had brick grottoes for the Blessed Virgin Mary.

My mother left us all briefly to go into the brassiere shop for a maternity girdle and we talked to Carmela, the gypsy lady. She had some *carduni* left, even though it was late in the season for them. We bought them for Grandma Donitella. My parents said Carmela was a holy person. They enumerated all her accurate predictions to date.

Before we returned to Grandma Coniglio's, we had to stop at Grandma Donitella's to give her the *carduni*. She started to pull strings from the stalks right away with a sharp knife. We all sat around the kitchen table and talked. My fathers' sisters Marialia, Angela, Santa, Rosalia, and Antoinette made us stay for lunch and fed us well. How was Grandma Coniglio treating us? they asked.

149

Did she cook enough *pastasciutta* for us? What a shame she cut Maria/Teresa's hair. Then they switched to Sicilian, which meant we children were not to listen. They talked about how my mother's parents worried too much about money, especially Grandma, *un piccatu*. But she probably had a lot of Arab blood. She was not like Grandma Donitella, who sat quietly pulling strings from the *carduni*, generous, quiet, and good as gold.

We started walking back home and my parents said to us kids, "Don't mention to Grandma and Grandpa that we stopped at Grandma Donitella's." That meant we'd have to eat lunch again when we got to Grandma Coniglio's. I already knew we didn't tell one side about the other side.

But Frankie had to ask why.

"Because sometimes you don't let your left hand know what your right hand is doing," said my mother.

Frankie said, "But I thought that one hand washed the other." My father slapped Frankie and said, "You ask too many questions."

Back at Grandma's I realized I had run out of places to dig for secrets and couldn't bear the thought of eating all next day and sitting around with relatives. But Vinnie and Cousin Alfonso saved me from certain death of boredom.

Alfonso had supper Saturday night with us and I could tell that he, Lucy, and Vinnie were up to something. Frankie ran off to see the girls and I asked Lucy what was up. "Meet us in the attic in 15 minutes," she whispered.

I sat in the kitchen and watched my mother and Grandma make dough for the *cavatelli*. When they left to put the cut macaroni on white linens on Grandma's bed to dry out overnight, I slipped through the attic door.

Alfonso stood on a chair hanging a bulb at the end of a wire from a hook on the ceiling. Only Lucy spoke, "Vinnie's gotten hold of one of Mario's textbooks—we're going to operate on a snake."

Walking in the swampland, Mario and Vinnie had found a garter snake and brought it back in a shoe box. Mario told Vinnie how he used to dissect snakes. So Vinnie and Alfonso got this idea to operate on it. I knew it was Vinnie's idea—he wanted to be able to tell Dana he could do something that Mario could do.

"We are about to perform the operation," he said. Lucy held the box with the snake while Vinnie gathered the instruments he needed. She opened the lid and showed me the snake. It wriggled slightly.

"Carmine, get the steelyard scale over on the ledge by the staircase." Vinnie tried to sound professional. I ran over and could just reach it. I froze. Someone was coming up the steps. It was Maddelena. She was getting to be a pain. Lately, she wanted to play stick ball with us boys, and she followed me and Frankie to Squire Island. She and Rena wanted to deliver newspapers and come to Lee's Sweet Shoppe with us.

But I owed her a favor this time. She had bailed me out just before we had gone down the shore. My father had stood at the bottom of the stairs and called me out of my room for reading his newspaper before he had. He demanded Frankie and I recite that poem about some Indian who loves God best. We couldn't remember a single line of it. I knew we were going to get licked at the wall. Maddelena hid behind the door to her room and whispered all the lines to us. We stumbled through the whole thing and then he made us recite again. Good thing Maddelena knew the title and author, too.

I made her go back down and guard the door for us. "Whistle real loud if you see grown-ups coming. We'll show you later what we find."

Vinnie brought down a pastry board, a mortar and pestle, and a ravioli cutter. He took a cigar box with sewing things from a drawer. He pulled out the pin cushion with needles and straight pins in it. He had lined up a white styptic pencil, a bottle of rubbing alcohol, and a single-edge razor. Lucy brought out white linen napkin bibs that the men wore to keep from staining their white shirts. We all had to wrap one around our mouths so we wouldn't breathe the anesthesia. For extra precaution Lucy pulled a shawl from the black trunk and told me to hold it up to my face along with her when Vinnie opened up the anesthesia. We were suffocatingly hot.

Lucy held out rubber dishwashing gloves so that Vinnie could slip his hands into them. Then he reached behind a set of cannisters on a high shelf and pulled down a sealed apothecary jar. He opened the jar and I pulled the shawl to my face as I smelled the sharp odor. He dipped a wad of cotton into the ether in the jar and held the cotton up to the snake's nostrils. I heard the snake briefly wiggle against the box, then go very still.

Vinnie hung the snake over the shorter arm of the scale. He slid the weight along the graduated longer end until the arm balanced perfectly and then announced the weight, "Three point seven four." Alfonso repeated as if the number meant something.

As Vinnie stretched the limp snake out on its back on the pastry board, Alfonso pounded the styptic pencil to a fine chalk in the ceramic mortar with the pestle. Lucy poured rubbing alcohol onto a cotton ball and wiped the snake's belly. Vinnie rolled the ravioli cutter in the powder and traced a line of white down the reptile's belly.

Lucy cleaned the single-edged razor with alcohol and handed it to Vinnie. He slid the razor down the snake's belly, opening up his leathery skin. He tacked the snake's skin to the pastry board with sterilized straight pins that Alfonso handed him.

We all stared for a few moments at the snake's insides laid bare right there. His organs were gathered in odd, misshapen clumps. They looked like bits of clay molded by a child and stuck together. Would this snake ever be the same again once we sewed him up? For a moment I wished Frankie was there to ask questions.

Lucy heaved a little and Alfonso laughed. Vinnie looked at the insides and then sliced a tiny piece of an organ and wiped it into a little dish, which Lucy handed him. Yellowish fluid ran from where the snake was cut.

"Remove the pins, Funzie," Vinnie said. "Be sure to put them back into the pin cushion. They're from my mother's sewing kit."

Vinnie stitched and stitched with olive green thread. Lucy had to hold the flaps of skin down for him. When he was done he wiped the belly clean with alcohol again. He weighed the sleeping snake again and read, "Three point seven six." Alfonso repeated after him.

"Heavy thread," said Vinnie. "He'll be out for at least ten hours."

"You sure?" asked Lucy.

"Yeah, I think so. We can leave him up here in the box. We should be able to remove his stitches in about three days."

Alfonso brought out a bottle of a liqueur called *Fernet Branca*, which he had stolen from Grandma's cabinet. He poured some into a whisky glass and passed it around. It was brown and bitter. I tried to drink a shot real fast, the way cowboys in movies did. It burned on its way down.

"Let's do last rites, just in case," whispered Lucy. She knew right where the Sick Hall was. She set up the candles in the base of the crucifix. She lit them with matches. She opened the little bottle of oil and rubbed some on the snake's head with her index finger. Vinnie muttered some prayers in Latin that he knew from being an altar boy. He moved his hands in the sign of the cross. We all bowed our heads. We sang *Tantum ergum sacramentum, veneremur cernui...*When we heard Vinnie say, "*In nomine patri, et filio, et spiritu sanctu,*" we blessed ourselves and said Amen.

We got back downstairs just as people were starting to miss us. Maddelena bugged me for a while about what we found. I told her, "Someday when you're older I'll tell you."

On Sunday, all except for Grandma and Grandpa went to early mass so we could prepare for the company. My grandparents were up even earlier than usual but they never went to Sunday mass. "God understand," they would say. They had too much work to do. Grandma stood on footstools in the kitchen to reach things in her cabinets or worked at the stove. Nonnie pitched in and helped. The stove was completely covered with huge metal pots of food. In one the tomato sauce simmered. First Vinnie, then Mario, then Lucy came by with a hunk of bread and dipped it into the sauce. Each time Grandma laughed and said, "God bless! Can't you wait?"

My mother busied herself peeling and seeding roasted peppers. Lucy prepared big trays of antipasto. Grandpa carved the rabbit into small pieces. It would be marinated in basil, olive oil, garlic, and wine vinegar, then baked. Grandma dressed and stuffed the pheasants with fresh oregano from the garden. They would be baked in tomato sauce. My father stayed out of her way.

153

Mario drove Vinnie, Frankie, and me in his Lincoln with the top down to Bella Palermo Bakery around the corner. We had to pick up the cannoli, baba rhum, other pastries, and cookies. As Jennie the saleslady wrapped and tied the boxes with string, she said, "You're the Donitella boys."

"You've heard so much about, People stop and stare at us whenever we go out," sang Frankie. Mario shoved him.

"My how you've all grown! I've known your Mom and Pop since they was little kids."

I asked Jenny what was a *tiramisù*. She took me to a glass case and explained the layers of liqueur-soaked sponge cake with chocolate and vanilla custard and cocoa-dusted cream.

"Tiramisù means pick-me-up in Sicilian.You want a *tiramisù?"* she said.

"No thank-you," I said, "we're just having a small gathering. This will be enough. I was just wondering what it looked like." My brothers and I left, each dangling two boxes of baked goods from our fingers.

My mother was giving last minute orders when we returned. "Hide all the blankets, sheets, and pillows in the attic. Girls, set the table—don't forget to set a separate salad bowl out for your father. Boys, get the chairs."

"Where are we going to put everybody?" Vinnie asked.

"Borrow a few chairs from Mercy next door. We're having just the aunts, uncles, and cousins, about 22 people. Put all the little kids in the kitchen. Set up the card tables. Put the bigger kids in the parlor. Set up the aluminum table. Adults can all fit around the long dining room table. Find enough chairs, make enough places. Go ahead, you can do it."

Uncle Pete, my mother's brother, sucked his teeth loudly after we were through with the first course, the cavatel'. He reminded me of my seventh grade teacher, Sr. Grace Marie, who'd wait until the class was falling asleep after lunch and start sucking her teeth clean.

"When are we going to have the rabbits and pheasant?" he asked.

"You just finish one course and already you worry about the next," his mother chided him. Uncle Pete sold real estate in North Jersey. But Grandma wouldn't let him help her with her own property. Everybody said she didn't even trust her own son.

"Let's relax a bit. In a couple hours we'll have the bird and the rabbit," said my mother. "Here, have some more of Pop's wine." She passed him the crystal-glass decanter. He uncorked it and poured and offered to fill an empty glass for Uncle Rickie, his brother, too.

"You look like you got the Stigmata, Pete, with that big gravy stain over your heart," teased Uncle Rickie.

"You may call me Jesus," he answered, removing his sauce-spattered white bib and crumpling it on his lap.

"Whatta you talk about, Jesus?" asked Grandma Coniglio. "You take the Lord name in vain." Nobody ventured to explain.

"Good pasta, Ma," my father said.

"What else you expect?"

Just as everybody seemed to be wondering what next, Aunt Santa said, "Mario, why don't you play some piano. My kids will sing the songs they learned in dancing school."

He opened Grandma's old piano in the dining room. It used to belong to my mother when she was a young girl. Now she only remembered how to play one song on it, *Isle of Capri*.

The little kids danced around as Mario warmed up. My aunts Santa and Antoinette made their kids get up and sing songs as Mario played for them. Cousin Jimmy who was seven sang *Mammy* and cousin Anna who was six sang *Diamonds Are a Girl's Best Friend*. And everybody clapped and yelled "Encore."

Uncle Bernie opened the black case containing his accordion and slung the straps over his shoulders. He started to play *Hey Cumpari*. Grandma Donitella clapped and sang along. Mario played along on piano. Grandma Coniglio joined in. Grandma sang the solo part of *Funiculì, Funiculà* and everyone joined in answering her. We clapped and the aunts danced with each other and with the little kids.

155

"I wish Pop was here, he loved that song," my father said, wiping his face. "He'd be so proud of his grandchildren."

It didn't stay quiet for two minutes. Someone said, "How about *Oh Marie*?" And my father and Grandma Coniglio sang together to Maria.

"Vinnie, show your aunts how you dance," said my mother. "Lucy, dance with Vinnie."

"Move the table! Give them floor space!"

"OK," said Vinnie. "Play the boogie woogie beat, Mario." Lucy danced with him as my aunts and uncles clapped and snapped their fingers and little kids tried to imitate them.

"Can you play *Siracusa*?" asked Aunt Angela. "Too bad Francesca's not here to lead us, Magdalena." She and my mother used to be in a secret girls club together and that was their secret song.

It was hot and Mario ran his fingers up and down the keys, signaling that he was done playing. Someone started the *Giufà* stories. I think it was Uncle Alfonso, telling half in English and half in Sicilian the one about *Giufà* taking the kitchen door to market on his back because his mother told him to pull the door tight behind him as they left to go shopping.

Then someone remembered the one where *Giufà* tells his mother he wants to be a pilot when he grows up. His mother, who has all but given up hope for her son, rejoices and glows with pride. "Is that right, *Giufà*? " she asks.

"Oh yes, Ma! I'm going to make a lot of money. And I'm going to pile-it here and pile-it there!"

Everybody roared with laughter. The next story was about *Giufà* the priest.

"A parishioner comes to Father *Giufà* and asks him what kind of sermon can he give for $50. Father *Giufà* says, "For $50 I can give a sermon that only the most devout will understand."

"And for $100?"

"Ah, for $100 I can give a sermon that no one in the parish, only his Holiness the Archbishop, will understand!"

"And for $200, Father *Giufà*?"

"Now for $200 I can give a sermon that I myself won't under-stand."

"Finally, Father *Giufà* what can you do for $500?"

"For $500 my son, I can give a sermon that God Himself won't understand."

Before anyone could laugh at the punchline, Grandpa Coniglio let out a loud snore. Vinnie brought out his *Mad Magazine* and placed it on Grandpa's chest as if he were reading it. Aunt Angela brought out her Kodak camera and snapped his picture.

The inevitable happened just as it began to get a little quiet. People ran out of steam and fell into chairs like overstuffed sausage. Uncle Pete opened a cabinet and turned on Grandma's small television. Eastside Kids was on and some people watched it, some fell asleep right where they sat.

Maria's blouse had lost a button. My mother went into Nonnie's former bedroom to find her sewing kit. She screamed so loud, I'm sure Mrs. Lear back in Rahway heard it. Conversations stopped mid-sentence. No one had time to run to her because she re-traced her steps so quickly back down the hall. My father met her.

"A snake! A snake!" she gasped, jumping up on a chair, her hands framing its size, "This big!" She stretched her arms out to five feet. Vinnie, Mario, and I ran into the bedroom, my uncles fol-lowing behind us as my aunts shrieked.

We saw nothing. Mario said to my mother, "Now tell me about this snake. Did it offer you a bite of an apple?"

My mother laughed nervously and said, "Stop that! You're try-ing to make me think I'm crazy. There's a snake on the loose here. I saw it crawling across Mary's feet. "

Vinnie told my mother that the snake had turned to stone and pointed to the serpent carved in relief on the stone base at Mary's feet."

"But if you find me a staff, I'll turn it back into a snake," he teased.

"I was looking for my sewing kit and I saw this snake sliding across the floor. You kids! You'll drive me to drink!"

After a while everyone settled down, deciding that if it really was a snake it had escaped. My mother settled down to sew on the button. Teresa said, "I don't like snakes. They're bad, they bite. Bad snake. I see it, too."

My mother ignored Teresa and threaded a needle. But Uncle Alfonso sank his big hands up to his muscle-bound forearms into his deep pockets, raised his shoulders, and whistled. "*Madonna, chistu ccà*...she was not exaggerating!"

And then my Uncles Bernie, Vito, Pete, Jimmie, Rickie, and my father all saw it, too. The snake was in the dining room under the raised liquor cabinet. Suddenly all the men were huddled over the snake in one corner, while the women were standing on chairs and footstools in the other. The conversation was a chorus of echoes hard to separate out:

"It might be someone's spirit, shhh!"

"*Talé, talé chistu ccà è bruttu*! *E' masculu o fimmina*?"

"Let mom stuff and cook it! She used to make rattlesnake in Cammarata, right Mom? Or was it snails?"

"Alfonso, why are you laughing so hard, you bring that thing in here? Make him dance the tarantella. Bernie g'head play the accordion!"

"Chop him up and put him in the *cucuzzi*!"

"No, it's no *bruttu, iddu è beddu*! Look how beautiful!"

"Just get that damn thing out of here. Someone grab a fly swatter."

Uncle Bernie played the tarantella and Uncles Al and Rickie danced around it with each other. Grandpa slept through the whole thing.

"Pop must've left a cellar window open."

"Don't feed it, you'll never get rid of it!"

"How you know it's a *he*?"

"Cause if it was *she*, it would have two big bumps, *accussì*, hah, hah!"

Maddelena tugged my sleeve and whispered in my ear, "Is that what you were doing last night?" I didn't answer because Grandma Coniglio returned to the room with her broom in one hand, her dustpan in the other. Wordlessly, she parted the men, the way she parted pasta dough. She swept the snake onto the dustpan and gave it to me to take out back to the garden.

Soon everybody forgot the snake and was hungry again and my grandmother and mother served the pheasant and the rabbit and the side dishes. Grandpa woke up and we told him about the snake and he said it was good luck to have a snake enter your house.

That evening into the next day I had a bad case of the runs. I asked my mother what was in that *Fernet Branca* stuff Grandma had in her liquor cabinet. She said, "Your grandparents like to drink some of that before they go to bed. Helps them go to the bathroom next morning. You wouldn't like it, it's too bitter."

"Right," I said and walked slowly down to the garden.

Vinnie was downstairs trying to read one of Mario's biology textbooks. I asked him what he had cut from the snake's insides.

"I cut out his bile duct, his gland of evil."

"His what?"

"You know the gland that makes a snake crawl on his belly and tempt people to eat of the forbidden fruit."

"Vinnie, don't talk to me like a punk," I said, realizing I should know better than to ask questions. I went off to see if the snake was still in the garden. Grandma was there weaving dandelions into crowns for Maddelena and Rena to wear in their hair. I pretended to look for more dandelions for them, and saw neither hide nor hair of that snake ever again.

Summer wore on and we all began to feel cramped at Grandma and Grandpa's. We kids got tired of answering the same questions from the neighbors, of listening to our parents brag about us to everyone. I had long ago given up looking for anything new and interesting.

Then one day right before we were to move back to our house on Creek Street, I noticed that the padlock on Grandpa's locked stall was dangling loose. Grandpa was nowhere in sight. I quietly lifted the lock off the door and grabbed the doorknob. The door was stuck and I had to pull and pull until it swung open so hard it banged into a nearby table. I walked inside. There was no wine, but there were dozens of tools in boxes and hanging on hooks on one wall. Two of the walls were covered with old calendars and color photographs of women from magazines. The women were either half-clothed or fully naked and were posing on chairs, benches, sofas, beds, or beaches. Some wore just net stockings and garterbelts, or feathers and high heels. They had large bare breasts. The only breasts I had seen before were those nursing babies. These looked very different.

I got an idea. I unhooked the calendar closest to me from the wall. It was from 1957. I rolled it up, hid it inside my shirt, and closed the padlock on the door. I ran up to the attic and went to the drawer where I had seen the glass doorknob. I spread a shawl on the floor by one of the windows and lay on my back. I began looking through the doorknob at the women on the calendar for each month. August was something but February was the best. I watched their breasts and nipples multiply. I twirled the knob and the women moved and contorted different ways. I don't know how long I lay there. I began to understand more about my grandfather and his quiet smile. He was an observer like me. And he had a room full of women who never got old and who were never, ever fussy.

I almost invited Frankie up to see them. But he must've been out chasing those girls from South Street. So I kept my secret to myself. The best part was that to Grandpa's girls, it didn't matter a bit that I couldn't dance and had nothing to tell them.

Rena (1965-67)

The race is not to the swift, nor the battle to the strong, or however the damn saying goes, Frankie. Your brother Mario can recite the entire quote for you. God knows I'm no Solomon, my memory is not what it used to be, damn it, Frankie, but I'm your father, you know my rules. I could've told you a few things about battle. You should've talked to me first. Are you doing this to prove something?

It was early summer when Frankie announced his decision. I was the first one to wake up and hear the odd softness of my father's voice drifting into our bedroom from across the hallway. Lucy and Madeleine were still sound asleep next to me. Maria and Teresa were snoring, one on the upbeat, one on the downbeat in the cot at our feet. They slept head to foot like a push-me pull-me. I hoped baby Carmela hadn't gotten lost again last night. If she had, we knew where to look first.

The creek had captured a hard summer rain the day before and I could hear its fullness humming by. Sound travels well on humidity, Carmine had told me. The moist air also seemed to trap all the odors that rose off the earth, the sharp smell of vegetation near the creek's banks, the sweetness of the honeysuckle. The mix of smells was a familiar mark of summer. Crickets still crooned. Slow waxing and waning drones. Some of their chorus was out of sync, like the voice next door.

I wiped the sweat from my neck and strained to listen to the voices traveling on the still, humid air.

Are you sure this is what you want? I can get you out of it.

The softness was hard to figure. My father's words always carried their weight.

Except for the voices across in the boys' dormer, no one else stirred yet. School had let out a week ago and Mario had just returned home from graduate school. He and Lucy had a party the night before and Madeleine and I tried to pick out the girl who had beat her boyfriend with the cue stick and the one who had a baby. When Madeleine and I were sent to bed at 3 a.m. people were still up. Some had probably spent the night sleeping on our parlor floor.

Lucy and her husband Joe and baby Joey were living with us for a few months until Joe started a new job. Lucy slept with Madeleine and me sometimes, because Joe wanted to sleep down the cellar where it was cooler. Lucy hated the cellar. It was fun to have Lucy back home. She helped us catch up with the washing, ironing, and cleaning. We had fallen way behind since my mother had taken a job at the outlet factory around the corner on Elizabeth Avenue. This had a foul effect on the whole household. Little things piled up and everybody got agitated.

No Dad! I'm not trying to one-up you! I'm not trying to be better than my father...

Frankie's voice came loud, firm, strange. As if he was the parent. It stopped mid-air. I couldn't hear my father now. But I waited for the explosion. Frankie would be beat at the wall for yelling like that. You didn't raise your voice to my father. But nothing happened. By all laws of the universe, it should have. I imagined I heard a wind. But everything was still.

I tried to remember how many ah-wing-ah-wetts we had agreed on the other night. Lucy and Madeleine stirred and I could tell they were awake, listening, trying to make sense of the conversation next door.

The night before had been like the weekend nights when Mario's band practiced at our house, before he went away to school. We danced and sang and had fun. But then I remembered Frankie hadn't danced. He was unusually quiet.

Lucy's friend, Patty, who had a crush on Mario for years, was falling all over him. So were two other girls and I couldn't tell which one he liked best. I told Dana, "I wish Mario would marry you."

She laughed and said, "We're too good of friends." Then she added, "...and I'd have to bleach my hair first."

Dana kept an eye on baby Carmela, who could not go to sleep with all the commotion. Last time we'd had a party with all of Mario's and Lucy's friends we lost Carmela. But no one noticed until the next morning. Officer Baciagalupe came to our house to start a search party. He was the one who heard the crying from the cellar. She had fallen asleep in a bushel of ironing in the cellar and someone had piled more clothes on top of her. No one had thought to look there.

"This is a kick in the teeth to your mother and me, Frankie... What did we do to deserve this?"

My father had enjoyed himself at the party last night, bragging and telling stories to the company. He and my mother had shown Mario and Lucy's friends how they danced in their day. They put on their old scratchy music, the Ink Spots, the Mills Brothers, Benny Goodman, and Glenn Miller. My father said, "You kids will never have music this good." When *Stardust Melody* came on he grabbed my mother from the kitchen again—she frowned, because she was trying to make an urn of coffee, slice cake, and serve people. And then my father said it was getting harder and harder to get all his kids together and insisted we sing the family song. We all groaned but we knew it was better to get it over with. Dana and the others who knew it all joined in and sang, *We Are the Donitellas*. He and my mother danced again in the parlor and he cried. But he always cried when he felt good. So what was going on?

Didn't I raise you right? Maybe I didn't do such a good job on you younger guys...you should've talked to me first...

I sat up against the headboard. Our patrons on our vanity caught my eye: a paint-by-number portrait of the Blessed Virgin done by Maria; holy pictures of Jesus of Nazarene—for me—and Mary Magdalena—for Madeleine, who had changed her name from

Maddelena when she started learning French; St. Theresa the Little Flower for Teresa; a dog-eared snapshot of Lucy dressed as St. Lucy for a grammar school play years ago, holding her eyeballs, two black olives, in the palms of her hands. Over the years we had added our scapulars, statues, holy water fonts, rosaries to this altar. I contemplated its disorder and made a mental note to dust and rearrange it before my mother said, "What a pigsty. This place needs a thorough cleaning."

"What's going on in the boys' room?" asked Lucy. "I feel like I just got to sleep." She stared straight ahead at the patron saints.

"Me too," I said. I was wide awake now. That pleading in my father's voice had caught her attention, too. I had heard his voice echo with passion and anger, with emotion of every flavor. All shades of feelings came through his voice.

Maria and Theresa stirred but didn't wake up.

Lucy put on her housecoat, saying "I'll get to the bottom of this." She went downstairs to ask our mother what was going on. She returned about 15 minutes later and told us, "You're not going to believe it. Frankie joined the Army."

"What's the big deal?" asked Madeleine. "Dad would go to Vietnam himself if he didn't have all of us to support."

"Well, Frankie tricked Mom. He told her he needed her signature on a paper to approve his graduation gown rental. Frankie told her the truth last night before he went to bed—and she just told Dad this morning."

"Is Mom upset, too?"

"Not nearly as much as Dad. He's angry because Frankie didn't behave like a good Sicilian son and consult with him before making a decision."

"Does this mean he won't be living at home anymore?" I asked.

"You can't attend bootcamp from home, Rena."

"Uggghhh, the food's awful in the Army. Ruined Dad's stomach," Madeleine said. "Where will he go? They wouldn't send Frankie to Vietnam...would they?" asked Madeleine.

"I don't know," Lucy said, "I think he's too young."

"We could watch him fight on TV every night, if they did," I said. "That way we could root for the good guys!"

"Rena!" said Lucy, "This is real life, not a movie."

"So's the Huntley-Brinkley news, Lucy," said Madeleine.

"Well anyway, he'll probably just go to Fort Dix first or some-place down south. I think he has to leave on Monday, so he'll miss his graduation ceremony next week."

"He didn't like school anyway," said Madeleine.

"Just his friends there," Lucy said.

Everybody seemed depressed. My father quietly descended the stairs. I noticed the crickets were out of tune. Joe had said that meant they were mating.

I went downstairs and stepped over sleeping bodies on our par-lor floor. I put on a pot of coffee and others began to wake up. Ev-erybody moved like zombies because no one had slept very much. I saw there were plenty of leftovers for breakfast—pizza, doughnuts with sugar and cinnamon, and sausage and peppers made after mid-night when we could eat meat again.

I ran next door to wake Dana, stepping over the half-finished canvasses in her room. "Wow. That Francorino," was all she said in a scratchy voice from bed, her eyes still closed. I thought I saw the huge hands move in the painting over her bed. I felt the big eyes of another on me. When Dana moved out someday, she said she would give me that hand painting. I said I'd hang it on the wall above our altar of patron saints because the hands looked like they be-longed to Jesus or a saint.

I went outside on Creek Street for a while, since it was Satur-day and after breakfast I'd be inside cleaning all day. I walked to the corner in the shade of leafed out maples. I wanted to see if there were any tar bubbles at the corner. When it got this hot the tar bub-bled into tempting humps. Carmine had shown Madeleine and me how to burst them and make the hot water inside squirt up. He was no longer interested in tar bubbles, so Madeleine and I claimed them for ourselves.

As I poked at the black gummy hills of tar I thought of Frankie going to war. I remembered when Madeleine and I were just eight and nine and we helped him deliver his afternoon newspapers. He had 60 customers, so Madeleine and I each took 15 papers. She took the Raleigh Road customers and I took Whittier Street, where I could pass Squire Island and see the boys playing. We'd have to run home from St. Mary's through Wheatena Park to get the papers delivered on time.

Frankie always took us to Lee's Soda Shoppe after we were done delivering newspapers and bought us a soda or a hot chocolate. Lee liked Frankie a lot so sometimes he'd give us seconds on the house. Everybody liked Frankie because he was a funny wiseguy. Only my father said he had a rebellious streak that had to be tamed. My mother said, "Don't pick on him, he has a good heart."

Frankie gave Madeleine and me 75 cents allowance each week for helping him. We delivered papers for almost a year. Then Frankie's paper route manager said we girls couldn't deliver papers anymore. Someone had reported us to the circulation department and the circulation manager said that he had never heard of girls delivering newspapers. He would get in trouble if we didn't quit. But Madeleine and I still helped Frankie fold all 60 papers. He had shown us how to do it real fast, sticking one end of the paper in the other, hitting it on your leg and bending it so it stayed folded. Madeleine and I had contests to see who could fold the most papers. If a paper fell apart when Frankie threw it on a porch, it didn't count.

I felt sorry for Frankie in the winter out there alone until after dark. He had asked my mother if he could quit, because he was tired of the route. My father overheard him and said, "You're tired? Did I hear you right? There is no such thing as a tired Donitella. Act like a man. A man doesn't complain over trifles. Besides, you're too young to be tired."

Frankie had to stop our allowance. He would have continued it, but he had to turn over all the profits he made to the household fund. We needed a new family car. He helped buy the big station wagon that was the first car we ever had that was big enough for all our groceries during the weekly shopping. I had spent every cent of my allowance. But Madeleine had saved almost all of hers and hid it in her corner of the drawer. She did not want to hand it over to the household fund, so she never talked about the money, even though everyone sort of knew. My parents said that Madeleine would never have money problems, because she took after Grandma Coniglio.

When I returned to the house, I dunked pizza in my coffee for breakfast, then put on cut-offs for housecleaning. Vinnie and Dana took Carmela, Teresa, and Maria to the park. Mario worked in his lab with Carmine. Frankie went shopping with my parents for socks and underwear. We were going to have a big going-away party for Frankie on Sunday and my parents had to prepare the ravioli, Frankie's favorite dish, the sauce, meatballs, and sausage. My mother was going to make cannoli even though we only had home-made ones at Thanksgiving.

My father said, "I want all my people here, my cousins, my *cumpari,* everybody." All day long, between shopping and cooking, they called the aunts, uncles, cousins, and friends in Peterstown.

Madeleine and I had to do three bushel baskets of ironing before the party. Lucy had a great idea. She, Madeleine, and I could get the heaps of wrinkled clothes done if we stayed up all through the night. It was too hot to plug in irons until dusk. We'd listen to 45s—hers, Mario's, and Vinnie's— on the old HiFi, and she would tell us good stories about her old friends. Time would pass quickly, she said. We didn't have much choice, I thought.

I was suspicious at first, because the last time we had all stayed up late with Lucy, she had told us how girls between the ages of 9 and 12 start bleeding each month. And then they get hips and breasts, which means their bodies are ready for childbirth. "That doesn't mean the rest of them is ready, right, Lucy," I had pressed. I had seen old photos of my mother before she had 10 kids and it always seemed to me that she was once somebody else in those photos. Our mother was pregnant for almost eight years, Madeleine and I had calculated.

Our mother, for all her experience with these mysteries, did not have time to address them. If she had any spare time it was put to use taking out wrinkles, puckers, removing dust, and otherwise staving off dirt and disorder.

Every Saturday we tore the house apart and put it back together. We wiped, sprayed, oiled, and polished away the week's accumulation of dirt and disorder. We had the double strength of Pream, Lemon Pledge, Lestoil, Mr. Clean, and Spic 'n Span—and our own eagerness to be done. We scrubbed floors, tubs, counter tops, and sinks; moved toasters, tables, refrigerators, furniture; swished toilet bowls; changed bedding, and removed whole settlements of dust from under beds and dressers.

Since Nonnie had died we had to do all the sweeping, too. Her sturdy broom had outlasted her and all the ones we had bought from Woolworths and Grants. "That broom'll get up and move itself if you don't use it once in a while," my father said. So, one night after I had swept with her broom, I dreamed that Madeleine and I were tickling Nonnie's ankles and making her laugh. And then she started to chase us with her broom. She was getting back at us. I woke up with a haunting feeling, because my mother always said it meant something important when you dreamed about the dead. "They're trying to tell you something," she warned. But I was relieved to hear Lucy humming *Blue Moon* in her sleep and I fell back asleep. If my great-grandmother had a message to deliver, let her appear in my mother's dreams.

By Saturday afternoon, my father acted as if he himself had talked Frankie into enlisting in the Army. When Frankie's girlfriend Charlene Maloney came over to help us prepare food, my father told her, "You've lucked out, Charlene. You've got the bravest Donitella son."

After cleaning house I helped my mother make the cannoli. We poured the flour and salt on the counter and hollowed out a well in the center. I added a couple tablespoons of red wine and mixed, first with a fork, then with my hands. My mother made a cross in the dough and whispered something.

"What was that about?" I asked.

"I blessed the dough like we used to do. You don't remember."

"Why?" I asked tearing off a piece and popping it into my mouth.

"Because wheat is the staff of life. That's why we eat bread at every meal."

"I thought it was because we couldn't afford enough meat," I said, tearing off another piece of dough to nibble on.

Between phone calls my father came over to where we were working to report his progress in getting hold of everybody. One time he said to my mother, "Hon, what do you think about putting some ground fennel in the cannoli dough?" My mother got very impatient and said, "Would you get out of my hair and let me cook! I don't want to put ground fennel in the dough. I never heard of ground fennel in cannoli!" I thought, Here we go, they're going to have one of their big yelling fights. But I was wrong. My father scampered off and said, "OK, OK, you know what you're doing. Sorry, sorry, just thought it might be nice."

When he was back on the phone again, she said to me, "He can't ever leave me alone! Him and his fennel! I gotta keep my eye on him or he'll be putting it in the sauce, in the meatballs, in the salad!" She scooped the ricotta cheese, cream, and sugar for the cannoli filling into a bowl and began mixing it vigorously. I sprinkled in some cinnamon and nutmeg. For once I felt sorry for my father.

"I guess he's all nervous about Frankie going away," I said.

"He's always nervous about something!" she snapped. "I don't know what it's going to be like when he retires and all you kids are gone and he has nothing to worry about."

I stirred the cheese mixture as she grated in the chocolate. She preferred grated chocolate over the chocolate chips that Bella Palermo used. And we never put in the dried citron candy because everyone only spit it out. She was grating so fast and I was stirring so fast as we talked that we both saw what happened about a second too late. We had folded in a piece of her skin and a drop of her blood. She flinched and sucked her skinned knuckle.

"Ouch!" I said for her. "That grater's sharp!"

"Oh well," she said, wrapping her bleeding knuckle in a Kleenex. "At one time I'd have thrown the whole damn thing out and started over. Now, I say to hell with it. Life's not perfect, someone's going to have to eat my flesh and blood."

"Well at least we blessed the dough," I said, "Maybe it'll add extra flavor."

We laughed and she seemed to feel better. So I told her about the salad that Madeleine and I had dropped into a sink full of dishwater last Thanksgiving when the whole family had come over.

"We rinsed off each leaf and re-dressed the salad and no one seemed to notice. Especially not Uncle Al, who ate three servings."

"Is that so?" she asked as we heated a quart of olive oil for deep frying the shells. I attached the thermometer to watch for when it registered 375 degrees. The cannoli shell was the most important part. Too thin and it got mushy. Too thick and it was impossible to bite into, without it cracking into pieces. Madeleine came over to help us roll the dough into perfect six-inch circles for frying.

"Rena," she said, "I thought we had sworn on our patron saints never to tell anybody about the salad." We each wrapped a circle of wine-darkened dough around a metal cylinder and sealed its end with a bit of egg white.

"Don't swear," said my mother, adding some chopped toasted almonds and vanilla and almond extracts to the filling. "Besides, God sees everything. You can't hide from Him."

"It's over six months since we swore to secrecy," I said, "and we didn't renew the oath. So it doesn't count anymore."

At 9:30 that evening we set up two ironing boards. One of us would have to iron on a sheet spread over a thick pile of towels on the cloverleaf table. At one time my mother never would have allowed this. But times had changed since she started working.

It took Lucy, Madeleine, and me almost a half hour to agree on which records to play. The music we ironed to was very important. We still had mostly oldies, since Vogel's record shop always had a sale on them. But Madeleine and I had bought a few new ones with allowance money: I had just bought *Sugar Pie, Honey Bunch* by the Four Tops, *Ain't Too Proud to Beg* by the Temptations, *Piece of My Heart* by Janis Joplin, *Groovin'* by the Young Rascals. Madeleine had bought *Different Drum* by Linda Ronstadt and the Stone Ponies, *Sunday Will Never Be the Same* by Randy and the Rainbows.

Lucy put on *Chains* by the Cookies, *Up on the Roof* by the Drifters, *Dedicated to the One I Love* by the Shirelles, *Tears on My*

Pillow by Little Anthony and the Imperials, *Hully Gully Callin'*
Time by the Jive Five. These were just for starters. We'd need a lot
more to get us through the evening.

We heated up the three irons, one of them with fancy spray
steam and the other two old and taped where they were cracked or
falling apart. We all hated the old ones because the adhesive from
the masking tape melted when the iron got hot and made your hand
sticky. To keep on top of things, we washed a couple loads of towels, sheets, and baby clothes. We listened for the automatic washer
to vibrate five feet across the cellar floor on its final spin-dry cycle.
That's how we knew a load was done and ready to hang. We hung
the sheets and towels on the line out back under a yellow porchlight
that was not supposed to draw mosquitoes and moths. We had a new
product called spray starch. So instead of having to mix the blue liquid starch in a tub to soak the shirts, we could simply spray it on.

We stared at the heaps of shirts, blouses, kid clothes, handkerchiefs, pillowcases. We closed our eyes and counted to three. Each
pulled a corner of a garment from a basket. Whoever pulled the biggest item got to start with the fancy new iron. I pulled a long-sleeved
shirt and had the honor of winning.

I had ironed a lot faster when I first learned. But my mother
said that I missed all the important wrinkles. She made me redo everything so I would learn right. "Your fathers and brothers can't
leave the house in these shirts!" she exclaimed. She said we put in
more wrinkles than we took out. We would never have her ironing
skills. Her hands seemed to disappear into the iron and glide over
shirts effortlessly. The three of us together, Lucy, Madeleine, and I,
didn't add up to the speed and efficiency of our mother.

But we had fun dragging out our task, listening to Lucy's stories about hers and Mario's friends whom they had known since
high school.

We made her tell us again about the girl who threw her boyfriend's ring down the sewer and ran into Lee's Sweet Shoppe,
grabbed the pool cue and started beating on her boyfriend in front of
everybody. Four people had to restrain her. The girl said the boy
had lied to her.

"But why did she beat him?" I asked. "Couldn't she just talk to him, call him names, and publicly humiliate him that way?"

"Hell hath no fury like a woman scorned," said Lucy, standing the cracked iron up. She wiped her sweaty, sticky palm on her Bermuda shorts and said, "The boy had not taken her seriously and she had to make a point."

"On his head?" I asked.

"Would you ever beat Joe like that?" asked Madeleine.

"Joe would never do anything that bad."

"Yeah, most boys aren't like Joe. He's one in a million," I agreed.

"Tell us a story about girls who didn't make fools of themselves," asked Madeleine. "I'd never make a fool of myself over a boy. Never."

"Well, we'll see," said Lucy, pulling out a pillowcase, something easy, to iron. "Even in the stories where the boys make fools of themselves it's still the girls who suffer in the end."

"Like how?" we asked.

"Like this girl who came to my Sweet Sixteen party years ago. Betty, the one that got drunk at a party in her senior year. Some boys, real jerks, took advantage of her."

I asked Lucy if you could get pregnant from toilet seats or from swimming in a public pool like the one in Rahway Park, or from getting too close to boys in bathing suits. Lucy said it was highly unlikely, which contradicted what Sister Mary Elise had told my class.

"Lucy, you're gonna have to have all the babies for me and Rena," said Madeleine. "Even if we wanted to we can't now."

Lucy looked worried until I explained, "We took an oath of blood. We pricked our pointer fingers and exchanged blood and precious stones, which we buried, when we were eight and nine."

We explained to Lucy how we had found stones in Wheatena Park across from Quinn and Boden by River Road where you see clear across to Old Lady Koose's house. The day we found them we could see Old Lady Koose's shadows through her window as she conjured up potions and cooked a child who had disappeared. We decided it was an omen and we should make a vow. This was one we knew we could keep. We buried our stones in the banks of the creek out back.

"You'll probably break that vow when you get older," said Lucy, going for a short-sleeved shirt.

"I doubt it," I said. "We feel like we've had enough of motherhood now."

We asked Lucy to tell us some good stories about Mario and his girlfriends. Mario liked having a lot of girlfriends and didn't keep one for long. If she was blonde her chances of being around awhile were better. And if he really liked her, he'd bring her home to meet the family at Sunday dinner. Everybody—neighbors, my parents, and aunts—all knew perfect girls for Mario. He'd meet them once and that was it. He didn't call many girls twice. My father, who thought he should have found a wife by now, would remind him, "You've gotta give me grandsons, Mario."

Madeleine and I had one burning question we had begun to discuss between ourselves. I looked at her and she looked me. "Madeleine, you ask it?"

"OK, I will. Lucy, did Mario and Dana ever...?"

Lucy looked down at the ruffle on the small Madras blouse of Maria's she was trying to iron and began putting in more wrinkles than she was taking out. She smiled and said, "I can't say."

"Well then they did go all the way!" I said and Madeleine and I jumped for joy and said we knew it, we knew it. We loved Dana Krause. We'd pick her to marry any of our brothers. Every time she helped me design a poster for a school contest, it won first place. Dana was too cool. She even designed a fulcrum for Carmine.

Then I dared to ask, "What about Vinnie?"

"And Dana?" asked Lucy. trying to get out the new wrinkles in the ruffle. "I can't say..."

"Yahoo!" we shouted together.

"Shhhh," said Lucy, "you'll wake up little Joey and he'll want to be fed."

"Well then Frankie, too, must have...," said Madeleine.

"Frankie's only 17," I said. "Dana's 22!"

"Doesn't matter," said Lucy, "Dana likes Italian boys."

"Let's face it," said Madeleine. "Carmine's gotta be the only Donitella boy she missed. His bad luck."

"He's such a weirdo," I said, "You think he'll ever find a wife?"

"She'd have to be just as weird," said Madeleine.

"Now, let's not be too hard on Carmine," said Lucy, who always came to everyone's defense.

"But he's such a Chatsworth Oswald, Jr., you know that brainy guy who used to be on Doby Gillis," I said.

"Yeah, can't you just see Mr. and Mrs. Carmine Weirdo and their little baby Weirdoes going around, collecting junk from drawers and saying, 'Hmmm, this looks like a good way to catch sound waves.'" Even Lucy giggled at the image of baby Carmines.

"I guess I shouldn't mock him," said Madeleine. "If he didn't help me with a science project, I might have gone into science myself. I'm going to study French—more sophisticated."

Madeleine told the story of how she had wanted so badly to enter a project in the big sixth grade science fair last month. Only one student from each class of 60 would have his or her project displayed. Madeleine stayed up past midnight for weeks and Carmine helped her. Her project was to show all the ways that we use electricity. She used her allowance to buy dry cells, wire, and other equipment. For heat, she made a radiator out of tin foil and cardboard. For light, she hooked a small light bulb to one dry cell. For motion, she made a motorized armature with a two-by-four, long nails, and coils. She was worried this wasn't good enough. So she took apart a battery-operated game we had called Master Mind, which lit up when you slid the right answer written on a metal card into the right slot. Carmine helped make up addition and subtraction questions and answers and re-assembled the game as a hand-held math computer. Finally, the day before the project was due, Madeleine and Carmine stayed up until very late painting a large piece of oak tag with oil paints for the background. It was supposed to be a huge waterfall, indicating hydroelectric power.

I helped Madeleine carry the entire project all the way to St. Mary's. I followed her to her classroom and we set it up at the front of the classroom. We were sure hers was the best and would be picked for the fair. But when the homeroom teacher Mrs. Mayer came into the classroom, she stared at the project and said, "What's this?" Madeleine seemed to be struck dumb, so I said, "It's Madeleine's science project for the fair." Mrs. Mayer put her books on her desk, sighed, and said, "Well, can you please get it out of my way? Larry Chunklin's mother brought his project in days ago and I've already selected it. It's a weathervane, a lot neater than that mess. Now let's get started, class, roll call!"

Madeleine told the story, laughing as if she was glad the way things turned out. But I remembered that day well. She wouldn't let me walk home from school with her, she ran by herself. I told her to tell Mom what happened, and she said Mom didn't have time to do anything about it anyway. Larry Chunklin was an only kid and we hated him.

We took a break from ironing halfway through the night and Lucy showed us how to dance the Hully Gully. We made cherry Kool-Aid and cold meatball sandwiches. We all had a full mouth when the awful realization dawned on us. "We're eating meat! It's Friday morning!" We tried to talk with full mouths. Should we swallow? Spit it out? Or throw the sandwiches out? Lucy pushed the food inside her left cheek and said we should finish. It was not a sin because we had innocently forgotten. She would call the rectory in the morning to make sure.

By dawn we could see the bottom of the last basket of ironing. Lucy ran out of stories and to stave off sleepiness we all started counting "ah-wing-ah-wetts" again. How many were there in *The Lion Sleeps Tonight?* As usual we had to play the song over and over, about five times, until all three of us agreed on the exact number. That took us up to finishing time. We put clothes away in closets and drawers so they couldn't be inspected for any missed spots the next day. We tiptoed past all the rooms where people slept. We stood in front of the fan in the parlor a few minutes to dry our sweat and then we went to sleep for a few hours.

Sunday morning my father insisted we all go to 10 o'clock mass and Communion together. I was hungry and didn't feel like fasting, but I did, for Frankie's sake. Madeleine and I drove to St.

Mary's with Vinnie, Carmine, Frankie, Joe, and Lucy in Mario's Lincoln with the top down. We took the long way—St. George Avenue—so the boys could smoke cigarettes. But we had to hurry and get to church early to save four pews so the family could all sit together. Madeleine and I saw that Father Herman would be saying mass. "Whoever taps the other first the first time Herman says 'We must strive' gets the favor of her choice from the other," we agreed. We waited a long time it seemed, and I began to toss my dime for the collection basket in the air. It fell and rolled away from where we were sitting. Lucy gave me a look.

The organ music started just as my parents showed up with Maria, Teresa, Carmela, and Joey. We all stood and sang:

Give praise to Mary, Queen above,

Oh Maria

Hail mother of mercy and of love

Oh Maria

Triumph all ye Cherubim

Sing with us Ye Seraphim

Heaven and earth resound the hymn

Salve, Salve, Salve Regina

My father had gotten into his pew on the last Salve Regina part and handed Joey to Lucy. He joined in singing very loudly. He drowned out everyone around him. He started to sing the second verse and didn't notice that everyone had stopped singing and had sat down. He was staring into the music booklet. The organist had stopped playing but began again to accompany him, playing even louder than he sang. The priest and altar boys waited for him to finish, frozen in the middle of the altar. He sang the whole second verse by himself, until he got to the Salve Regina. He stopped suddenly, his voice catching in his throat. He knelt and buried his face in his palms. Madeleine and I were both hoping the same thing: Dear God, let no one from our fifth and sixth grade classes be at this mass. We pulled our white mantillas close around the sides of our faces.

The collection basket came and I was embarrassed to have nothing to put in. We all went to Communion together, Joey and baby Carmela talking loudly as we did. As soon as I swallowed the host my stomach growled so loudly, I knew the boy next to me could hear it.

After mass, my father made us wait in the courtyard while he went to the rectory to talk to Fathers Murphy and Herman about making a special intention for Frankie at the rest of the masses on Sunday. That afternoon, we knew who had gone to 11 and 12 o'clock masses and heard that they needed to remember Frankie Donitella in their prayers. The phone rang all day with people wishing us luck.

The relatives and friends trickled in. Aunt Francesca, mom's secret pal and Madeleine's godmother, arrived first. Grandma Donitella cried and prayed in Sicilian. Grandma Coniglio gave Frankie a greeting card with $3 in it, unaware that she had chosen a sympathy card. My cousins who were studying dance and music in New York got up and sang *Over There* to Frankie. Someone had a camera with a new flash cube on it and took lots of pictures of Charlene and Frankie. My father made all the boys pose alone for one. Then my brothers put Frankie on their shoulders and ran down Creek Street singing *For He's a Jolly Good Fellow* and the neighborhood kids all joined in.

Lucy tried to get Mario and all of us together to sing *Blue Moon* like we used to when they babysat for us years ago. But my father's voice was getting very loud and disruptive. Everyone quieted down as if something were about to happen.

"Vincent, calm down, you're getting too sentimental in your old age," said Uncle Vito. "I know he's your son, my heart goes out to you..."

My father kept yelling over him, "He's my son, you don't know, no one knows what it's like to have a son going off to war!"

"He's only going off to Fort Dix just now," a small voice came from the crowd. But my father's outburst had nothing to do with the facts at hand and it was as if he heard no one, saw no one present.

We all went down the cellar, where we kept our TV, to cool off. He looked at the blank screen, but it was as if he was watching the 7 p.m. weekday news he sat in front of every evening. He was disgusted with the reports of students on campuses demonstrating against the war and he had shown his disgust recently by throwing his half-full beer can at the screen. He said the demonstrators and those who burned their draft cards and the American flag should all be put in a big open pit and have hot paraffin poured on them. He hated these intellectuals who were ruining the country and any of his children who went to college were never to discuss the war with any of them. He called the peace sign the footprint of the American chicken. Madeleine and I could not wear our rawhide-strung peace medallions around him on pain of punishment or worse.

Blood or red wine poured down the side of his mouth and stained his shirt. He stared at the TV screen and said, "Those bastards, they don't know nothing about gore...gangrene...seeing your buddy blown to bits..." And then his voice disintegrated into parts of speech, no complete sentences. The relatives saw it made no difference what they said, so they ignored him and went back to talking to each other. The last coherent thing he said was, "If my father was here..."

We all said good-bye to Frankie early Monday morning as my father and Mario drove him to the bus.

"Each key is a lifetime," Mario said one Saturday evening toward the end of summer. "A hammer hits a string and a world of sound lives until it dies. And another. And another."

I had asked Mario how a piano works as he sat on his piano bench idly hitting one key at a time, holding it down until all its sound was lived out. He kept repeating the pattern. He slid open the doors and I looked inside at the strings and hammers as he picked one to activate. Madeleine and I looked at each other. We had already taken the doors off and lifted the top off the player piano when Mario wasn't around.

Our parents had taken the little kids and gone to Peterstown to visit the grandparents. Madeleine and I preferred to stay home with the older kids. Mario was saying good-bye to his piano. He ran his thumb up and down the keys as we all sat around in the cool cellar and chatted. I tried to do it and hurt my thumb. But Mario had big, tough hands, "piano hands," my parents said.

Mario had just told Lucy he was quitting the band. Lucy was upset and protested, "But you'll really miss the music! You need the music, Mario, to help you relax and study better."

Mario said he knew he would miss it, but that a voice in his head kept saying it was time to buckle down and get serious. And the voice wouldn't go away. He hadn't told Dad yet, but he was dropping out of medical school and switching to the study of astronomy and physics. He wouldn't have time for music anymore. But he said that the Catalysts, his new band, had cut an R&B version of *Impossible Dream* and he would present it to Mom and Dad this Christmas.

Everybody seemed melancholy so we all went for a walk down Creek Street. It was already getting dark at 7:30 and I noticed that the maples had begun to crinkle and turn color. Summer's end was painfully near. I hated summer for being swift and short. We went as far as the concrete bridge over the creek halfway around the corner, where it wound through the backyard of Tony the tax collector. We sat on the bridge and threw pebbles into the creek. We could see the window in Tony's backyard that Frankie had sent a ball crashing through last summer during a game of stick ball. Frankie had to contribute a month's allowance to pay for its repair.

Vinnie pointed to the window and said, "I'll tell you a secret about Tony's window. Frankie didn't do it."

"What do you mean?" asked Lucy.

"Eddie Newman did it."

"Why'd Frankie take the rap?" asked Mario.

"Cause Eddie started bawling and saying his father would kill him," said Vinnie, tossing pebble after pebble into the shallow brook.

"Oh man," groaned Mario, "Eddie's always done his crying bit. What about Frankie? Didn't he get beat then?"

"Who remembers. He was probably getting taken to the wall for something else anyway and figured what the hay..."

Lucy looked bothered but was silent. Then she said, "Things are sure dull without Frankie around." She started to cry. Madeleine and I looked at each other as if to say, don't go soft like her.

My parents received more surprises that summer. Mario softened the blow to my father about medical school by announcing that he was also getting married. To a girl name Sheila Campbell. My father was a bit glum about the name until he met the face that went with it and she said all the right things and wrapped him around her finger. Besides, by quizzing her on her family tree, he discovered a strong possibility of Italian blood somewhere along the line. Campbell, he said, must have originally been Campobello.

Carmine got accepted to Harvard, which really came as no surprise. But he also received full a scholarship. My mother said her rosaries, which she had less and less time for, had worked. Lucy announced that she was pregnant again. She and Joe would be moving out in a month. But before school started, she, Madeleine, and I had one more ironing marathon. Madeleine and I got to ask Lucy another burning question: whether or not she and Joe were virgins when they got married. She said yes, their honeymoon in Atlantic City was the very first time for both of them. We believed her, because she couldn't tell a lie if she tried.

I never got off Creek Street that summer. My mother's job got more demanding and Madeleine and I had to do more and more housework. We split the house chores between us. I was responsible for the parlor and the two dormers and bathroom upstairs. Madeleine had the kitchen, downstairs bathroom, the babies' bedroom, and my parents' bedroom. She said she liked having our parents bedroom to do because if they weren't around we could look through the secret compartments in their dressers.

Only once did we find something of interest. As we dusted the cedar chest where Mom kept her wedding gown and our First Communion veils, we opened it wide. There, buried deep beneath all the folds of white voile, satin, and lace, we found boxes with old photos of bare-breasted dark women, probably from New Guinea. In another box we found an old manuscript of the stories my father used to tell us when we were younger and everybody was home. He had written them all out in ballpoint pen. Each story had a title: *In the Beginning Love Lay Frozen, Four Directions, Simple Pleasures, Feasts, In the Province of Agrigento...* The last one he had started but not finished was called *The Last Cannoli*. The writing was almost indecipherable, but it looked like, *the evening after he called the evil men ham 'n eggers and told them to go pound salt, Mario Anthony Donitella returned to the same spot on his beloved mountain*...And that was all we could figure out.

We showed the stories to Lucy and said we thought it might be a nice idea to send them to Frankie to read. But then we decided if Dad ever found out we had not respected his privacy, he'd be very angry. We put them away and forgot about them. Until Christmas. A strange thing happened to my father when he heard Mario's recording of *Impossible Dream*. He cried, which was not so strange anymore. But, then he made us all sit and listen to the stories over and over, until my mother stepped in and said enough.

My father began to work fewer hours at his produce stand and took on the job of worrying about Frankie. He wrote him long letters and sent pictures. Frankie called every Sunday after 11 p.m. when the phone rates were very cheap.

Sometimes my father made us kids write something at the end of the letter and sign it. He had my mother bake cookies. They wrapped them in lots of tin foil and mailed them. They waited by the phone for Frankie to call the following Sunday to assure them he had received the cookies intact. One time I answered the phone first when he called and Frankie told me that the cookies had arrived a big pile of crumbs, but not to tell Mom and Dad. "They still tasted good moistened with a teaspoon of coffee," he said. He told my parents the guys in the barracks loved the cookies. So they baked and sent a bunch more.

God was sending us messages all through the rest of 1966 to remind us how lucky we were that Frankie had not gotten orders for Vietnam. First, one of my father's fourth or fifth cousins who lived in Peterstown had a son killed in Vietnam. He was a Marine. Our whole family went to the wake at Cardoni's Funeral Home and then to the funeral the next day. When the Marines did the 21-gun salute around his flag-draped coffin, his mother fell to her knees wailing. I heard some guy next to us say, "That Chester, he was crazy, probably walked in front of the bullet."

Then the brother of a girl in one of the ninth grade classes was injured badly in Vietnam. We prayed for him for weeks at morning prayers in St. Mary's until he came home in a coffin. My class had to go to the funeral at Lehrer Funeral Home on Elm Street. The boy's name was Gary and he was laid out in his uniform with his white hat on. He didn't look like someone who had been in a battle and I wished I knew exactly why he had died. No one talked about his wounds, hidden by his uniform and the casket.

I was glad that Frankie was not being sent to Vietnam. My father continued to watch the news and the riots and demonstrations and to yell at the TV screen. Madeleine and I had started hanging around Lee's Sweet Shoppe after school, staying away from home whenever possible. We learned how to play pinball and saw friends of Frankie's there in leather jackets. They would come over to us and tell us to send their best to Frankie and that they hoped he didn't go to Nam. One of them, Pete Jenner, liked preaching to us. He'd say things like, "Yeah man, I tell you, Domino Theory sucks. We ought to just get our troops out of there. Dropped enough bombs and napalm." Neither of us said anything. We heard enough opinions on the war when we got home. And besides, we had been told never to discuss the war.

Then one Sunday after mass, Madeleine and I wanted to go to Lee's Sweet Shoppe to play pinball and my mother said we had to stay home. We started to argue with her and she said. "Go get dressed up. We're all going to Fort Dix to see Frankie. He leaves for Vietnam Monday."

Madeleine and I put on our matching pink searsucker skirts and our matching white cotton ruffled blouses. Charlene was coming with us. She had made a tray of manicotti, the way my mother had taught her Frankie liked it—with a marinara, not a meat, sauce.

It was a nice spring day just a year after Frankie had joined. As we drove in the big station wagon that Frankie had helped pay for down the New Jersey turnpike, everything looked so new to me, so different from the more familiar northern part of the state where the Humble Refinery torched the sky at night, where industry fringed the major highway. To the south there were farms and country roads and much more greenery. It was a long ride, but I had brought the little transistor radio which I had gotten for Christmas. I was listening to WABC on my earphone so I wouldn't have to hear my parents' music on WNEW. Charlene asked me to tell her if *Leaving on a Jet Plane* came on—that was Frankie and her newest song.

We found Frankie's barracks and I didn't recognize him. His pile of long hair was gone, mowed down. What was left were just dark twigs on his snow white scalp. He looked very tall and very thin and very different without his black leather jacket. He was all teeth, scalp, and eyes, and the drab olive uniform made him look sallow. My father walked over to him and hugged him and I realized that my father was now shorter than all my brothers. We all hugged Frankie and said, "You look great!"

We looked for the perfect picnic spot to have our lunch. Frankie showed us a grassy hillside where we could spread out our blankets and our food and heat the manicotti and everything on a grill.

I put out the antipasto and some cold leftover broccoli frittata. My father and Frankie got the fire going and talked Army talk. My father said they ate hardtack in the South Pacific. They swallowed their ration of it, then drank a bunch of water and watched their bellies distend as the hardtack expanded.

We heated the sausage and peppers. Madeleine and I sliced the tomatoes and dressed them. We put out sesame-seeded bread, Frankie's favorite, from Saraceno's in Peterstown. My mother and father had a little fight before we ate because she had forgot to bring a separate salad bowl. Frankie said he could run back to his barracks and get one, but my father said don't worry about it, he'd just throw his salad on top of everything just as he did with his mess kit during the war and probably get *àcitu*.

As we dunked our Stella D'oro cookies in our coffee for dessert, someone brought out the Kodak Instamatic and took pictures. Charlene gave Frankie a small photo of him and her together. It was laminated to a heart-shaped piece of metal, just like the one that saved my father's life in World War II. When it was time to leave, my father got very emotional and wanted some time alone with Frankie. I could tell by the way Frankie gestured he was playing the parent again, saying, "Calm down, Dad, everything's going to be

OK." *Leaving on a Jet Plane* came on and I gave the radio to Charlene to listen to. She cried and so did Lucy and my mother.

It must have been two years to the day from when Frankie joined to the Saturday morning the phone call came. Just like two years before, I was awakened too early for a Saturday. It was hot and humid and I smelled the sweet honeysuckle and the sharp weeds of the overflowing creek, full again after a hard rain. The crickets crooned out of sync. Then I realized the phone had been ringing and ringing and it was only 6 a.m. Finally someone answered it.

The voices on the phone downstairs were soft. I heard my mother's first, then I heard her call clearly, gently, "Vincent." I heard my father's footsteps, then his voice, low and annoyingly soft.

I thought of my wardrobe and what a rummage sale it was, how bitter I felt about not being dressed for the times like my classmates. By the time I got a new style, it was three seasons out of date, and it never fit right because it came from someone else's closet, a cousin, a neighbor. I thought of the 21-gun salute funeral a year ago and how I'd had nothing decent to wear to such an event.

Next, I thought of Frankie's letters from Vietnam, always signed "Your dutiful son." I thought of how little about the war his letters told us, not nearly as much as Huntley-Brinkley reports. I thought about the dead boy Gary and how unlived-in his body had looked in the casket.

Madeleine, Maria, and Teresa were awake, then, and we all looked at each other with the same thought. Who else would call this early on a Saturday morning? I wished Lucy was there. She'd know what to say to the voice coming through the wires.

"I'm gonna go downstairs and see what's going on," said Maria, jumping out of her cot. Without saying a word, Madeleine and I scrambled behind her banging down the stairs like horses. Normally such noise would have cost us plenty.

Here, I have to improvise because my mind's shutter closed when my feet hit the last stair and I saw my parents' faces. And it was all because of that black wall-phone, with its long tangling wire that stretched into the bathroom for privacy. I saw the hole kicked through the bathroom door. Frankie's foot had made it years ago when he was chasing me and I ran into the bathroom.

Sometime by noon the shutter must have opened and I knew this: He could come home in a few weeks after his condition had improved. Who knew what happened there in the land of smoke, sandbags, and strange wet green vegetation?

I never could envision what a mine looked like, if it was a mine. Grenades reminded me of artichokes. So, the details, if I ever knew them, remain camouflaged in TV frames of swamp, sand, and jungle.

Frankie wasn't dead. His tour cost a leg and some superficial wounds of the flesh. But he had his life, the voice on the phone said. We should be proud, the voice also said. He'd get a medal of sorts, some big honors.

My parents stayed calm. Not only because the worst was over, but because they were best at handling big things. Lucy came by later in the day and was the first one to cry. We put roses in front of the statue of the Blessed Virgin Mary. Dana Krause came over and I saw her cry for the first time ever, probably as much for the news about Mario getting married as for Frankie. She gave me her big canvas with the Holy Hands and the one with eyes all over it. I hung them both above the altar in our room. She was moving to Greenwich Village.

That Sunday, Madeleine and I went to mass and Communion and then to Lee's Sweet Shoppe. We didn't talk much. We always knew what each other was thinking. I tried to picture Frankie walking around on Vinnie's stilts and felt embarrassed. I realized that missing a leg would present all kinds of problems, but I was just not ready to figure them out. Madeleine and I didn't risk talking about the phone call. We had to be strong the way Frankie must have been.

To keep from talking we played game after game of pinball until Pete Jenner came over to ask the usual questions. He said he was going to a big anti-war march in Washington next weekend. For a moment I ached to go. Dana had gone to one and said she got high on the music and energy alone. But I knew I wasn't leaving Creek Street for a while.

Pete leaned against the other pinball machine and carelessly let his cigarette ash fall onto our machine. The gray ash went rolling down the glass, leaving a tiny trail. The Beatles were singing *A Day in the Life* on the juke box and Pete nervously tapped to it.

Madeleine and I stared straight ahead at the silver balls and just listened to him and the bells ringing as we racked up points.

"How is your big brother? What do you hear from Nam?"

"He's fine," said Madeleine, tilting her game and turning the machine over to me.

Pete seemed to be waiting for more of an answer and I got impatient with the dead air, so I said, "Yeah, Frankie's fine, Pete. He's coming home in a couple weeks."

We could've told him how right he was. War, this war in particular, didn't seem to be good for anyone. Not for Frankie, not for my mother or father, not the demonstrators who had to put in a lot of unhappy hours. And not for my summer. It was probably wrecking people's summers all over the place.

But I didn't tell him. I kept my eye on the smooth silver ball, knowing it would be a cold day in Hell before we talked about family wounds with outsiders.

"Remember what a jeanbuster he was, that Frankie?" I said to my daughter Lucy. She was getting too serious. She sat at the kitchen table with the kids' riddle book opened, showing her youngest, Peggy, how to connect the dots.

"You have to follow the numbers in order, Peggy," she said, "then stand back and you see what you've got." She held my granddaughter's hand with the black crayon and helped her move from point to point.

I opened the Tupperware container and took out some biscott' and continued, "That Frankie, he used to make me laugh. He'd walk around on his knees in big shoes with the big overcoat, then he'd get on those old stilts and be a giant. I caught him in the garden once about to kill a praying mantis when it was a $50 fine. He'd grab a banana and do Jimmy Durante. Always busting my jeans!"

Lucy didn't laugh. She said, "Ma, that was Vinnie who did the midget trick, not Frankie. Don't talk like he's dead."

I closed the Tupperware and burped the air out of it. I squinted inside my head and I remembered. She was right. I'd confused my own sons. Frankie wasn't dead, but he wasn't home where he belonged.

"Well, what do you expect?" I sighed. "I can't even get my own kids' names straight sometimes. I'm getting old. C'mon, Carrie." I picked up Peggy's older sister and put her on my lap.

"Grandma, is Uncle Frankie flying?" asked Lucy's son, Joe-Joe. "My dad is flying somewhere, too, right Mom?"

Then I saw that puzzled look. My grandson's face looked like an unfinished paint-by-number. Ever since my youngest son returned from Vietnam and then left again, it was like we all had riddles we couldn't solve, cravings we couldn't satisfy.

Lucy didn't answer her son, but told him to finish his pastina with the butter and eggs and help her and Peggy figure out the animal. "Look! What do we have?" She held the drawing book back a ways so we could all guess. Eyes and a muzzle. A dog? Lion? Bear? I saw some beast, but none I recognized.

"Daddy!" said Peggy. It broke me up that Lucy smiled. I wanted to scream at her, "Whoever told you waiting was a virtue?" Then I realized she probably learned it from me. I knew. She knew. We all knew. Her husband was not at some Tupperware convention for the weekend. Not every three weeks, he wasn't.

She had just come by and said she and the kids were moving in for the week. She was quiet about her condition, but I knew the early stages of pregnancy. She didn't touch coffee.

She was taking some night classes in child development psychology at Union College. So I thought of what my mother used to say, *Cussì si fannu di cursaru a cursaru…*It meant something like a tit for a tat. I dropped hints, asking if she had any nice fellows in her class. I only encouraged her to flirt, to take her mind off Joe. Her father had more extreme ideas. He wanted to gather his four sons and all take Joe for a ride and give him a talking to old-country style. I told him nothing doing.

I said to Lucy, "I guess Frankie's like Joe. When he's good and ready…" I knew, as Frankie's mother, I was supposed to worry about the child with the biggest hurt. His first year home, I soothed, dressed, bandaged. I cried alone in my rocking chair at night. Then I saw that he survived, he managed with one leg, sometimes better than the rest of us with two. By the time he left, I had finished grieving for my son's pain. I prayed for him, too, but I knew that when he had taken care of his business, he'd return to us. I told myself this: A part of him escaped through that wound. I'd heard this happens after they open you for surgery. The spirit of my comedian son vanished. Perhaps Frankie went off to find his ghost.

It was the rest of us I worried about, who ached for something we couldn't touch. Riddles we couldn't solve. Hunger we couldn't feed. Perhaps I was getting too philosophical in my old age. I was turning 50. I could see things in a way I didn't have time for in my younger days when my husband and I were raising a house full of little ones. Now I could connect the dots and see something recognizable.

For example, the stone and the blood. I remember like it was yesterday. We used to say to our kids, "You can't get blood from a stone." But then we did. How? We believed that there would be enough to feed, clothe, and shelter us, a little left over to make us laugh, and there was. Our faith was so strong I could boil that stone in water and call it chicken soup and meatballs and my kids would tell me, "Ma, this soup is delicious!" In the old days, we sometimes went to bed hungry, but never with these cravings.

Now, we had extra money, thanks to Frankie. He sent us his whole disability check each month. But the things we bought did not satisfy us. We used to get more satisfaction from plain pasta and beans than we now did out of the thick juicy steaks.

Lucy sent the kids to the parlor to pick up Joe-Joe's dinosaur collection. "Put it away nice on a shelf," she said, "Your great-grandma and great-aunts are coming over for cake and coffee."

When the kids were gone she said, "Ma, I was in the cellar checking the furnace yesterday to see if you need to call the oil man before winter sets in. I saw a bayonet and billie club sticking out of the rafters in the ceiling behind it."

"You never knew your father still had some of his war weapons?" I looked at her sideways. "Your brother Mario never told you?"

"Told me what?"

So I told her the story how after Frankie got home from Vietnam, Vincent took his four sons for a ride. He told them he was *Capo* now and what it meant. He said you could no longer trust a country to protect the women when it let its sons take bullets like sitting ducks.

"Just as he's pulling down Creek Street with the four boys that day after riding them around in circles, he sees some teenage boys stopped in their car in the middle of the street talking to Madeleine and Rena. He jumps out of the car, asks the girls who the boys were. The girls say they don't know them. He jumps back in the car with your brothers and chases the boys for five blocks. At a red light he gets out with the billie club he'd been keeping under the car seat and asks the boys what they wanted with his daughters. Of course, the boys told him they mistook the girls for someone else. Him with the club in his hand, thank God he didn't make a scene. He let them go."

"Poor Mario, Vinnie, Carmine, and Frankie, they must've been mortified," said Lucy, shaking her head.

"That's the worst part about him and his big ideas. Mostly they're embarrassing. Mario said they found an old handgun in his glove compartment, I don't know if he even knew how to use it. I have no idea where he got it. Mario and Vinnie took it apart with a penknife and threw it in the Rahway River."

"Before he really went too far," said Lucy.

"Just in case, I took the billie club and the bayonet, which was in the cellar, and hid them both. He didn't even miss them."

Lucy said, "Someday I'll tell my kids these stories. They'd never believe it now about their grandfather who spoils them."

"I think he wishes he was as soft on his own kids as he is with his grandkids."

"He thinks he's to blame for Frankie, doesn't he?"

"*Ma, chissà?*" I sighed. "Like my mother says, Who knows?"

"Let's go shopping after Grandma and the aunts leave," said Lucy. "My clothes are getting tight."

"Sure," I said, we'll go to Klein's or Corvette's, or maybe Daffy Dan's. I think they still have summer clearance." My daughters and I—except Madeleine, who ran away to San Francisco—were all suckers for clothes with the designer labels torn out.

"What about the kids?" Lucy said. "Maria and Teresa are out. Will *he* ever wake up?" She nodded toward my bedroom.

"Your father? He'll wake up." To myself I said, Although he's half asleep even when he's awake these days. He worked harder than ever. When he was down, like today in bed, it was only after weeks of working around the clock. We'd put an addition onto the produce stand and our business was booming. But my husband slept without resting and ate without tasting.

So, like my daughter I waited for my husband to come around.

Waiting did have its helpful side. Now I could laugh about the way Frankie had left three years ago, after his father had gone to the Veterans Hospital in Newark with one of his great ideas. He drew a

190

line with black marker on his right leg. He wanted to have his leg re-moved and re-attached to his son. He told the doctor he'd read there was a way. I could hear him ordering the doctor around, not hearing the doctor's answer. The nurse called me later to talk to me about the VA's in-patient alcohol treatment program.

I told her my husband wasn't really an alcoholic. Italian men didn't become alcoholics. He just drank too much once in a while when he had something on his mind.

Like the evening before. He started talking about trying to track down Frankie. We'd just received a card from him, post-marked Los Angeles, saying he was fine, he'd keep in touch. I tried to tell Vincent how I felt. Our son is a man now. You can't treat him like a child. But no matter what I said, he said the opposite. I was an easy battlefield for him.

Just before going to bed he threw tomatoes, squash, eggplant, string beans at the wall, talking about the things he should have done another way. First he said he'd been too hard, then he was too soft; then he blamed his father for dying too young.

He didn't like being the one who had to wait. But like it or not, he was learning to do it.

We weren't the only ones Frankie left behind. Charlene he left at the altar. She never shed a tear in front of us. I wouldn't have minded if she had, though I admired her *bella figura*. She saw that her father-in-law-to-be cried enough for all of us. She was calm as she, Lucy, and I called 250 guests to tell them the wedding was off. We had two days to do it.

I was especially sad about the wedding cake. Charlene and I had spent weeks designing it ourselves. We took a cake decorating class together and learned to make roses and petals and lacy trim. It was to have all white decorations. We'd make it a huge tier cake, four feet high. We learned how to separate the tiers with wooden dowels. We bought a beautiful battery-operated fountain to set be-tween the two top tiers. We made the bride and groom ourselves out of icing. As I packed away all our equipment I realized how peaceful I'd felt involved in such a project.

Perhaps I'd sew some new maternity clothes for Lucy.

Then Vincent decided he was moving to Sicily, back to his father's village. He was going to try to find his people there. He thought he'd find his peace.

I'd say, "Vincent, why don't you just tell the younger girls the stories you used to tell about Sicily." No, he was moving to Sicily, that week anyway.

He chided me for being embarrassed when he spoke in Sicilian in front of storekeepers, neighbors, customers. I answered him in English and he got loud and indignant, saying *"Minni futtu! Minni futtu!* I don't give a damn what anybody thinks about me."

My youngest, Carmela, brought home a form from grammar school to fill out. In the space for nationality, he made her write *Sicilian*. When the older kids were young, he'd reminded them over and over, You are American first, of Sicilian extraction. He'd make them memorize exactly how to say it until it had the weight of a prayer. He'd discipline them if they got it backwards, making them stand in the corner to jog their memory.

Now, he said he intended to renounce his American citizenship when he got to Sicily. He said this country was a disgrace. The Treaty just inflamed him more. But, in my heart I believed if there'd been no Vietnam, he'd have found another reason to be *Capo*. Because in my heart, where I knew my husband like my own soul, I knew his agony was something old always looking for a tough face to mask it.

When my mother-in-law and sisters-in-law arrived we let the kids sit with us awhile. Then we put the girls in the tub, with the bathroom door open so we could keep an eye on them. We set Joe-Joe up on the bathroom floor to play with his dinosaurs and watch them, too.

Grandma Donitella got up in the middle of the kitchen floor and showed us how Lucy used to do the hula hoop and win contests. We all got hysterical, seeing this quiet old lady roll her hips from side to side. Lucy laughed and laughed so hard, big tears rolled down her face.

"Hey, Ma, that's sexy!" squealed Rosalia and got up to try it. Then the rest of them, Angela, Marialia, Antoinette, and Santa, and

Lucy and I all stood around that clover-leaf table and pretended we were doing the hula. We put on some old music, *Mack the Knife,* and some old rock and roll.

Lucy said, "Joe-Joe, big boy, run down the cellar and find that old hula hoop, it's lying around somewhere."

The scene reminded me of the Nickelettes, the girls' club I belonged to years ago, before I had a family. My secret pal, Francesca, who sent me French paintings over the years, should've been here. But Francesca was the only one who would not have had the patience with the *bella figura* we all put on next.

You always keep a *bella figura* in your family. You never say you don't have the money to do this, go here, buy that. You make up some other reason—you don't want it, don't like it, prefer to stay home. You never tell anyone you can't get blood from a stone.

We all knew the best way to keep a beautiful face was to brag about our kids.

I said, "Madeleine called last week, to say she was enrolled in first year of college in San Francisco. She's in some arts program, I think." I didn't say I had no idea how she was living. She hadn't taken a cent from us. "Rena has a very nice boyfriend," I went on to say. "He even has a little Italian blood." I didn't tell them she wanted to get married next month at the age of 17 and threatened to elope.

I said that my baby Carmela, who just turned eight, was at her Grandma Coniglio's until this evening because I had been working overtime at the factory. I said how she loved to visit with her grandparents. I didn't say she wanted to stay home because her aunts were coming. I sent her there because I knew that her father and I would have words last night about Frankie and there'd be fruits and vegetables flying.

When I felt my *bella figura* going to hell as I remembered the look on Carmela's face, I jumped up and pulled out the teapot. I put on some tea water for Lucy.

"Look at what my Carmine invented, girls!" I showed them the teapot with a steam-operated music box that he finally perfected and how it played a little song when the water boiled.

When Carmine had dropped out of Harvard, I never mentioned that it broke my heart. I told people my son was too smart, smarter than the professors there, who bored him to tears. He was so smart no one but he knew what he was talking about. Now he was moving to Arizona. I said we were happy for him—not worried at all that he'd never find a wife.

When my sisters-in-law talked glowingly about their kids, I looked between the lines and saw what was hidden. They pulled out graduation snapshots. I saw the truancy, the underage drinking on Staten Island, the arrest for trespassing on a freighter in Secaucus with pot, the one son dating a colored girl. We didn't live in Peterstown anymore, but gossip has no boundaries.

I didn't push. I respected their secrets the way they respected mine. We were silent a bit and I put on another pot of coffee, arranged some more pastries and cookies on the platter. Santa asked Lucy about Joe.

"Away on business," I answered for her.

"Again?" asked Marialia.

"He's working toward a big bonus," I said, not skipping a beat. I was better at this than Lucy. It wasn't exactly lying. Before they could ask about Frankie, I said, "We heard from Frankie again, he's job training in Los Angeles."

Job training, that's what we had told all the relatives three years ago, "They're young, Frankie and Charlene. They just want to save a little bit up first; Frankie's gone to a government program in South Carolina, in New Orleans, in St. Paul, in Dallas." I never said we couldn't write back because he sent no return address.

I didn't go into how I could see that Vinnie, Carmine, and Mario were worn down trying to be their father's sons. I could see them all running to other states, even as they said to me, "Ma, you gotta *talk* to him."

"My son, Mario, they want him to head a lab in Chicago," I bragged. "They're looking for the first cause of the universe there. If anyone can find it my Mario can."

With Mario, as with Carmine, it was always easy to cut a *bella figura.* I could go on about the degrees, one after the other, medicine, astronomy, physics, chemistry. Mario had job offers from big labs around the country. I didn't say how I wished for his own sake he'd just bang away once on the piano he hadn't touched in years. What a mother sees in her children's eyes is not always to be expressed in public.

"They walk on the moon, they can do anything now, I tell you," said Rosalia.

Marialia snorted, "Who they fooling? They didn't put a man on no moon. They filmed the whole thing in a studio. They wanted to scare the be-Jesus out of the Commies."

"Everything's a conspiracy by the government," said Rosalia, "Or so my big sister says." She pushed her cup and saucer in and leaned on her elbows as if getting positioned for confrontation. But Marialia waved her off with her hand and one high-pitched syllable from her throat.

I told them how happy Mario was with his wife. Angela remembered the fiasco at his wedding, the cooked rice someone threw at the bride. I didn't say some of my own kids were expressing disapproval of Mario's choice. Mario had, thank God, removed the bubble gum planted on the bottom of Sheila's shoes before she walked on the bridal carpet down the aisle.

I went on, what a perfect couple Vinnie and Dana. I didn't say they were living in sin, out of wedlock in Greenwich Village. Or that I prayed she had gotten Mario out of her heart. It was out of loyalty to her that *they* threw the rice at Mario's bride.

"Hey, Aunt Toni," said Maria, "What's black and white, black and white, black and white?" Their Aunt Toni loved their act. Maria and Teresa, my teenagers—twin-agers everybody called them—had come home, both wearing wrinkled skirts. I knew that underneath those skirts, which had just been pulled out of paper bags at the corner of Creek Street, were the hotpants their father had forbidden them to wear. I smelled smoke on their clothes and knew they must have been at the sweet shoppe playing pinball. I knew they were committing mortal sins, skipping Sunday mass. I would ask Lucy if she had talked to those two about boys yet. Lucy was better at that than I was.

"Give up?" chimed in Teresa, "A nun rolling down a hill." Maria did the fake drum roll.

Antoinette could laugh from deep down in her gut like nobody's business. "You two are a pair!" she howled, "You take after your brothers, Vinnie and Frankie!"

"Aunt Toni," began Teresa again, "What's a specimen?"

"A urine sample?" she wrinkled her face.

"An Italian astronaut," said Maria. Aunt Toni didn't laugh, so Teresa said, "Get it? Space-a-man?" Maria did the boos.

When Vincent's sisters asked where their brother was, I painted such a portrait of him sleeping peacefully after hard work, I almost believed it. He'd worked a late shift and then stayed up through the night doing paperwork, I said. I left out the part about the smashed tomatoes and disfigured squash in the garbage can from his getting worked up over Frankie.

After Grandma Donitella and the aunts left, my daughters and I sat with the empty coffee cups, picking crumbs off the same biscot' in the middle of the table. We picked stingily, the way you pick when you're not hungry for what you're eating. It always seemed so quiet after company left and in the ringing silence you could hear the parts of stories you'd held back.

Maria and Teresa wanted to get Lucy going again.

"Lucy, did you hear about the guy who had five penises?" asked Maria. Teresa continued, "When he went to the doctor, the doctor asked him, how do your pants fit?" Maria finished, "Like a glove, he says."

"Hey!" I yelled at them, "there are little kids with big ears around, watch that!"

Suddenly a big crash came from inside the bathroom, where Peggy and Carrie were playing in the bathtub. "The kids!" We all jumped up and turned our attention to the bathroom. Joe-Joe stood holding his brontosaurus in one hand, looking down at a king-size bottle of Jack 'n Jill baby oil. It was leaking oil out one side. He looked up innocently and said, "Ma, look at that! It said 'un-break-a-ble' on the label, but it broke!"

I wasn't worried about the baby oil. I was looking at my two grandchildren, Peggy and Carrie, in dark gray bathwater, and I wanted to say, I used to use the same bathwater to bathe all you kids. I used one big towel to dry you. At the dinner table someone would always say, "Pass the napkin." We wiped our mouths on the same cloth. We were happy.

"Joey, why'd you do that, you dropped that on purpose?" asked Lucy.

"Ma, Dad said not to believe everything I read. He was right!" Joe-Joe was so gleeful at his discovery, but his mother had a hard time seeing that.

She was about to scold him when we all realized why the bath water looked so dark. Peggy and Carrie looked up with big eyes and said, "We help you, Grandma." They had emptied the whole hamper of dirty clothes—bras, girdles, boxer shorts, smelly socks, dirty shirts—into the tub with them and were washing everything with Ivory soap.

Lucy turned red, her anger with her husband making an appearance at the wrong time.

"You kids!" she hissed, "All three of you! You made all this extra work for Grandma and me. I'm going to spank you!"

"DON'T SPANK THEM!"

"Hi Grandpa," said Joe-Joe.

It was the voice of my husband, standing behind us, waking briefly from the dead. "Especially not when their little tushies are wet. It really hurts," he added, this former expert on how and when to spank.

"I broke the baby oil," said Joe-Joe. His grandfather rubbed his head.

Lucy couldn't help but restrain herself. "You kids," her voice was weaker now, "are not supposed to make extra work."

Vincent went back to the bedroom, saying "It's not good to hit kids. Just explain nicely and show them love. Don't you learn that in your psychology classes. Kids just need love."

"And discipline," said Lucy.

"From their father," he yelled from the bedroom. "The father teaches the discipline." But he said it in Sicilian dialect and I had to translate.

I felt the start of my own little craving—the sweet peaches from my father's old tree soaked in his sour wine. The last barrel he'd made tasted close to vinegar, but still I savored this treat more than anything.

"Maria and Teresa, could you watch the little ones? I want to take Lucy shopping, stop by the stand, and pick up baby Carmela at Grandma's." I heard silence, so I added, "I'll buy you both jeans at Daffy Dan's."

"Don't get them too baggy," they yelled in unison.

Lucy and I stopped by the stand first to see how Fletcher and Hampton were doing. I was still getting used to how big and modern it looked now, part of it glassed in with heating, air conditioning, nice new awnings, real bathrooms, instead of the backhouse we used to have. The refrigerated trucks brought all kinds of produce from California and Florida, stuff we'd never heard of until the Cuban, Puerto Rican, and Colombian population around here exploded. We were starting to have some produce year-round.

But I'll tell you this. The fruits and vegetables reminded me of everything else. Outside they were prettier than ever, greener, redder, more golden. Inside they were begging for something, empty of flavor, lacking in sweetness, juice, and texture. It was a sin, some of that stuff we sold, waxy and beautiful, like an embalmed corpse. We should have buried it.

I told Fletcher and Hampton to fill crates and take all they wanted before closing up tonight. They asked about Vincent and I said he was doing great.

I said the same to my mother and father when I got to their house. It seemed like everyone was waiting for a crack in our *bella figura*. Carmela came running out of the parlor to hug us, hoping Lucy had brought her kids. She was disappointed, but I told her they'd be even happier to see her when she got home.

"Did you bring me a pastry from the aunts' visit? You said you would save me one, Mom. You said." I could tell from her voice she had already guessed that I had forgotten. The Bella Palermo pastries were all gone. "We'll stop by a bakery on the way home and pick one up," I said, knowing it was not the same as if I'd remembered to show her she was out of sight but not out of mind.

I could see she was angry and wanted to cry, but I watched my youngest hold back her tears. She buried her nose in her blanket, for which she was too old. She went back to the living room and sat alone.

I reached into the cabinet for some of the wine-soaked peaches. I knew what I'd just seen. Already, my baby knew when to keep a *bella figura*.

Maddelena (1982)

A bathroom in San Francisco—a water closet to be precise—was where I decided I was the one who would go to Sicily. As I sat there a voice out of the blue teased—Even the rocks, even the wind sang. Well, what did they say?

This could never have happened back home on Creek Street. Back home you had to make an appointment to get in the bathroom. But the inspired architect of my Victorian apartment had put the toilet in a separate closet, a layout that could have saved my family untold grief—maybe even Frankie's foot going through the door.

In San Francisco I also had my own bedroom and job. Well, a mattress and a part-time job as tourguide at the Stanford Linear Accelerator. But the novelty of living out West wore off after a few years. Then the lack of seasons began to bother me, along with what seemed like too many smiling faces.

I called Lucy to commiserate. "Remember how we used to pass an evening when the TV didn't work, seeing who could come up with the cleverest insult or wisecrack? I miss that." Lucy, who took endless psychology classes to keep her mind off her marriage, said Californians were simply stuck in persona the way Easterners were stuck in shadow. Whatever the diagnosis, it annoyed me no end that every last stranger was so cordial.

I'd last seen Lucy at Thanksgiving on Creek Street. At the last minute Mario couldn't make it back—he had to speak at an international consortium on new particles or anti-particles, something that barely existed. Neither could Vinnie and Dana, who had taken up Switched-On Ballroom and were at the Atlantic City dance finals. Nine years ago it had been me who didn't go. I was too pissed off at Rena for breaking our promise never to marry and getting hitched to that guy from Hoboken. In fact, the last time the whole family had sat around the clover-leaf table was ten years ago, before Frankie went to Vietnam. Would it take another war to complete the family circle? Looking at the empty places this last Thanksgiving, my father cried about his failure to reunite us, and without so much as touching a ravioli, developed a spectacular attack of *àcitu.*

Knowing the agony of heartburn, I felt sorry for him. I really did, although I couldn't understand why he wasn't content. His name had been passed on to a dozen grandchildren, with more on the way. Perhaps the empty seats at each failed reunion reminded him he'd lost a son. He really missed Frankie. We all did.

I thought that day on the throne about what my father had said about Sicily. In Sicily, fathers could keep a better eye on their sons. Maybe they could wander just so far from each other there. In America, he said, fathers could lose their sons. What kind of promised land was that?

Well, what kind of promised land was Sicily? The longer I lived away from Creek Street, the more I wanted to know what my father's stories omitted. It fell to me to find out. My brothers were dutifully passing on his name. My sisters were wrapped up in their husbands and their kids. In the spring of '82 I packed up and stored my blue crates, my gray cinder blocks, and my unfinished pine boards. I went down to Fly-By-Night Travel and bought a cheap ticket. "I'm leaving my future on pause," I told my San Francisco friends. "Family business."

"A cultural exchange program in France! Italy, too!" I told my parents, giving them only sketchy details—just as I had 10 years ago when I ran away to San Francisco. They gave me their blessing without asking too many questions. So, I didn't have to let them know I was looking for something they never gave us.

I stopped in Paris first where I stayed at a hostel near St. Germain des Prés. I wrote home to my mother that on a rainy day Paris is just like the Belle Epoque paintings Aunt Francesca used to buy at Woolworth's. No need to come, I told her, because I knew my mother never would.

Once I reached Italy, I found myself like Zeno's hare, perpetually cutting in half the remaining distance between me and my destination. Italian filled my ears, recalling my grandparents and their quaint Old World chatter. I took baby steps down Italy's boot, stopping in Venice, Florence, Pisa, Lucca, even Savona. In Assisi, I strode the hilly streets with the spry Franciscan friars in their coarse robes with triple-knotted cords. The surrounding plains pulsed in soft pink and mystical blue and almost beckoned me back into the fold. I even stretched my skimpy budget in Assisi and hauled away a pair of olive-wood rosaries with beads the size of eggs. The size of eggs! But as soon as I had paid for them I knew where they belonged— in my mother's hands.

Traveling down the boot was like marching down the bridal carpet. Sicily was the altar. At times I could hardly wait to get there, to hear what the wind and rocks would tell me. Other times I was not sure. I boarded a succession of second-class trains, finally settling in for a long ride on the all-night train from Rome to Palermo. I called it the Steam Special. It was hot and humid, and the passengers were jam-packed like loaves of rising dough. The wheels clacked and clicked like an old skeleton.

At the Messina Strait I sat still in the stopped train as it waited to cleave into two like a Sicilian widow's bosom. I saw mountains in the distance over the thin line of water separating the *dancing boot* from the *dancing hat*. Rising rugged and majestic, they seemed to hold promise, if not a discernible message in their peaks. Were those wispy words I saw in the steamy exhalation of Mount Aetna?

I crossed the Messina Strait to the island of my forebears. I felt the earth tremble, but it was not the firepit of an island this time, just the excitement of getting so close.

Exhausted in Palermo, I took a bus to the countryside to pass time waiting for the local train to Cammarata and San Giovanni-Gemini. The hillsides smelled sweet and sharp. The ubiquitous cactus, the fig of India, displayed a coquettish blush that belied its hide and thorns. I sighed and began to walk back to the train station. The pavement boiled, but I shivered. So close to the work of knocking on doors, I buckled under the weight of my plan. What in Mother Mary's name was I doing here?

It might have been enough that at last I'd seen the jigsaw puzzle of land. Here the sun scorched life out of grassy mounds, there it was defiantly lush from irrigation, the land's savage heart tamed and coaxed to fruitfulness. Yet its crusty volcanic remnants held brutal memories of the fire within—like my father.

Wearing my knapsack, I began to walk down a road that glistened like licorice in the unforgiving Mediterranean sun. A young woman stopped in the middle of the road, flung open her car door, and stared at my cut-offs and T-shirt "*Attenta ai ladri!*" she exclaimed. Robbers everywhere. "Everyday a person is assassinated here." She shook her finger at me and said Sicily is not for *na signurina sula*—a woman alone. I hopped in her car and she drove me back to the train station in Palermo.

There I boarded the local train for the mountain villages, Cammarata and San Giovanni-Gemini. The car was airy and quiet compared with the train from Rome. When I took my seat, a weathered *contadina*—a peasant—saw my hunger and wordlessly fed me crackers and lemon slices. Big-paned windows framed the countryside that scrolled by after the last imprint of industry in the province of Palermo. I felt a quiver and thought it meant we had crossed into the next province. "Agrigento" I asked the *contadina*. "Sì," she replied. Civilization seemed to be getting thinner out the window.

Three hours later the train deposited me at Cammarata station, a small one-room depot in the valley surrounded by rumpled hills. Still nine kilometers from the village proper, I could have turned around. Instead I stood silently in the empty depot. In the distance, Cammarata tumbled down the foot of Monte Cammarata in tiers of streaked and dirty rock. A narrow road joined it to the lower San Giovanni-Gemini. On either side of the road lay the bones of my mother's and father's people.

The last passengers off the train were a family of five, the Ferraros. Half curious, half pitying, they said, "We won't leave you alone in the train station, *na signurina sula*." Mr. Ferraro folded me into the back seat of their car along with my few possessions.

"I have to knock on doors," I recited feebly in Sicilian. I had no addresses because Grandma Donitella had taken hers to the grave last year. Grandma Coniglio wouldn't help me, refusing to believe I'd dress properly enough to impress her side—she was right. There'd been no correspondence between the relatives in my parents' generation.

"Shut up and eat first," Mrs. Ferraro said back at their house, which helped me relax. They fed me pasta fazool, bread, and lettuce greens dipped in green olive oil and vinegar. They anointed me with hot bath water, then marched me though my father's village, chanting my four grandparents' names until they sounded like a church benediction.

One Jimmy LaRosa, a bespectacled man on a stool in Caffe Sport in the village square, rose at the sound to greet me. Jimmy worked at the *Municipio*, where he filed the names of Cammaratesi and the dates they were born, christened, married, laid to rest. He had tried on American life, living in Bayonne, New Jersey. After five years he had cast if off, thumbed his nose, and returned to Sicily. "I can help you put your finger on your relatives," he told me.

I slept fitfully in the Ferraro's spare bed. Next day, on the way to the municipal building I saw widows in black climbing the steps of alleys glossed by hard sun. They were spry women, *molto in gamba*, alive with energy tempered hard as steel by the death of husbands, brothers, and fathers. Donkeys pulled crayon-colored carrette. Narrow, craggy, winding streets rose and fell without rhyme or reason. They were built for cloven-hoofed beasts, not the cars that honked with no restraint at pedestrians and animals.

In a dusty office on the lower floor of the municipal building, Jimmy LaRosa patiently ran his earth-brown finger up and down hundreds of handwritten registries. He licked his finger from time to time and asked me questions I couldn't always answer. *Donitella* repeated itself on page after page in the *Indice dei morti*. I could clearly hear all the stories my father had told over the years, but now it was my ancestors singing them.

After two hours I developed a splitting headache and longed to give up. Jimmy made a phone call, spoke rapid-fire dialect like an eggbeater transforming limp egg whites. He turned to me with an all-white smile brought back from America.

Together we went and knocked on a village door. When the door opened, he spoke rapidly again to the young swarthy man, then turned to me and asked, "Did your father sell fruits and vegetables?" "Sì," I said, "This is your *famiglia*, go into their home." He left me there, surrounded by the Provenzanos—four boys, two girls, and the parents, Pietro and Concetta, who hugged me and chattered in that same sing-song dialect.

The village that had looked old, dirty, dour, and distantly courteous began to shine and soften as it opened its heart to me.

I twirled macaroni with the Provenzanos, Grandpa Donitella's nieces and nephews. They compared my face to faces in an old photo. I recognized the decades-old smiles of Grandma and Grandpa Donitella. Initiating me with pats, pummels, and chucks, they pinched my flesh, shook their heads, and set out to fatten me up. I feasted on simple pleasures—*pasta al forno*, eggplant in tomato sauce with many toes of soft garlic, farm vegetables slathered thick and fragrant with emerald olive oil, pizza with anchovies, cacciatore made with rabbits fattened in cages on cousin Rosalia Mangiapane's roof. They fed me pastries that preserved the old memory of hardship and suffering—the eyes of St. Lucy, the breasts of St. Agatha, and the bones of St. Rosalia. The virgin's creamy breasts were too rich, the sugary marzipan bones best left to ossify as platter ornaments. But St. Lucy's dry, crumbly eyes were perfect dunked in espresso, a marriage of sweet and bitter that tasted familiar.

I loved how their faces lit up like candles when I told of the new bloom of Donitellas in America. I produced a dozen photos of swaddling infants indistinguishable even to me. I understood well Pietro Provenzano's quick explanation for why there were more girls than boys—Anyone can make a water bucket, the trick is to put a spout on it. Substitute "oil can" for "water bucket" and you had my father's saying. Grandpa's son, my father, was the central character in many family stories, famous for siring ten children who all lived past infancy. As they sang his praises I remembered his failings and saw that they might not have been failings had he been born here.

The Provenzanos put me up in the Albergo Lucia, which they owned. I slept on an iron-frame bed in a high-ceilinged room. Young Rita Provenzano told me to keep the room shuttered or "little animals— scorpione" would climb in. In defiance I left the window unshuttered. I awoke to no intruders, only Church bells pealing sweetly in the dead hours before dawn.

Rita's father Pietro had strong opinions about everything. It didn't matter to him or the other cousins that my Sicilian was raw. I had only to utter a string of words and they responded. So when the opportunity presented itself, I said to him that I'd heard that once, in Sicily, the rocks and the wind sang.

Pietro didn't miss his cue. Chapter and verse poured forth. I listened in rapt attention.

Everything we know in Sicily we learned from the rocks and wind. For once that was all we had and if it hadn't been for them we'd not have given the world so much—even Nobel prize winners. There was so much poetry in Sicilian rocks and wind we had to invent the sonnet. Spring, the season of fertility we invented it here in Agrigento. The world sees only our politici buffuni, un piccatu... *But fortune does not wear one face. Because the rocks and wind sang we Sicilians taught the world to see and hear. We inspired music and art of the Renaissance and lent our language to Dante. Our forebears taught us to taste and we taught the world when an ancient Sicilian wrote the first cookbook 400 years before Christ. We shared the soul of our rocks and wind with the rest of Italy because they needed one.*

Pietro sighed and ended balefully. *But then the tower came and the rocks and wind no longer sang.*

The tower? Pietro said he'd take me to see it. Word spread swiftly that Pietro was taking me to the top of the mountain. He packed me and a half dozen cousins, old and young, into a Fiat and chugged in second gear to the 5,177-foot summit of Monte Cammarata. At the peak we stepped out and stretched in a circle. Here where the chaparral was sweet and gave its aroma away unstintingly, where the pinyons dropped their burden, where wild porcini burst into view after rain with the finesse of a magician's hand, there rose a TV antenna.

They were silent, the big-eyed children and the black-dad women with broken-comb smiles and gray hair. They craned their necks, then looked to see if I shared their awe. Pietro admitted that the tower that picked up waves had brought them TV images of the mainland, but so far not much more in the way of material wealth.

I looked down below to the medieval Castelli dei Branciforte on its promontory and the yellow stucco Norman Church Santa Maria that swallowed the spry widows in its darkened vestibule.

When the time was right I would wander alone to these glorious stone monuments and listen for the winds of antiquity.

It so happened that my visit overlapped with a *festa*, the feast of Jesus of Nazarena. Perhaps this would give me an opportunity to see something left out of my father's stories. But *la nave*, the huge boat-float festooned with gold and red velvet, and statues of wood that looked ready to shed human blood and tears matched my father's words exactly. *La nave* made its ceremonious week-long voyage down a steep incline on wooden rollers. Men, like pall-bearers, had practiced for months moving the rollers with a show of great piety. The promenade and the square were packed each evening with strollers locking arms, flirts of both sexes, mimes, and cannoli vendors. The townspeople sang and danced without restraint in cafes or by stone fountains, whose grotesque gargoyles spat water.

Carlo, a cousin whose nut-brown skin and wiry hair framed one pastel blue eye and one black eye, showed me around the festivities. He laughed at my rudimentary Sicilian, singing, *O Maddalena!* and clapping his palms together over his chest. One night he took me through a makeshift funhouse where an ultra-violet black light made confetti out of lint on his sweater and a flashlight out of his pale eye.

During the day, Carlo took me knocking on more doors in my quest to meet all my cousins in this foreign land.

I sat in one-room homes and drank vermouth or red wine with cousins allowed to age without the help of bridges, caps, crowns, and hair dye. I broke broke bread with widows too young to be toothless and withered, who piled gnawed pizza crusts on their plates. I was captivated by the familiar rhythm in their soul, their pitch of expression. Had I seen them before, perhaps at the Peterstown market in New Jersey?

Wherever I was I knew when to laugh or cry or be silent. My cousins' attitudes toward life, work, death, God, and children were inside me, whether I embraced them or not. I understood their dialect best when I didn't try. All their words stopped short of the final syllable as if it were superfluous weight on the tongue.

One day Carlo took me halfway up the mountain to drink Bianco Sarte in a bar-discoteca. We talked about my Grandfather Donitella, until I had to look away from Carlo's mixed-up gaze.

When I asked him to take me to the top of the mountain again, he said "Some other day, when it isn't dark." He told me there were dark spirits on the mountain, that my own grandfather's cousin, Tino, had been cursed by one.

It happened one summer evening, Carlo said, *Tino decided to take his* innamorata *up there, when all of a sudden he found his little black dog at his feet. Tino yanked the dog home by the collar, locked him inside the house, and set out again. Halfway up the dog's at his feet again. Tino took him back locked doors, windows and halfway up the mountain, again the dog reappears. This happened two more times and finally Tino let the dog stay. When he and his* innamorata *started down the mountain, Tino saw a black figure following them. The dog barked, but all the same the figure came so close, Tino jumped to protect himself and struck himself on the nose with his finger. The next day a hole appeared in his nose and this became cancer. Tino died within a year.*

What did Carlo make of this old curse, I wondered. *Chissà,* Carlo shrugged. Perhaps it happened this way. Or perhaps Tino ate *u pani boja chissà...*

"*U pani boja?*" I asked. "Please explain."

Carlo explained about executioner's bread. In olden times, when the baker forgot to save bread for the executioner, the baker's wife felt sorry and turned one bread upside down for him to pick up each evening when he returned from the gallows. That's why upside-down bread was considered bad luck.

Dark figures or hangman's bread—all the same, I would have liked to climb the mountain where my grandfather's cousin was stricken. But I saw that Carlo was firm in his resolve not to do so.

After several weeks the pomp subsided and the Provenzanos invited me to stay in my room at the *Albergo Lucia* as long as I liked. There would always be a place for Grandpa Donitella's blood, they told me. But the hoe and tiller, pastry board and wine press could not sit idle too long. Someone had to catch the olives before they hit the ground. Someone had to sing monotonous couplets to the jackass who turned the stone around and around a pole to press the olive harvest. Someone had to steady the grapevines. Someone had to stir the crimson mass of *strattu*, swarmed by flies, on its wooden plank, the essential remains of the abundant apple of gold, peeled, seeded, and drying in the sun.

Someone had to discipline the unruly land into orchard rows for olive, citrus, and almond. Wild land is like a young girl reaching puberty—you need to keep her chaste or she'll become promiscuous. So said Pietro, whose roughened hands worked the land from dawn to dusk. The furrows must be parted carefully and moistened to hold the seed that would swell into food. He blessed himself before he plowed and I felt I had known him for much longer than a few weeks.

I asked Pietro to show me the land up close, the land that fed him and his family, but left nothing for profit. He gathered up a swarm of cousins and a dog and we started at the grapevines bulging with fat purple and frosty green fruit. From vines and trees, Pietro fed me clusters of black raspberries, peaches, honey-sweet fresh figs with bleeding red interiors, prickly pears oozing purple juice. He and the cousins filled cloth bags with *fagiolini*, plum tomatoes, violet and white striped eggplant, tentacles of *cucuzza*. At a shed with threshed wheat and drying almonds we found old cousin Calogero. His kind hazel eyes peered through bronze, lined skin. "*Du' cosi no potti addrizzari u Signuri: i cucuzzi e i testi duri,* " he said solemnly, drawing himself up to his full height. By the time I figured out he'd said, "Two things the Lord couldn't straighten out—*cucuzzi* and hard heads," we'd left him behind with his *burro*. I glanced back to see him grinning, humming, and dancing the tarantella in his tattered clothes.

I was too intent on soaking up ancient wisdom to know for sure if I was being mocked. I wanted desperately to take something away from my Sicilian relatives. I had questions, and there were answers everywhere—not that I always recognized them. I remembered the joke about the man who lost his hat on a dark street but tried to find it many blocks away because the light was brighter there. I wondered if I was doing the same.

I searched in hot, bright places and cool, dark ones. One Sunday afternoon I had dinner at the home of cousin Rosalia Mangiapane, Carlo's mother. After dinner everybody fell into a stupor, so I stole out on my own through the streamers that kept out flies. I found an alley where jasmine, bougainvillea, wild fennel, and geraniums caressed the hard stone. I turned a blind corner, skirted a blind man's walking stick, and listened carefully to what fell from the lips of the old women. They stood perpetual guard in front of altars sunken in walls. I heard only *Ave Maria* and *Pater Noster*. Lingering in the cool interiors of an Arab archway, I suddenly saw a symbol carved on its belltower. Engraved by a long-ago hand was the skull and crossbone, the sign of death, a footnote everywhere.

Between the gray stone walls of the Mangiapane's home, I sat with a group of women and shelled into a bucket the nutty embryos within fagioli. As they did whenever they worked, they sang little couplets, chattered without purpose, or prayed aloud to pass time. Thunder rolled on distant hills. One woman started with fright and blessed herself with closed eyes and the ceremony of rosary beads. *The scirocco, the south wind from Africa, is blowing*, sang Rosalia Mangiapane.

"What does it sing, this wind?" I asked, seizing the opportunity. I threw hulls on the floor like everyone else, hiding my hope that Rosalia's wind was the same as my father's. One cousin adjusted her shawl more tightly around her as if to protect all the knowledge she carried within her heart. As in any family there were those who would not speak of the past and those who felt called to do so.

If you want to know what the wind sings you have to be very still, Rosalia sang back, popping the sweet raw interior of the bean into her mouth.

I first heard the wind sing when I lost my second husband to a burst appendix, Rosalia began. *Oh, how I grieved. This was after my first two children had died of pneumonia, my little ones taken by angels. I stayed in black past the obligation: four years. I had only despair. My grief was so great, I could not move for a long time. Until one day I heard the wind sing a tune written by ancient Sicilians. It sang of fierce times before the men cut down all the forests in Sicily, shaved her clean, when women hunted and spit-cooked goats and wild boars. It sang of sacred springs that bubbled everywhere in*

Sicily, perhaps on Monte Cammarata even. It sang of the stone temples of Agrigento where two goddesses still whispered the secrets of fertility. It sang of the riches that once poured into our rocky harbors and a ship that sailed far when the wind blew hard on the backs of blue waves.

I wondered if I were the only one in the room who understood that Rosalia spoke of pagan times, until the indignant voice of the woman wrapped tightly in her shawl asked: *Did it sing of the grace of God?*

Oh yes, and of the Madonna, and the saints.

The shawled one looked appeased and went back to hulling. But Rosalia chanted, *It sang of other graces, too, not just those of God. Christ stopped at Napoli all Sicilians know. He never paid a personal call this far south, but many are the other gods and goddesses, devils, hooligans, and ballbusters the wind has blown onto our shores. We have always been blown the chaff with the wheat.*

Rosalia stopped hulling a moment and squeezed the gold corno and hand of Fatima charms on the chain around her neck. Although she was Carlo's mother she had two dark eyes with wrinkles that splayed out from them like a cat's whiskers.

Statti zitta! Be quiet, urged the shawled one of deeply furrowed brow. She rose abruptly and began sweeping and sweeping the hulls into a neat pile.

I loved Rosalia's free verse—it reminded me of my father's. But what did it tell me of my people? As I sat hulling bean after bean with the women in a circle, I realized I had merely done my grandparents' voyage in reverse. I had stepped back over the centuries, watching houses squeeze closer together and go from wood to stone. I heard some of what the rocks and wind had sung. But I didn't have an ending to the stories or answers to why the Donitellas remained dispersed.

Having come this far, I decided I couldn't leave without a family tree. Perhaps a tree would reveal some secrets.

I stepped aside for the donkey-pulled cart, then rushed through the gate that swung both ways to the municipal building. I knocked hard. Jimmy LaRosa opened the door, expecting me.

"Jimmy, you've got to help me draw up a family tree," I pleaded, excited at who I might find on it. He was ready to do the research. And so I returned daily, hurried through the gate, knocked until Jimmy let me in. We sat for hours paging through the registries for all the Donitellas related to me.

It was not hard to draw a tree of Donitellas going back four centuries. We unearthed dozens of *capostipite*—heads of family—named either Mario or Vincenzo, just like my grandfather, father, and two oldest brothers. They sired many children, sometimes as many as 17. I couldn't help but see that fewer children lived than died and that a dead infant's name was often conferred onto a new child who lived a little longer. But we were stymied by my mother's side. "Did your great-grandfather have two wives?" Jimmy asked.

"Not a chance," I responded. As far as I knew no one had preceded any of my grandmothers to the altar, least of all Nonnie. Jimmy scratched his head, perplexed.

That evening I called my mother on Creek Street. Many months had passed without any news passing between us. I told her about the many cousins, the family tree, how her side was impossible to draw. All Jimmy could find was someone with Grandpa's name who had married a second wife with Nonnie's first name...

Even as my mother spoke, "That *was* Nonnie," I realized, of course, it had to be. "But Ma, you never spoke of divorce in your family! I'm shocked!"

"Not divorce," she yelled from Creek Street. "Fire." She explained how Great-Grandpa's first wife had died pregnant with their first child in an awful conflagration. Her nightgown caught fire at the hearth, the same hearth where she had baked bread. She also told me how Nonnie's brother felt cursed by the *malocchiu* until it drove him so crazy he shot himself in the head to silence his demons forever.

While I was taking in this astonishing revelation, my mother spoke quickly of the news on Creek Street. My sister Lucy had delivered her sixth child a few months back and named him Franco, because my brother Franco was home for good, living down the shore. When was I coming home to Creek Street, when was anyone coming home to Creek Street? I knew she was echoing my father's plaintive wail.

"Soon; I'm coming home soon," I said, feeling my heart beat in my chest with the same rhythm my hand had played on so many doors. So eager was I to complete the tree now, I barely acknowledged that a vital piece of information I'd traveled so far to find was provided by my mother, who seldom left Creek Street.

Next morning, I ran back to the municipal building, through the swinging gate, knocked on the door, and told Jimmy of the breakthrough on my mother's side. He smiled quietly, as if unsurprised, and we passed the whole day finishing up a tree going back three centuries on the Coniglio side. I stared at my two bounteous family trees and asked Jimmy, "Who were they?"

Jimmy was a patient man, but he had only one answer for this question. "Peasants. They were all peasants," he asserted. "Always and forever."

Is that all there was? Would I never find out who was wise or cursed? What made them laugh or cry? Why they lived and died?

Jimmy palmed his chin as if he had whiskers. He rolled a cigarette, lighted it, and sat back. He took me to the door of the building and pointed to the mountain top. He had a story to tell me, which his father had told him long ago.

For years every week, Momo from the next village passed over that mountain through Cammarata, leading his donkey. The village carabinieri, *always suspicious of outsiders, would stop Momo every week. They checked every inch of that donkey. They lifted his feet, checked his hooves and his shoes, his saddle, his bridle; they looked in his ears, through the hay, they even checked his droppings. Every week for years they found nothing. When old Momo was on his death bed, the chief* carabiniere *went to see him and said, "Momo, I know you been smuggling something all these years. Tell me now that your days are numbered, what was it?" Dying Momo smiled, took a deep breath, pulled the* carabiniere *to him, and whispered in his ear,* "Donkeys."

Jimmy flicked his cigarette butt on the floor, smothered it with his foot, and looked to see whether I had understood. He looked up at the mountain and back at the municipal building. He added, "The family secret is not what comes through this gate. The precious family secret is what hides in your own heart."

I rolled up my family tree into a tight cylinder, beat my thigh with it, and took it back to my high-ceilinged room. I lay on the iron-frame bed and stared at the unshuttered window, wishing a little animal would dare to come through it.

Finally, I thought about my Great Grandma, old Nonnie with the dark secrets of fire and death within her heart. As she sat calmly rolling her beads, pinching her snuff, waiting for her own death, she must have longed to tell her stories. I thought of all the widows in black, lively shadows with their own stories of death and suffering. I thought of my family on Creek Street, the black we wore invisible to the naked eye.

I put a number on the days I would remain in Cammarata. I took Rosalia's advice and listened to what came and went if I just sat still. I sat with the women in a circle hulling fagioli, singing or praying, I couldn't tell which. I helped knead dough, crank pasta, stir the rich tomato paste on its wooden plank. I learned a few couplets to sing to the jackass. I made him dance around that pole. Once, after I had looked away for a moment, I thought I glimpsed him standing on his hind legs.

Someday I'd tell my father about that jackass—he'd love it.

By and by comes Fletcher. Thin silver twigs spray from the nest of dark beard on his mocha chin. Laughter precedes his words.

"I know what you're doing, girl!"

I stand still, hunched over a produce bin. I turn just my head.

"Caught red-handed fondling the eggplant," I confess. I pat the buttocks bottom of the purple vegetable, stand it up and face him. Except for the silver in his beard, Fletcher has hardly aged.

"Don't seem so long ago I did same for your Daddy. Damned if he didn't come check every time make sure I got them girl eggplants separate from the boy ones."

"How you been Fletcher? You haven't been around in ages."

"Fine, fine, Carmela," he nods. "Little older, tireder for the wear. But fine." Nods his head again. "I want some greens, some good bitter greens. Stuff in Peterstown ain't worth a damn with all the old farmers gone."

I toss Fletcher a fat eggplant. He catches it squarely, grunts. He bends slightly and says, "Don't go testing my reflexes without you give me some warning."

"Which is that one, Fletcher? I can't tell if it warps in or out."

Two thumbs press, his smile relaxes, brow knits. He stares at the sky. His whole concentration and he doesn't know.

"It ain't neither," he says. "Do some strange things, growers these days. When I worked for your dad, we knew a male from a female and weren't no two ways about it. Not like today..."

"I know, I know," I cut in. "But life was a lot simpler in the old, old days, long gone..." I croon, roll the eggplant around, put it aside. When Fletcher leaves I'll score it, dress it up with peppers, carrots, mushrooms. Make some character for my godchild, Caitlin, Lucy's youngest.

"But in the good ol' days, you didn't have carambola, the fruit that sounds like an island dance, or guava—the sand plum." I point to each fruit on my roll call. "Or the furry sapodilla, or tangy tamarillo. Or plantains, or ugli fruit or toasty breadfruit. Or my favorite, the fruit that has an identity crisis like me—the apple pear."

"My, my, aren't you one for words, Baby Carmela. And you haven't even gotten to the vegetables." Fletcher scratches his head, amazed anyone knows names for all those things. "Some of these newfangled things do look like they're gonna get up and perform," he says.

But never mind the family of exotics, Fletcher wants to know about my family. He does a mental reckoning—been almost 10 years.

I pull Fletcher by the arm and make him sit on a crate, a sturdy one.

"You ask about family, you've gotta have a whole lotta time on your hands. It's not busy, so sit."

I'm as versed in the lives of my siblings as I am in the lives of the funny new produce I sell at the family stand. My bane and blessing. I recite botanical history, family recipes, family history with equal conviction daily for some customers. Some days it has more meaning than others.

I like having the company of someone with knowledge of earlier chapters of my family. And here's Fletcher, known them longer than I have.

Fletcher has a vivid memory of Creek Street. Though it's a place he's never been to, he'd seen it daily for years through the eyes of my father.

He sits and listens, sit and listens. "Yeah," he says. An old set of images floats in front of his eyes. I tell him about my parents… You could say they're happy now; just had their twenty-fourth grandchild. Carmine and his wife Sandy. Having passed on his name, my father passes time. In the garden mostly. Just tomatoes and fennel now. One gives him acid, other gets rid of it. He and my mother preserve them both a dozen different ways, Fletcher ought to try some of the pickled fennel. My mother rocks in her rocker, says her rosary three times a day. She has lots of beads. Especially likes the big olive wood ones—each bead, all fifty-something of them, is the size of an egg.

An egg? asks Fletcher. Yeah, an egg, I say. Madeleine
—Fletcher remembers Maddelena, she's the one got wander-
lust—bought those over-sized beads on impulse. Saved her quarters
and went to Paris. Then Italy. In Assisi she said she couldn't resist
those beads—needed a shopping bag just for them. On the plane
home Madeleine met a Franciscan friar who tried to help her back
into the fold. She told him, just bless the beads, Brother, and when
she got home she sent them to Mom. And then she moved back to
San Francisco. Why so far away? Probably because there's no
Creek Street or Rahway there, explains Carmela. Tries to get the
rest of us out there. No she doesn't say rosary, not her. Not anymore. Says nothing. Just does some silent meditation, every morning and evening on a round black cushion.

Weird, says Fletcher. He'd rather vedge-a-tate than meditate,
he laughs.

I tell him don't knock it. Least Madeleine knows who she is.
She's here for her summer visit this whole month and she's showing
me how to be still and silent on this black cushion. Isn't so bad.

Still sounds like some kooky San Francisco practice, says
Fletcher.

Well, I say. I score the eggplant and using toothpicks attach
carrot legs, mushroom eyes. I envision the ears—crinkled red peppers, no, broccoli florets—and nose—a small hot chili, maybe a
string-bean.

Someone's supposed to have a calling, maybe it's Madeleine,
who knows, I add. Maybe it's me. Depends on what you call a
higher calling. Maybe it's Carmine. He's the only one who doesn't
live on a coast. Called to the mountains, some high desert town in
Arizona. Likes the hot winds and brilliant sun and the electromag-
netic fields of the red rocks there. Now Rena. Her calling was
dance—the Rose Hips Troupe in New York City. You have to have
hips of a certain dimension. Which doesn't sound so bad to Fletcher.
Rena says Madeleine moved way out West because of her.

Maria and Teresa, yeah, they have a bunch, too, five between
them, can't tell who's whose. They're the ones no one could ever
tell apart, everybody thought Maria and Teresa were twins. So they
began to act like twins. Answered to each other's name, married

brothers. Bob and Gene Sullivan. Share a teaching job at St. Mary's. Never seems to bother them not knowing which one they are from day to day.

I put vegetable shoes on the eggplant, which is becoming something with personality if not gender. Joe left Lucy, most everyone knows, but not until after their eighth child. She's better off, even she says—his repressed shadow began to show up, she says. Got her doctorate in psychology and is an expert on shadow material of the psyche. Lucy says we all have to get in bed with our shadow one day...

This time Fletcher interrupts me. Says his son became a psychologist, too, and he respects the profession but sometimes this modern pee-sychology lacks common sense. I say no shit, my father says exact same thing. Hates when Lucy talks about the family shadow. Lucy set up her office in the cellar to write her thesis there. Something on the care and feeding of shadows.

Fletcher reckons Mario's still an astrophysicist and Carmine an inventor. I nod. Mario and his stars. Carmine and his music traps, big ones, tiny ones, even made one using Grandma Coniglio's old ringer machine. Bunch of kids, both. And Vinnie? Married. The girl next door. Three, no four, kids. Fletcher knows that must be Dana. They live in Greenwich Village, dance, go to art shows. Vincent disowned them for a while cause she didn't change her name. Got over it. Like everything.

Left someone out...Frankie? Frankie, Fletcher says his name again as if he's remembering a forgotten dream. Broke his heart, he says, the way he came back from the War, though he seemed to manage.

The War, I think, the War. What War? He must mean the War I have no memory of, not like others around me, for whom there was no war before and none since. One more thing I missed out on.

"Yeah, was a shame," I say. I remember not wanting this brother named Frankie to come home. There were enough around to take my mother and father from me. I remember one day late in adolescence realizing that Frankie was not born with a wooden leg. And at the same time realizing Frankie never talked about The War. He never talked about his wounds. Everyone else did.

"He still making a bundle down the shore, with his restaurants?" asks Fletcher.

"You bet. Casa Vincenzo, Casa Magdalena, and a new Casa soon. Lives in this big old house that belonged to Mario's godfather, lives there alone. Sends his money to Vincent and Magdalena."

"Never married, huh?" Fletcher does not mention the wedding that wasn't, when Frankie left Charlene at the altar. And he knows how my father turned to spirits after that when Frankie wouldn't contact anyone for years.

"No. No wives. Just dates. Blonde after blonde, I tell him. My father says they came with the house. Charlene, you remember her, keeps in touch with Lucy."

Fletcher shakes his head. "Sad to see a war, a useless war, break up a romance. Was a good romance, too."

The fire of war, the fire of love, the fire of others. I would take any if I could. Don't know why I have to ache for others, for what I missed out on. I even missed the scary fires that burned holes in the house and a baby's mattress long ago. Madeleine says fire's a thing to watch for, the island we came from still smokes.

Fletcher raves about Vincent. His fiery nature, which I see modulated to a low simmer. It was like he always had fire going, says Fletcher. Depending on which way the wind'd be blowing, he'd be raging happy or raging mad. No in-between. Fletcher says he and Hampton—God bless his soul—and Vincent always had a great time. Never a dull moment. They'd hear a jumpin' song on WNEW—Minnie the Moocher—they'd all have to dance—if there were no customers waiting. Unless of the course the customer wanted to dance, too.

"He ever show you his shim sham? He had Hampton and me teach him that, we told him not bad for a white boy."

One of the few things I have seen with my own eyes. I know the move. I show him. "Shuffle step, shuffle step, shuffle ball change, shuffle step. Repeat other side. He hasn't done it for a while," I say.

"I wouldn't worry, girl," says Fletcher.

"You show me, Fletcher. Double time."

"Can't you see who all you're talking to?" he asks. "These grey hairs are for real. What about you, young lady? You're the baby, right? You haven't told me what you're up to when you're not minding the stand."

I draw a blank. The baby lives at home, minds the stand. How can such stale words have such a strong flavor? I could share some silly verses from my *Half Lives of the Family of Fruits*. This old man would not find my love of words silly. When I'm not assembling vegetable personalities, I assemble verses. And sometimes they come out so fine, I feel I must be destined for greatness after all! I could recite *How to Treat a Persimmon*: An oriental god might have designed it/That clean bell curve, that lacquered finish/Orange-red of sunrise...Maybe I'd be a poet yet. If I ever put my mind to striving. Like the others.

"Speakin' of the devil," says Fletcher. "Ol' Prince of Darkness himself is here! Lord! Don't believe my eyes!"

I've waited too long to speak of myself. Fletcher will not hear my verse.

My father's smile precedes him to his old workplace. Just as always his smile has a soundtrack. Some string of Sicilian words that neither Fletcher nor I understand, but we both know to be gritty terms of affection, You son of a gun, you this, you that! You mile-high pile of thus and such! My father hugs Fletcher hard, then leans back on his cane to get a sidelong look at his old buddy. My father asks if I've taken care of him.

"You get all you need, you hear? Carmela, fill up some bags for Mr. Johnson. Cherries are good, throw in a crate."

I note that my father has much more grey than Fletcher, but their skin's about the same color.

"Blimpy," Vincent says, "Blimpy." On days when I really wonder who I am, I wish I wasn't the only sister with a nickname. Blimpy does not sound like the endearment I know it is. I used to say I didn't like my name and my parents would tell me how I was named for a woman of unsurpassed and penetrating vision. But I still wanted another name. So they started calling me Blimpy. Not because of my physique—I was the tallest sister and the thinnest. But I had been born with a special mole on my back—from God—that looked like a blimp until it was removed. For a long time I kind of wished they hadn't taken it from me.

"Blimpy, Lucy wants to talk to you and all your sisters tonight at Grandma Coniglio's."

I finish up Mr. Eggplant with some packing straw for hair.

My father says he and Fletcher are going to have a drink. A soda, I know. As they head away I hear a play on their old routine. Fletcher asks, "Everything copacetic by you, Boss?" and Vincent answers "Ohhhh, Fletch! Too late in the game to be re-dis-con-nun-giated!"

Caitlin is going to receive her First Holy Communion at the end of June. I want to show her the veil I wore when I made mine. I have to dig down through soft layers of time in the chest in my parents' bedroom. Each has its own smell of sharp and sweet, infused with earthy cedar wood.

Time and time again I find a reason to come upon the stories, faded ink on crackling dry papers. I pull them from beneath the veils, voile, wedding and baptismal gowns. I read them one more time even though I know the words by heart. Rena and Madeleine first showed them to me. They were baby-sitting for me and Maria and Teresa. They dug up the stories and read them to me and my sisters. I loved the stories. I was mad they didn't have an ending. I was mad I hadn't been made to stay inside on warm summer nights and listen to them like my nine older siblings. I longed to have been there with the big kids hearing my father tell them as we all sat in the parlor. I have missed out. Mario, Lucy, Vinnie, Carmine, Frankie, Rena, Madeleine all say otherwise. But I know.

Everything I know is someone else's memory. It is unfair being the last. Maria and Teresa don't care one way or the other. But then they don't care who they are from day to day.

I am last to arrive at Grandma's. I ring the bell and stand under the freshly hung laundry. Grandma resists the automatic dryer everyone says she must buy. As I wait for someone to come down two flights and open the door, I pull the weeds choking the fennel and tomato plants and herbs in Grandma's garden.

Upstairs 30 hugs and kisses take place before the six of us can sit and eat and talk and eat. I give Lucy the bag with the veil and the Mr. Eggplant for Caitlin.

Grandma's refrigerator has already been raided. The table is spread with leftover meatballs larded with fresh parsley and mint, Swiss chard afloat with cloves of garlic in amber puddles of olive oil; broccoli rabe frittata, tomato and basil salad dripping with olive oil and vinegar, wedges of provolone, cracked green olives, fried sweet peppers, bread, whipped butter.

We're eating light, someone says, it's too hot. Gram's in the back room, we'll bring her in for coffee and biscot' after we talk.

Four sisters and I look to Lucy and ask why has she gathered us here. Yeah, why? Lucy. What's up? Lucy is silent. She breaks off the tiniest crumb of bread, rolls it between two fingers, and places it on her tongue like a Communion Host.

"It's Frankie," she says. She nibbles. A fork slices through cold meatball and hits the plate noisily. Impatience, suspense ask to be fed. Before Lucy can say more, Rena teases, Is it his shadow? Acting up again?

"Him and Charlene," Lucy says.

"Their shadows are both acting up?" asks Madeleine.

"They're getting married, don't tell a soul."

"To each other?" asks Rena.

Lucy pops an olive into her mouth.

This sounds familiar, we all say, forking bundles of greens onto plates, dabbing bread into dressing. Didn't this almost happen 24 years ago? Charlene should have her head examined, someone notes. Someone else affirms the notion. Bread is passed and torn asunder, dripping olive oil, dripping juices. Three forks spear a meatball, another three slice the frittata, dishes pass, naked olive pits accrue in a bowl.

"Mom and Dad are calling the brothers tonight to tell them, but no one else," says Lucy. "Absolutely no one else. It'll be a small wedding this time. Just us." Lucy sandwiches a hunk of frittata between crusts of bread.

"Just us. That's forty-something small if you count just us," says Madeleine.

"It'll be at St. Anthony's this time in Peterstown," says Lucy.

"I guess no one wants to return to the scene of the crime at St. Mary's," says Rena.

"Could be bad luck," I say.

"Sooner or later...," says Maria between chews.

"...it was bound to happen," finishes Teresa, also chewing.

"Yeah. It just goes to show," say Maria and Teresa together.

"What?" asks Madeleine.

"Never too late...," says Maria.

"...for love to bloom again," finishes Teresa.

"You realize we haven't had a complete family get together since Frankie came back from Vietnam," says Rena.

Before anyone can chew on this, a bottle of Cent'anni surfaces, the last one. It is uncorked and poured for a round of toasts. Gramps' best vintage, we all agree, too bad he's not here, that Gramps. Maybe he is.

"To Frankie and Charlene," we toast.

To Frankie. Stealing the show again, I think, ejecting an olive pit from my lips. I love the cracked greens. I eat three more.

Lucy knows she's not getting away without divulging details. Between bites we press her. That Frankie and Charlene had seen each other over the years on and off is no surprise. But then it was off for a couple years. Then Frankie shows up one night under Charlene's window, says Lucy. He brings a friend who plays trumpet. Serenades her, singing that Johnny Mathis song, how he "...needed someone all the time...And all the time it was Charlene."

Maria and Teresa say they're going to cry. Everyone in the room agrees it is the thing to do. The dishes are almost empty.

It gets better, says Lucy. He throws something through Charlene's open window. The laminated heart photo she had given him years ago before he went to Vietnam. I remember being told about it. A note was pinned to the heart, asking her to marry him, says Lucy.

"I know it's for real this time," Lucy sniffs and reminds us, "don't tell a soul."

Mom and Dad are through the roof, beside themselves happy, Lucy says. Got so excited they had a little fight.

"Mom said she had the premonition. And Dad said it was his premonition this time. Mom said it was her dream. She dreamed that Nonnie was rocking in her rocker telling her to prepare the almond cookies. We must prepare the almond cookies, Nonnie said over and over to Mom. Nonnie was dressed in black. She had an almond blossom wreath in her hair. Mom said Nonnie was absolutely radiant, even though in black. In the olden days, someone always came to weddings dressed in black. The almond meant union. Mom knew this. She knew it wasn't death this time. Not like when her father had come to her in a dream with a baby in his hands and Grandma Donitella had died.

"So Dad says his father appeared to him, too, and was telling him to prepare for something. So Dad realizes Grandpa must have been telling him to prepare for his youngest son's wedding."

I wonder why my grandfather doesn't ever say anything about my father's youngest daughter's wedding.

Lucy says Mom and Dad argued over who had received the real premonition. Then Mom told Dad to take a short walk off a long pier, getting it backwards again. And they had laughed and agreed that they were probably both getting sent a message. After all these years together, it wasn't so unusual.

Frankie and Charlene set the date for next December 15, Mom and Dad's Golden Anniversary.

We all chuckle, me not least of all. My secret, an idea of who I might be—the one with the calling?—begins to come to light. A little internal fire, not indigestion. We bring Grandma Coniglio in from the back room. I notice how small Grandma has gotten. Grandma began her life small and is even smaller now. But her eyes are bigger and her skin is pulled over her shrunken frame tight as parchment.

Parchment. I ask for the key to the attic and run up. Like all my siblings, I have done my attic time, snooping and exploring where kids once were not allowed. I know right where to find the stained onion skin and Grandma's old correspondence from Sicily, with the fancy old script. I love that old, hard-to-decipher script. I find my mother's long-abandoned fountain pens from her steno course at Battin High School. My mother had put them away when she got engaged. She would have no use nor time for written words.

Lucy comes up to the attic and shows me what she has found. An art deco frame with a pin-up girl from the 1940s. For Frankie? asks Carmela. No, Carmine. He was the one used to follow Grandpa around. Found it in Grandpa's bin after he died. Sheds some light on his perpetual grin, we agree. Lucy leaves, I slip the letters, pens, and paper downstairs to my car.

The secret news of Frankie and Charlene's wedding spreads like wildfire in a dry forest. The Donitella list runs to two hundred something by the time word has spread to my aunts and uncles and all the cousins, first, second, and third; great aunts and great uncles; close family friends. And all the *cumpari* and their families. Charlene is an only child. The Maloneys, gracious as ever, have kept their guest list to 16.

Late June, here's Frankie coming home for a visit down Creek Street with the brothers. There's Frankie still horsing around on Vinnie's stilts, brothers on either side. I note how the dappled shadow and sun through the maple leaves make his color good and healthy. Lucy just shakes her head as she and Charlene stroll behind. I know Lucy's theory about Frankie's striving, striving to be the funniest, the most successful, the best. Someone should light such a fire under me. Rena, Madeleine, Maria, Teresa, and I join them all and they go to the bridge where the late bloom of lilacs is still sweetly fragrant. We skim stones in the brook, talk about the wedding, ask who let the word out.

I continue to mind the stand and add verses to my *Half Lives of the Family of Fruits* that no one will see. And to keep my secret. I am cooking. With real fire.

Everybody seems to have a secret. I catch my father dancing the shim sham in the kitchen. I catch Vinnie writing something and he says he is working on a short story he'd written years ago, "Odd

Og." I find Dana and Rena teaching big Carmine to dance. I hear Madeleine asking Carmine Jr. to explain a text on quantum physics. One day Maria and Teresa are digging down in the cedar chest for their birth certificates—they want to know for sure who was born first. My mother rocks vigorously, races through her olive wood rosaries and listens to French tapes as Mario plays some old tunes on his old piano. Before this summer he hadn't touched the piano in almost as many years as I have to my name. Now he comes by often to play this old version of *Impossible Dream*. Lucy drops by and sleeps down in the cool cellar once a week all through the summer.

I notice how little it bothers me when I hear "Lucy, my psychotherapist; Mario, my astrophysicist; Carmine, my inventor; Rena, my dancer. Carmela, my baby."

I smile, keep on working. I try the silent meditation Madeleine showed me.

Silence precedes wisdom.

The day after the feast of St. Lucy it starts. Everyone is saying have you heard that Dad's going to finish the stories. He has an ending to those stories he used to tell us and since we're all together he wants us early the day of the wedding on Creek Street to tell us all of them again.

It is just like old times before I was born. Early morning Sunday. There's cold pizza on the clover-leaf kitchen table for breakfast. Someone puts a pot of coffee on. Someone catches it just before it boils over. Lucy and Mario wake up early, stepping over sleeping bodies. Mario wakes everyone up playing his piano in the cellar. Lucy sings *Blue Moon*. I awake to find three nieces in my room, two in my bed, one curled up on the floor. Spouses who can't hack crowds have stayed in town. Five, possibly six, nephews are kibbitzing in the dormer across the hall. Out-of-town relatives and friends are sleeping everywhere, anywhere, on couches, rugs, in the bathtubs, of which there are two now, one up and one downstairs.

"Lucy!" calls my mother. "Carmine!"

I run downstairs and follow Lucy, who runs dutifully as ever when called. Carmine's still asleep. My mother's call comes from the backyard.

"Who's teaching Lucy's two youngest to thumb their noses? Which one of my adult kids would do this?" my mother wants to know, stifling a little smile.

Lucy must know we have just gotten on good terms with Mrs. Lear. After all my mother's prayers over these years. Trying to get that woman to accept us! Mrs. Lear is attending Frankie's wedding, says my mother, and it was almost all ruined when she saw Caitlin and Sean thumbing their noses at her. My mother tells Lucy she scolded them in front of Mrs. Lear for picking their noses and then Sean said *vaffanculo* and my mother had to lie again and tell Mrs. Lear he was saying, My fin-ger, my fin-ger. And on top of that she turned around and found little Carmine with his magnifying glass trying to set Mrs. Lear's hedges on fire. Where's his father?

"We mustn't get on her bad side again!" pleads my mother.

My father comes outside and says not to worry, not to worry. His words will make anything right again. Everybody is to gather in the parlor for the stories and then they will go to Frankie and Charlene's wedding.

My mother worries about last minute details, the carnations, flowers at the altar, the band, who's carrying the cannoli to the hall, will all the relatives be happy with the seating? My father says he doesn't like to repeat himself, that there will never again be anything to worry about, just listen to his words. Words are all he has left for his children and their children. You're forever worrying about the little things, he says. Now inside. I have spoken. For cryin' out loud.

Only I hear and see what happens next.

My mother says, "Vincent, go take a long walk off a short pier." My father says nothing. He takes his wife's hand affectionately.

Such a small thing. But still it is momentous. Magdalena Coniglio Donitella has had the last word.

I smile and take my place and hold my godchild on my lap.

My father tells the stories, and he tells them again. He says his father appeared to him one last time—two days ago on the Feast of St. Lucy—and left this one behind, *The Tale of the Last Cannoli*. My father cries silently a moment and says, "I think Grandpa wrote this one down in his own hand."

The evening after he called the evil men ham 'n eggers and told them to go pound salt, Mario Anthony Donitella returned to the same spot on his beloved mountain. Unbeknownst to him, a hag and her husband lived close by in a dense part of the forest that was dark, deep green, and moist. The forest floor was like sponge, and only a dapple of sunshine ever penetrated the thick foliage and gnarled trunks.

The Hag, Faccia Brutta (Ugly Face), and her husband, Malocchiu (Evil Eye), thrived in the darkness and too much light blinded them. Faccia Brutta was as ugly as sin. She had warts three inches high and a long hooked nose and straggly hair. Her eyes bulged out of her rippled forehead. When she laughed it shook the mountain—like a terremoto. *When she cried a thick, sickly fog shrouded the village.*

Malocchiu was puny and ugly too. And smelled to high heaven.

There was a very strange thing about this couple. Neither one had a shadow even if they were caught for a fleeting moment in the light that stole in while they gathered berries and wild herbs to eat. No shadow. Perhaps they had simply absorbed too much darkness.

For a pastime Faccia Brutta and Malocchiu cast spells and meddled in the lives of the people of the village. One of their favorite pastimes was wreaking havoc upon the beautiful muse of men.

When the Hag spotted Mario laughing at his shadow in the light of the full moon, she rubbed her bony hands over her warty face. How dare he!

So, she said the words: "Ecco, from this day, Mario Donitella, I curse you and your offspring to be forever restless. All those poems in your head will stay there. You will never be able to write them down. Hah, hah, hah," she squealed. "You will get àcitu *every time you try!"*

It was her àcitu spell. No one in his family would experience a sense of peace, just restlessness and acid stomach upset. For many years.

Suddenly lightning flashed over the mountain, turning night to day for split seconds. A fierce warm, dry wind accompanied the sparks of electricity. Mario ran home safely, but the beautiful tree where he had been sitting was struck by a bolt and split cleanly down the middle. It smoldered for the night. Mario slept fitfully that evening and for many more to come.

The morning after this spell was cast Mario decided to leave his beloved homeland and sail to America with his mother. He told his old friend Gaetano and broke his heart.

And so, early in the very first year of the twentieth century, when Mario was just 17, he took his mother and followed the hordes of people crossing the Atlantic. The trip seemed to last forever and the seas swelled and settled and people were knocked about. At last all the passengers were dumbstruck when they saw this place, for which they had left everything behind. They landed first at Ellis Island. They poured onto this island with their many papers and stories for inspectors who had the power to let them stay or make them return. While he waited his turn to be checked over by the immigration officers he went outside and walked along the stone seawall. The smell of fish and diesel was strong and strange to him. So this was the place where they would find prosperity, happiness, and peace of mind.

In the west he saw the black smoke of progress belching into the skies. In the east he saw buildings so high and wide and heavy that surely they were sinking into the surrounding water!

Mario noticed there were no donkeys.

His mother noticed there were no hills.

It was so flat, they thought.

He watched the gulls over the Hudson and fell into a stupor. His voyage had indeed tired him. He plopped on the ground against the seawall and fell into a deep, dark sleep. It seemed only five minutes later he was awake and walking along the seawall. As he looked out over the water he noticed that the number of buildings seemed to have doubled, maybe tripled, since he arrived. And the smoke belched blacker and blacker. On the seawall he saw a long, unending copper plaque engraved with hundreds and hundreds of names. He noticed that these were all the names of his compari whom he had known in Sicilia. How strange, he thought. Then he came to his very own name...and he gasped, realizing this plaque was a memorial to dead immigrants. And as he gasped, he snored deeply and woke himself, his heart pounding like that of a frightened bird. He ran back into the Great Hall of the main building. He never told a soul about his unsettling dream.

Mario and his mother breathed a deep sigh as they received their stamp of approval. They were ferried to the New Jersey Central Railroad, where they boarded a train for the place where they had people, Peterstown, Elizabeth.

And there Mario lived, outdoing the Americans at their own work ethic, until he died at the age of 51 having worked so hard to make life good for his family.

It was only when Mario crossed back over to his dreamspot on the Mountain in Cammarata that he learned about the spell that had been cast upon his family so many years before, the spell that had kept them in a state of restlessness and indigestion.

Mario was very brave. He knew he had to confront Faccia Brutta. He first ran into her husband who had just had a brawl with her and was on his way to get drunk on his favorite herb.

"Where is she?" asked Mario.

"In there," Malocchio said, making an obscene gesture.

Hearing the voices, Faccia Brutta poked her hideous head out. Mario would have gotten goose bumps if he still had skin.

"Listen you, Mala Femmina," he started, gathering his courage. "I command you to end the spell you put on me and my children many years ago, you wicked witch."

She cackled and drooled, and Mario gagged. "Or else..." he choked.

"Or else what?" She let her one eyeball stare out at him.

"Or else, I'll hang a crucifix over your house," he said trying to think of the worst threat possible.

"Maybe I'll give you a chance to break the spell," she said. *"Here's what you must do: Go find the olive pits."*

"What olive pits?"

"The ones that belong to the 10 children." For the Hag knew that in the pits were their souls.

"Then do this: string them together with the hair of a saint. Then have them incorporated into rosary beads, blessed by a celibate man in brown robes, and finally have Magdalena say the rosary on them ten times. You have the next 50 years plus one for not arguing." She was gone with a bolt of lightning and clap of thunder before Mario could argue the schedule. But he knew this was his only chance for eternal peace for himself, too.

"Mannaggia!" he thought as he scratched his head and wondered where to start.

Because he was a spirit, he was able to slip into the ground and locate the olive pits, although it took him several years and a lot of digging in the nasty ground of New Jersey. He found the first seven in Peterstown. And then he found the last three in Rahway.

Finding the hair of a saint was his next task. How would he accomplish such a feat? It sounded like a sacrilege. Then he thought of his dear wife, Lucia. She was truly a saint. Everyone had always proclaimed her so. So Mario went to his wife one night as she slept. He prayed and snatched a strand of her silver hair long enough to hold the pits. He took a few extra strands, in case. Then he strung the olive pits together himself.

Now to get them set into a pair of rosary beads. By this time he had only a few years left.

But then he remembered that in Rome and Assisi and in many other holy cities of Italy holy friars often strung together and blessed rosary beads. So he delivered the string of 10 to Assisi. There would be a better chance of a holy friar blessing them there. For he could not recall one Sicilian who had ever taken—or kept—a vow of celibacy.

Eventually the olive pits were set into a pair of rosary beads made from smooth olive wood. Now he had to figure out how to get them blessed and, most difficult of all, to Magdalena to pray upon.

It so happened that one summer his granddaughter Maddelena was on a trip through Assisi. Although he could see she was no longer the religious type, he inspired her to buy some rosaries as souvenirs. It was not easy. She had so little money and almost bought scarves instead. But he managed to get her to buy the right pair.

She was on the plane home when Mario realized that he had neglected to have a friar bless the beads. As luck would have it, an American Franciscan, a celibate man in brown robes, happened to be on the plane, returning from a retreat in Assisi. Grazie a Dio, thought Mario. Now he had to make sure his granddaughter brought the beads to the friar to have them blessed. It took some coaxing but he succeeded in inspiring her to do so.

Soon the beads were on their way in the mail to Magdalena, who promptly put them aside in favor of the beads she had used for years. Despite Mario's urgent messages in her dreams, she failed to heed him. Years passed. Only a month before Mario's deadline, just as he was about to give up hope, his great-grandson, little Mario, pulled the beads out of her underwear drawer and began to play with them. Magdalena snatched them from his hands—"These are not toys, caro mio!"—and hung them on her rocking chair. In a month's time, she had prayed on them more than ten times. More than a 100 times, in fact.

On December 13, 1990, the fifty-first anniversary of his death, Mario returned to Cammarata. "I have done as you ordered," he announced proudly to Faccia Brutta and Malocchiu.

She started to laugh. And laugh. It was a screeching, hideous laugh, a sound so ugly that leaves dropped from trees. Poor Mario had no idea what was so funny.

"None of that had anything to with breaking the spell, you stupido. Fool!" she said with such meanness that Mario wondered if he had been judged and sent to eternal damnation in Hell. He could not believe his immortal ears. She had tricked him.

But then she stopped laughing and stood up. The blood seemed to drain from her face and she became ashen white. Smoke began to *issue from her ears, off her face, from her hair, then from her entire body as if she were burning up. The sky darkened, the ground shook, and there was the most explosive sound to come off that Mountain in thousands of years.*

As the light from the early morning sunrise appeared on the horizon, the smoke began to clear and rise. Mario could not believe his celestial eyes. What stood before him was not a Hag, but the most beautiful woman he had ever seen. A maiden with clear dark eyes, and flowing shiny black hair. Her skin was aglow with health and eternal youth.

"Do not be afraid any longer, Mario Anthony Donitella," she said. "For you have broken the spell, not just of the past 100 years, but of the last 2000 years. You have accomplished this by obeying the Hag's every whim. This spell was cast upon me and my fiancé just before we were to take our marriage vows. A witch from the village became very angry when a sorcerer upstaged her by causing mighty Mount Aetna to erupt. In revenge, she decided to bewitch one man and one woman. Through us, she has cast the spell of discontent on so many of our people. Why else would our people begin to leave this land of plenty?"

The brush rustled and there appeared a handsome youthful man with clear blue eyes, dark hair and skin. He came forward.

"Look!" he said, "We have shadows! The darkness is gone from us!"

They danced around in front of Mario.

"We are your relatives of the light and dark blood of many ages."

Mario thought he was looking in a mirror.

"Here's what you must do to make sure the spell is broken forever," he said. "On December 15, 1991, your children will be married for 50 years. That is the day the spell will be lifted. But, you must make sure that they gather with their 10 offspring on that day."

"Anything else?" asked Mario, rubbing his eyes. He was tired, too, what with all the running around he'd been doing for over half a century.

235

"Yes, there is," said the maiden. "When they gather, they must sing the Family Song. And every word of the family story must be written down. When all this is done, the spell will be broken and the àcitu curse on this family will be no more."

This last was music to Mario's ears.

"One more thing, Mario," said the maiden. "Don't try to inspire your son or one of your grandsons or great grandsons to do the job. Only a woman will hear you."

Mario had seven months to get his clan cracking. Forgetting what the couple had admonished, he first tried to inspire Mario, his grandson. His grandson kept interpreting the story in equations and logarithms.

Next he tried Lucy, his wife's namesake. Lucy listened well. But alas, she did not have time to write down the words, what with eight children.

After trying unsuccessfully with two other granddaughters, he noticed something. A granddaughter who sat very still upon a black cushion each morning and evening to empty her mind. Who tended the stand. Who made vegetable creatures for little children. She seemed to have all the time in the world.

He began to fill her empty mind with words, morning and evening. He began, "In the beginning there was terrible darkness..." She wrote. He continued, "Light, love, and all things good lay frozen in ice..." She wrote. A good month before the party, she had written down every word.

And then it came to pass. On the fifteenth day of December in the year 1991, Mario's offspring met and had a great feast.

Mario decided to put off going to eternal rest for the weekend. He wouldn't miss this celebration for the world. He danced the tarantella with his grandchildren and great grandchildren. Once, he bumped into his son who turned around and blamed his wife. He sang when they sang. He reminded his son to sing the Family Song and he sang forth with them, "We are the Donitellas, you've heard so much about, people stop and stare at us whenever we go out..."

He made sure they sang both verses. His grandchildren did not hide behind their mother as they had when they were young.

He tried some of each dish—the fennel and eggplant appetizers, the sausage and peppers, the cavatelli, ravioli, rabbit, and pheasant. And when no one was looking, he couldn't resist stealing the last cannoli. *Everyone blamed it on Grandma Coniglio. He savored every bite.*

And on that day, when one love in its Golden Year was celebrated, and another long-standing love was consummated, peace and happiness came to many. The spell was lifted and a tremendous calm prevailed. Perhaps there would be other spells to grapple with, but the àcitu *spell and the restlessness spell were history.*

And on the Mountain of Cammarata, where Mario Donitella finally saw the Light and the Dark, there grew the most beautiful fig tree, lush and green, with the juiciest, most succulent fruit imaginable. And there the beautiful maiden and the handsome young man were married and lived ever after, feeding each other fresh figs.

If you don't believe me, you can go visit Sicily yourself.

The silence and stillness on Creek Street are riveting. A crack opens the ice of the frozen brook out back. Frost melts off a branch. I hear through walls into the next-door neighbor's house. Mrs. Lear blows her nose loudly and I realize that she has been listening, too. The old bag, crying!

No one's looking at anyone's eyes. But I steal a glance. Frankie's eyes are awfully glassy. My mother rocks with ease. Mario cracks his 10 fingers like he used to whenever they itched to play piano. Lucy seems to be studying the family's shadow on the red rug. Carmine's foot is tapping away to its own beat.

With one last stolen glance I catch my father's comprehending stare. In his otherwise granite eyes I see the same glint as when he used to tell me I was named for a woman of unsurpassed vision.